I0582414

Alexander and Maria

SOULLA CHRISTODOULOU

First published in South Africa by Kingsley Publishers, 2023
Copyright © Soulla Christodoulou, 2023

The right of Soulla Christodoulou to be identified as author
of this work has been asserted.

Kingsley Publishers
Pretoria, South Africa
www.kingsleypublishers.com

www.kingsleypublishers.com
A catalogue copy of this book will be available from the
National Library of South Africa

Paperback ISBN: 978-1-7764254-9-5
eBook ISBN: 978-1-7764254-8-8

Also by Soulla Christodoulou

A Palette of Magpies
The Village House
The Summer Will Come
Broken Pieces of Tomorrow

This story is dedicated to a dear friend, Drew Thomas, who I would never have met had it not been for our love of words and poetry.

1
Alexander

I have a check-up at the clinic in Inverness, a few minutes' drive from home; a familiar burst of irritability fills my insides. The routine hasn't changed in over twenty years, the nurses have come and gone, but the procedures, even the conversations, have remained the same, as have the outcomes and diagnosis. Maybe today will be different.

'I'm just off now, Sandra sweetheart.' She barely gives me a sideways glance, flicking from one TV channel to the other, puffing on her cigarette.

I open the front door, Caramel slinks past me, the morning's icy blast lapping at my feet. She disappears, like a garden ghost, behind the emerald privet hedge, glistening with the morning frost, and emerging again, she dashes across the road. I envy her speed, her agility, her freedom to come and go. My envy is tinged green in the whites of my eyes and in the recesses of my mind, in my plodding steps.

An hour later, I'm dragging my left foot home across the drive, a spray of gravel clatters across my path. Swinging it forward is more painful than usual and my hip aches from the chill. My face feels weather-beaten, my skin dull and grey with an in-the-depth-of-winter pallor. My head is fuzzy; a headache pushes at my temples. I hope I'm not coming down with a cold.

'I'm back,' I call out, leaning on the banisters to catch my breath. I pull off my gloves and stuff them into my jacket pocket which hangs stiff with cold on the hook. The oak coat stand belonged to my mother, and with Dad gone too it's now mine. I couldn't part with it; too many childhood memories of tugging at my school coat and scarf, the times I pulled it over and lay under it, legs and arms splayed until my mother straightened it, and me, up. But she didn't raise her voice, not once; my patience is inherited.

'Put the kettle on, Alec. I'm gasping. You took your time.'

'Traffic across the main junction. They've changed the light sequence.'

'Always overthinking.'

'Not at all, sweetheart.'

In the kitchen I flick on the kettle. Sandra's piled the breakfast dishes into the sink. I roll up my shirt sleeves, turn on the tap.

'Leave those. I can do them.' She steps towards me, jostling me out of the way.

'I'm capable of doing a bit of washing up Sandra, sweetheart.'

'Nothing new from the clinic.' I dry my hands, red from coming into the warmth. I pour boiling water into her mug. 'Coffee, black, two sugars,' I say, sliding it across the worktop towards her.

'Nothing's going to change now, Alec. What were you

expecting? But you've got me. I can look after...'

'I'm not a child,' I say, sitting at the table with my tea. 'Sorry. I'm tired. I saw a locum, around for six months at least. Pauline went into early labour last week. She's on maternity leave.'

'Poor cow.'

'Twin boys apparently.'

'She'll have her work cut out.'

'Aye, she will. Hard enough with one. I should get a card... ask the receptionist to pass it on.'

'You're getting too personal. She won't be expecting a card from you.'

'Aye, I know, but I'd like to send one. She's always been attentive.'

'Just doing her job...'

Sandra's right. She will turn this simple conversation into a battle of who's going to have the last word. And from experience, she'll have the last word. She always does. Why do I let her?

I carry my tea into the sitting room and place it on the coffee table; my shaking grip on the cup is weak and I spill it over the coaster. Damn. I wipe it up with a scrunched-up tissue I pull out of my jeans pocket. I lower myself into my usual place on the couch. A whiff of the rose scented plug-in fills my nostrils; I taste it on my lips as I lean forward to sip my tea. I shuffle forward, lean to the side, reaching for my vibrating phone in my back pocket.

'Work?' Sandra asks, settling into the single seater. She crosses her legs at the ankles; the heels of her socks are skewed. Her jaw clenches as she lights a cigarette and takes a long drag. The smoke wafts, settling in a cloud over my mug. I've never liked the stench of nicotine, and as I've got older, I hate it even more.

'Twitter. Pete stayed back at the end of his shift and helped me set up an account.' I adjust my glasses which have slipped down my nose. 'He showed me how to tweet… connect with other people interested in what I'm interested in. Share news and views.'

I open the app trying to remember what he showed me; I don't worry too much about how to do everything, as long as I can tweet.

'What views? What sort of people? What a waste of time.'

'I like it, sweetheart. It'll open up a whole new world.'

I browse and follow a handful of new accounts; two artists, the local newspaper, the British Library, Keats' House in Hampstead, a couple of authors.

'New world? What new world Alec? All you ever do is read books and talk about museums.'

'Aye, you're right there, but this will get me thinking, learning new things… it's like being in a classroom with so many different people you don't know where to start.'

'They won't know where to start with you that's for sure.'

Her comment hurts; digs into my lower back, runs down my calf where it joins forces with the cold in causing me more discomfort. She glances at me massaging my leg, turns away, says nothing.

Caramel meows outside the front door. Why doesn't she go round the back and through the cat flap? Sandra doesn't move so I hoist myself off the sofa. I open the front door a crack. Caramel pushes through the gap, bringing in a slither of late winter with her. I pick up the drift of mail around the door; she's left a paw print on one of the letters.

'Hello, my pwecious, special pwecious.' She rubs up against my shin, meowing. I feel her cold fur through my trousers. 'You're freezing, aren't you? Aye, you are.' The tiny brown smudge above her nose is brighter today, the white stripes along the front of her legs whiter too.

Caramel slinks to the kitchen. I shuffle behind her, leaving the mail, unopened, on the kitchen table. Sandra likes to go through it; her little ritual.

I struggle, as usual, to tear open the food packet with my still cold, unbending fingers. She waits in anticipation. I squeeze half the contents into her bowl. She sidles over and sniffs, grabs a chunk of the jellied meat. She moves away from the dish to the corner of the kitchen where she shakes her head in her usual little way. She chews the morsel, flicking her tail. She licks her nose and returns for more, purring. She's satisfied.

'You're not feeding her again, are you Alec?' calls Sandra from the other room.

'Half a pouch, she's freezing.'

'You spoil her too much. It's ridiculous.'

Back in the sitting room, I try to block out Sandra's drone. She's always criticising. If it isn't me, it's the neighbours. If it isn't the neighbours, it's our son's latest girlfriend. I try to remember a time she didn't have this mean streak in her but admit it's always existed; I just hadn't paid it attention. As a younger man, I wasn't in tune with such matters when I thought I was in love.

I slurp my tea; it's tepid but I can't be bothered to boil the kettle again. My hip's aching. I'm going to struggle on my afternoon shift. My work is isolating. It rarely brings me into contact with others apart from standard handover conversations with Pete and limited exchanges with Danny, the young man I care for.

I focus on Twitter despite the dull ache pushing behind my eyes. I marvel at how many tweets have appeared in the space of a few hours. Three people have followed me and I clap with joy. I'm grateful to my colleague for helping me;

being a novice he showed me immense patience.

I want to feel more connected to people. It's amazing how you can be in the same room as someone and feel so alone and isolated yet in a room with no one and feel connected with so many. I recently read an article about people making great friends on social media. I question if my experience will be the same, recognise a fizzing in me. Oh, the wonder of technology, the wonder of social media. I'm hooked.

I post a picture of the fields behind our house, notice I've posted it twice, omitting to add a message or hashtag. Not sure how to delete it remains in duplicate on my feed. What an idiot. I'm not as tech savvy as I like to think. Booking train tickets and passes to museums is easy in comparison.

However, Twitter is opening a whole new world. I should remember more than I have but I'm not giving up. Pete's liked both pictures.

'What time are we having lunch, sweetheart? I've got my shift at half past two.'

'Whenever you make it.'

'Are you not eating?'

'I suppose I will if you're making something.'

'Aye, I'll open a tin of tomato soup and butter some bread.'

She nods her head as she stubs out another cigarette in the overflowing ashtray sitting on the arm of the chair.

We eat the soup in the front room, on our lap trays. Sandra behaves as if they're the best invention ever. They were a gift from our best friends, John and Elizabeth, so I can't do away with mine. The lap tray irritates me; ages me before my time, reminding me of the old people's home where my late uncle spent his last days.

Sandra slurps at her soup. I cringe at her loud sucking. I used to find it endearing, the way she glugged and gulped like a greedy child, but she's got louder over the years and I've become less tolerant of her eating habits. The soup leaves a greasy residue on her lips. She tears at her bread with her front teeth; two crumbs hang on the side of her mouth. I turn away.

We eat in silence. Caramel lies at my feet meowing, content she has a full belly. I like the weight of her on me; she feels real, solid. I like being wanted. I want to feel wanted. I want to feel more than a mundane existence made up of packet-soup lunches, trips to the supermarket and an empty sexless marriage. I feel older than fifty-three. When did the frown lines and wrinkles around my eyes happen? Is this what life is going to be like now? I try to imagine what my dad would have said.

I sink into the sofa, take off my glasses, rest my eyes. I'm going to have to take some headache pills; I can't shift the persistent pain behind my eyes, pushing at my temples.

'Mind the cushions Alec, you're puckering them.'

I ignore Sandra. I mean if cushions aren't meant for getting squashed out of shape, for support, what are they for? I recall my mother and Dad's relationship… remember them kissing at the foot of the tinsel Christmas tree, me a scrawny seven-year-old; their relationship always perfunctory and respectful yet loving and kind.

My phone pings, I open my eyes. Maria, an author from London, has followed me back. I like this Twitter thing.

'What are you smiling about?'

'Nothing my sweetheart. Just happy today.'

'What have you got to be happy about?'

'You. Life.'

'Soppy sod. Shouldn't you be getting ready for work?'

'Aye, another five minutes, and I'll be off. My overnight bag is packed. Just need to grab my phone charger and a couple of headache tablets.'

'Your phone's turning into your new toy.'

'It is, it is.'

2
Maria

'Woo-hoo. I've got 321 followers. I'm sooo happy.'

'Oh Mum, it's not like you've won the lottery.'

'Twitter's going to be the best.'

'What about Facebook?'

'It's all about Twitter now. It's more formal and where my focus should be, especially since sending my manuscript to four agents.'

'Oh good. You can buy a new car with your royalties. Your fiesta is, like, so naff. A Porsche. YOLO.'

'YOLO?'

'You. Only. Live. Once. Come on Mum. And there's you on Twitter.'

'Well in my day it was carpe diem.'

I change position, stretching my legs across the couch, ignoring her teenage sarcasm. I glance back at my Kindle, a smug little smile on my face. I've worked hard the past week to build my followers. I've trawled through countless other author accounts checking what they tweet and how often, I've read tips on how to maximise my account and downloaded numerous writer quotes for future tweeting.

'I've "met" some great people… writers, authors, artists, photographers, life coaches. Twitter feels more serious than Facebook which is all gossipy and show-offy. Life's about much more. I want to feel more fulfilled. I want to be authentic, real.'

'Yes, Mum.' Natalie is folded over the coffee table. Tubes of acrylic paint scatter its surface and the carpet. Her palette is filled with a multitude of red, blue and yellow blobs; two jars are full of murky water and stuffed with paintbrushes. By her cosy-socked feet, stacks of art books and sketch pads crowd the cramped space.

I sip my Jasmine green tea, plopping the teabag on the saucer to use again. The Sunday morning news programme is spilling over with a political debate about Trump and the latest flurry of development in his activities since he took office just over a week ago.

'Ooh, I've got another follower.'

Natalie rolls her eyes. 'You do realise you rolled your eyes out loud,' I say.

'Ha, ha, you're so funny. What d'you think?' she asks, holding up her art piece at the corners, her fingertips matted with dry paint.

'Wow, Nat. It's amazing. Monet should be your middle name.'

'Let's hope Mrs. "I'm so brilliant at art" thinks so too.'

The number "1" next to Messages distracts me.

Dear Maria. Thank you for following me back.

I look forward to connecting with you.

Thank you too. Lovely to "meet" you Alexander.

'Get packed up. Lunch will be ready soon.'

'Don't tell me roast chicken and potatoes again.'

'And broccoli and gravy. Now stop complaining.'

Natalie packs her art materials away. In the kitchen, the water splashes. She is rinsing her brushes in the sink; the usual paint splodges on the wall tiles send my nerves teetering.

'Hope you're not making a mess.' I instantly regret saying it. I'm beginning

to sound like a grumpy old so-and-so.

She ignores me. I lean over to tidy her paint tubes, flicking through her

sketchbook. Her work's good. She must get her talent from her grandmother and not from me. I was always a writer, history essays, geography projects. Art, for me, seemed a waste of my time, but I know now, what an accomplishment it must be to create pieces for others to enjoy.

I think about my story; a jab of disappointment stabs me in the chest. I've had one reply; a polite but standard rejection email.

'I've turned off the oven,' says Natalie, leaning on the door jamb.

'Thanks. Do you want to clear the rest of this, and we can eat in here?'

***

Over the next three days I tweet lots of writer related quotes and images. Initially, it is more time-consuming than I anticipate but I'm good at multi-tasking – tweet while cooking, while in front of the TV and while in bed first and last thing at night. I work out how to save tweets in draft, sending them out with one click. My followers are growing at a good pace, boosting my confidence. I tweet links to writer articles and research relating to my own writing. It's like having a new hobby, a new focus.

One evening Alexander sends me another message after liking a number of my tweets.

> *Hi Maria. How are you?*
> *I saw your tweet about writing a new book. What's it about?*

> **Hello. I'm playing with ideas. The last one, now finally finished is about a book club based partly on my own friends. Each member reveals a secret. How are you?**

> *I'm OK thanks. Having a wee dram to warm me up for the night. my cat is being particularly vocal.*

He tweets a photo of a fat, lazy looking cat snuggled in his lap with a message to me. He's new at this. I cringe at his mistake, but I like it anyway.

> *Maria meet Caramel.*

> **I might use her in my next book.**

> *If you do, I can share some stories about her.*

The following evening, I'm half-watching Emmerdale

while browsing Twitter. I try to block out Natalie's music, booming from her bedroom. The music is aggressive; lyrics filled with swear words and obscenities. When did she start listening to this heavy, rap? I stretch out a leg and push the sitting room door shut with my foot. The closed door muffles the racket a fraction. I increase the volume on the TV. I'm snuggled under the throw; its sweaty body kind of smell reminds me to wash it.

Hello. How was your day?

> Hello Alexander. Good thank you. I was at the office today. How are you?

I've had a quiet day. on shift tomorrow. What work do you do?

> I work in admin and marketing.

Sounds interesting.

> It's okay. It pays the bills. And I have time to write.

How's your writing coming along?

> When I'm not fighting writer's block it's going well, thank you.

I'm in awe of your writing. I don't have the concentration for it.

His comment leaves a fuzzy warm glow in me. The compliment seems genuine. I like it.

'Bloody hell, Nat. You frightened the life out of me.'

'Sorry. Where's my fleece? The burgundy one,' she asks, bursting in.

'Should be hanging in the hallway. If it's not there, check your wardrobe.'

'I can't find it. I need it for tomorrow.'

'Check the laundry basket. I think I stuck it in there.'

'Mum, I need it.'

'Calm down. I'll give it a quick wash for you tonight.'

'Muuum.'

She storms out, slamming the door behind her. I bite on my lower lip. What else can go in the same wash cycle? I grab the throw off the couch.

My Kindle pings.

Hello beautiful lady.
I am good, genuine man who like to know you.

I cringe. This GBrett isn't genuine, surely? I scroll through his profile, check who he's following, a long list of females. Surprise, surprise. I ignore him. Not so long ago I would have entertained him, flirted, but not now. I'm trying to move forward to a different place where I can be fulfilled and find my niche, both in my writing and my love life.

***

The following morning, extra early, I hang Natalie's fleece on the wooden clothes horse, a permanent fixture, erected by the kitchen radiator. I turn the pockets inside out so they can dry quicker and find a squished wrapper. I can't make out what it is.

I faff about making a cuppa, wait for the toaster to pop.

I lay out the peanut butter and the orange marmalade for Natalie, her favourite spreads. I lick the stickiness off my thumb and fingers; she's a right messy one. I empty the extra slim dishwasher, careful not to clank about too much, but when the power shower kicks into life with a deep groan, I clatter around with less care; Natalie is up.

I butter my toast and sip my tea. No more messages from GBrett, thank goodness. Nothing from Alexander either. I feel a little disappointed. I'm perturbed by my reaction; a sadness comes over me. I glance at the date on the baking calendar Natalie won at her school's Christmas fete. The cupcakes' soft colours smile back at me, in contrast with my own grey mood. My tears run unchecked, tears of relief, of loss. Yesterday, for the first time in years, I didn't remember my wedding anniversary and realise I'm thinking about Alexander.

3
Alexander

'What's wrong with you?' asks Sandra.

'What? Nothing.'

Wandering around the supermarket, I'm in a daze. I can't get the Twitter girl, Maria, out of my head. There's something about her profile picture, her long dark hair, olive skin and her dark sunglasses. Mysterious. Inviting. I feel blissful yet, at the same time, unsure of myself.

I sent her a direct message, *looking forward to connecting with you*. It sounds stupid now. What was the right terminology for making contact on Twitter? Tweeting with you? Messaging you? And then I tweeted the picture of Caramel with, *this is my cat Maria* instead of sending it as a private message. Did she spot my error? I've made too many mistakes; tagging the wrong person or forgetting to tag or use hashtags altogether.

'Stop dawdling, Alec.'

Sandra's posture is tight, her lips pursed, her hands clench the handlebar of the trolley; she's struggling to be patient with me; me too. A sudden urge to scream and abandon the noisy supermarket grabs hold of me. I want to check my phone; has Maria messaged me since last night?

Sandra pushes the trolley to the end of the aisle and stops, her shoulders stiff. She smiles to soften her stare; a sting of guilt bites at me.

We haven't always existed like this. I remember our connection in the early years of our marriage; my bond with her, the world. Having a family of my own made me feel normal, ordinary. Callum, our son, now twenty-eight, made me the dad I never thought I would ever have the chance to be. I believed I owed her everything for her love, for making me a father, for making me the happiest man in the world.

I feel a little sad at how different things have become but this is what my life is all about now; mundane routine, disconnection, loneliness. Is this the way it is for everyone after being married for all these years? Or is this empty nest syndrome now Callum has moved out?

Her routine, which once made me feel reassured and safe, now smothers me; sits heavy on my chest. How long can I continue to nurture myself?

I shuffle along the aisle, my hip aches; the cold weather and stress plague me. A sluggishness comes over me and my lower back is hurting. I try to massage the pain away; my arm won't reach the spot. I try to smooth the soreness out by bending back and forth.

Sandra swings right into the next aisle. Catching up with her I reach for a packet of tea.

'Green tea?'

'I tried it at work. It's nice.' I feel my cheeks go red and look away. Not wanting a confrontation, I put it back.

It's what Maria drinks. Maria steals into my thoughts again and I fumble for my mobile inside my jacket pocket. As Sandra moves away, I pull it out, press the Twitter icon, impatient for 4G to connect. Maria's tweeted.

No one can tell your #story so tell it yourself. No one can write your story so write it yourself.
There's a picture of a candy pink typewriter adorned with a big white gerbera and the words "WRITE" on a piece of paper coming out the top of the machine.

My secret of becoming a #writer is to write, write some more and keep on writing.
The picture is of a woman's hand holding a quill; words appear on the blank page as she writes.

It's an animated picture which I recently discovered is called a GIF. I must find an excuse to message her later.

'What's that stupid grin for?' Sandra asks as I catch up with her.

'Oh, for goodness sake Sandra, am I not allowed to smile?' I shift from one leg to the other, putting all my weight onto my right side, and wince. 'Sorry, sweetheart, the weather's playing havoc with my bones today.'

She gives me a sympathetic look, grabs a jar of her favourite instant coffee, plonks it in the trolley. My heart drops. I can't imagine Maria drinking coffee; her teeth are too white. What else does she like to drink other than green tea? I conjure up a scene; we are drinking cocktails and holding hands across a table, a candle flickers between us. Romance is something I've not engaged in with Sandra for a long time.

We reach the end of the last aisle; Sandra always insists we go down every aisle in case she has forgotten to add an item to her shopping list; she's anal like that. But in all our years of marriage she has rarely bought anything not listed.

At the checkout, she unloads the shopping; the items stare back at me in monochrome, boring nothingness fills me. How can I ever do anything extraordinary with such a mundane existence?

Suddenly I'm annoyed; leave Sandra standing. I return to the tea aisle, moving as fast as my legs, will let me. My walking stick echoes my pace as I take one step after the other, banging into shoppers and trolleys crowding the aisle, mumbling my apologies. When rushing I tend to walk toe-heel, my foot drags more noticeably. My mother always reminded me to pick my feet up as a child. I didn't understand what she meant, and my frustration caused me to drag my foot all the more, often tripping over, scarred knees, a slash on my forehead, engraved evidence of my clumsiness. I now know she didn't register the impact my condition had on me; physically, emotionally, socially; Sandra doesn't either and she doesn't seem to care.

I add two packets of tea, Jasmine green and pomegranate green, to the last of the groceries on the conveyor belt. Sandra frowns at me, the furrow deepening between her eyebrows. The pain in my back is worsening, making me cantankerous; I'm hot and bothered.

***

My hideout is a glorified shed, dusty and musty smelling, but it's insulated and has a working two bar electric heater. It's crowded with a jumble of boxes; belongings Sandra has banned from the house over the years. A framed poster of The Beatles hangs on the back wall; bought at the local car boot sale in 2007. Sandra barred it from the house, so it stayed, wrapped in newspaper, in a corner of the shed until I created my sanctuary. My dad's worn armchair and his triple shelf bookcase is stuffed with reading material I've collected over the years.

I place the chipped mug onto the old Formica table I use as a desk; it's the one mug I'm permitted to bring outside. I take a sip. I swallow. I'm not sure I relish the bitter taste. Will I get used to Maria's green tea?

I flick on the heater, shake the drizzle off my fleece. I let out a sigh. The ticking clock, which sat on my dad's desk for years, says half past three. Sandra won't miss me for at least another two hours. I lean back in my chair. I take out my mobile and reread Maria's tweets. I ♥ them both and send her a direct message conscious of my steady, even breathing.

> *Hello Maria. I bought some green tea.*
> *You tweeted about drinking it and it got me inquisitive as to its taste.*

Her profile picture is open in front of me again and I find myself daydreaming of her. I flick through John Betjeman's book, *London*, and fantasise about where in London she lives. I stretch my legs out in front of me, my feet resting on an upturned crate. I take another slurp, imagine her here drinking tea with me, sitting astride me, running my hands over her, playing with her breasts, stroking her legs.

My thoughts both shock and excite me. I feel a stir between my legs. I haven't experienced the sensation for years. My heart pounds in my chest. My mouth floods with saliva and within seconds I'm hot, too hot. I can't believe the effect this woman is having on me, and I want to know her, all of her. I want to "talk" with her but, checking my phone again, I'm disappointed.

I read for twenty minutes. Still no message. I feel let down yet, gazing at her profile picture, I feel another stir. I'm surprised the flaccid, useless thing even has a flicker of life all of its own. I'm excited to the point where I want to run around the garden, well run as best I can with my walking stick, and scream, *my cock is alive*. What is happening to me?

In my head I'm racing down the street waving goodbye to this half-existence. I don't have the answer to where I'm heading but I'm free; free of responsibility, of behaving in the right way, of having the right thoughts. But realisation hits me. I don't have the courage to change or leave Sandra or my job. My whole life is embedded here; in this house, this shed, in Inverness. I've had no other life. I'm getting carried away. I don't have it in me to do anything so erratic but part of me yearns to do something shocking, daring.

My dad's passing in August, five months ago, has left me contemplating my life and that of my parents. They too followed life in a straight line; predictable, unexciting. They lived in the same house all their life, Dad held down the same job as an insurance broker and my mother as a school dinner lady.

I'm struggling against the impulsive urge to break free; to do something radical and end the cycle of rigidity and expectedness. Dad's inheritance means I have the opportunity to live differently than before. I now have more money than I ever dreamed of.

This is what's unnerving; I want this "new" life not to be about carrying on; I've always bowed to convention and wonder what, if anything, I might dare do differently. Become a pilot, join a drama group, disappear on holiday on my own. Disappear altogether.

I realise with a jolt, years of resentment and regret have seeped into the walls, proof of happier times can only be glimpsed in the photographs littering the house.

I undo my jeans. A thought, long buried and long forgotten, pushes itself with severe clarity to the front of my mind, in full-blown colour. I shift in my chair, trying to control my urge to fondle myself. I slip my hand under the waistband of my boxer shorts. I'm nowhere near even semi hard compared to a normal man but I feel stiff all the same. I close my eyes, massaging, imagining. My phone pings. I pull out my hand, heat filling my face.

Enjoy.

The word courses through me — a lover's poison — and I feel dizzy with exhilaration. Enjoy. The message is a double entendre for me; enjoy touching my penis or enjoy my tea. What would she think if I told her what I'm doing? I think about how to respond.

Thank you. How are you?

I rest my hand over my thumping chest. Can she ignore my question? I reposition a few books on the shelf to tidy it, continue reading, and after an hour, just as I'm beginning to lose heart, my phone pings.

I'm good thank you Alexander. I hope you are too.

Reading one of my favourite poets, Betjeman. Do you

know him?

No. I will Google him.

He's written poetry and books on different parts of the country. I'm reading the one on London right now. Which part of London are you from?

Not far from the West End.

I've visited Hampstead and Highgate over the years. And the west end.

Lovely parts of London. I hope you have a nice evening.

I read through the thread over and over. She's being cautious. I suppose I could be anyone. How can I reassure her?

I drink my tea, now cold but I finish it anyway. I read on, copy and paste a poem from the internet and send it to her.

"When melancholy Autumn comes to Wembley
And electric trains are lighted after tea
The poplars near the stadium are trembly
With their tap and tap and whispering to me…"

This is a bit of a Betjeman poem. you probably recognise the place he mentions.

'Alec! Alec!'

'Yes?' I ask, sticking my head out of the shed door.

'Shall we do dinner? I'm getting hungry.'

'Coming. Give me five minutes.' I shiver against the icy

cold and my words disappear into a swirl of condensation in the chill.

'Well, don't take too long.'

I let the door bang against her drifting words, shut out the world and imagine a restaurant, having dinner with Maria. Our food is arranged on white gilt-edged plates framed with polished silver cutlery. She smiles; a gleaming white, infectious smile which leaves my knees trembling.

***

'I'll prepare dinner. You put the telly on,' I say, wanting to be alone.

Leaning onto the worktop for extra support, I peel and cut potatoes for roasting. The television blares and she's having a cigarette; the nicotine wafts, clogs my nostrils, the milky white spuds seem to change colour with the putrid smell.

'I wish you wouldn't smoke in the house,' I call. 'You never did while Callum lived at home… you could afford me the same courtesy.'

She's watching her favourite quiz programme, hollering out the wrong answers. I call out a correct answer; she pretends not to hear me. I call out another and again there's no response. I pull the kitchen door shut and turn on the radio; BBC Radio Scotland. There's a discussion about great Scottish albums.

I think about music and the words of different songs and the messages they send out. I'm not a dancer. Dancing is difficult with two left feet and even more so with my legs; jerky movements, muscle tightness, joint stiffness. Without the aid of my walking stick I'd lose my balance and cause myself serious injury.

It's part of my every day but not hers. Would Maria be

put off?

I chop red onions and slice tomatoes. An interview with a Scottish author, Jackie Baldwin, replaces the music. I drift in and out of the conversation… '*Gosh, that's a hard one,*' she says, when asked about her inspiration. '*I would have to say Jane Austen because she focuses not only on the action, but on the feelings of the character, which is the way I like to write, the way I like to draw my readers in. As I started off writing monologues, I was also influenced by the playwright Alan Bennett…*' I latch onto her words, and I begin a monologue of my own with Maria. Attentive, her eyes search beyond me, as if peering into my soul, and heartfelt words spill between us.

Jackie continues, '*I don't have a writing routine as everything has to fit round my work…*' Her comment has me questioning when and where Maria writes. Does she have a little desk, or does she write snuggled up in bed? I will have to ask her.

'*It explores such themes as redemption and nature versus nurture and also explores mental illness through the eyes of the main character, DI Frank Farrell. He is my favourite character because he is very conflicted and not quite comfortable in his own skin yet has a strong moral compass.*'

I have mislaid my own moral compass of late. The fact it isn't working is liberating; a rebellious teenager enjoying the freedom from the rules, expectations and responsibilities forced upon him.

I feel suffocated; out of nowhere an inexplicable fury surges through me. I lose concentration.

'Damn.'

'What's wrong?' asks Sandra flinging the kitchen door open.

'Almost chopped my bloody thumb off.'

'I hope you haven't bled all over the chopping board.'

'My thumb's fine. Thank you, sweetheart.'

Within seconds her tone softens. 'Shall I carry on while you get a plaster?'

***

We eat dinner at the kitchen table in near silence, broken only when Sandra twice asks whether I put salt in the salad dressing. I shake my head, not trusting myself to answer. We share a bottle of red wine; it's a good one, a Merlot, but it leaves a sour taste in my mouth. Sandra hacks into her steak, her chewing loud. Her mouth moves in a continuous washing machine type motion. I've stopped finding her mouth attractive. When did we last kiss?

I cut into my steak, cooked rare. How does Maria like hers? Or is she a vegetarian? I'll have to find out.

No sooner than I have taken my last bite Sandra clears the table and washes up. She's already asked about a dishwasher, now we have the means, and the thought of her spending Dad's inheritance riles me.

I tip the last dregs of the wine into my glass and in the front room, mute the telly. I'm not interested in the television. I'm on Twitter. There's no response from Maria, my heart drops. I hope she liked the poem. I browse my feed and ♥ two tweets; a painting by an Edinburgh artist of a caricature couple in bed surrounded by cats and another of yachts on the River Clyde.

Caramel, her sunrise-orange coat shining, appears at my feet; her meowing reprimands me for ignoring her. I lean forward and pat my lap; she springs onto me and buries her head under my arm, her purring soft, her body warming my thighs.

'You're my pwincess aren't you Caramel? Aren't you girl?' I rub her under the chin, and she stretches before settling. Her closeness, her weight, conjures up a vision of Maria's head in my lap, me stroking her long dark hair. I scroll through her tweets.

I read somewhere you are never too old to set another goal or to dream a new dream.
There's a beautiful picture of a woman in a sundress with her arms stretched wide either side of her as she faces a russet setting sky.

I ♥ it and I send her a message.

Hello Maria. How are you?

Hello Alexander. Good thanks.

I imagine you working at your little desk, a real Virginia Woolf.

Nowhere quite so nice I'm afraid. And thank you for the poem. How are you?

You're welcome. I'm fine thank you.
Watching telly with Caramel.

That's nice. I'm not a cat person. Or a dog person. We have a house bunny called Fluffy.

I feel my heart constrict. Who's "we"? Does she have a husband, a boyfriend? I want to ask her but refrain.

My son had a rabbit years ago, but it escaped the confines of his hutch and sadly my son has left home now too.

I kick myself for not asking her a question. Sandra comes in holding two steaming mugs.

'Here you go, your posh green one.'

'Thank you.' I give her a shaky smile.

'What shall we watch tonight or are you going to be on your phone and iPad? I might as well not be here.'

'I can still talk to you.'

'Go on then,' she snaps.

'Well, what do you want to talk about?' I ask with enforced optimism. Without Callum to entertain us we have little in common. Did we ever? I struggle to recall the last time we had a conversation, a proper conversation, about anything other than chores and cooking and cleaning and taking out the rubbish.

'You're hopeless. I might as well be sitting here on my own.'

I feel the same, but don't say anything.

Caramel stirs in my lap and yawns, she licks at her paws and rolls out a long purr. At least you love me, I think, as my fingers ruffle her ginger coat.

I continue browsing Twitter, refusing to dwell on Sandra's words. After a few weeks I'm addicted. It's a great way to fill time, fill the gaping silence that dwells between Sandra and me. It's always existed and connecting on Twitter has further accentuated the growing expanse of nothingness between us.

She's flicking through a magazine, her stockinged feet tucked under her and her skirt has inched above her thigh revealing a ladder in her tights. I find the translucent white of her skin, through the tear, arousing. She might let me tonight. Let me play with her until she comes; long enough for me to imagine I'm with Maria. I can't do anything else and though she doesn't satisfy me nowadays, I have this niggling, smouldering urge.

She's always shied away from what I want, needed coaxing to experiment; not interested in satisfying me.

On the one or two occasions, years ago, after my pathetic failings at getting and sustaining an erection I broached the subject of what might satisfy me since I couldn't make love to her. At first, she made the effort; though she made it plain to me she didn't enjoy anything I wanted to do. She tolerated it until one night she told me to stop being disgusting, accused me of being obsessed with "it" all the time.

Her reaction shamed me; made me feel perverted – reached up and strangled my throat. In the end, her lack of interest fostered in me a justification to ignore my condition, be ashamed of it, and her disinterest became a convenient scapegoat for my own hang-ups. It mattered less, and then it mattered lesser still.

Sandra's lack of sexual appetite has gone from being a blessing since I can't, to an absolute frustration since my acquaintance with Maria. Maria has heightened my sexual awareness, created a forceful, rising tide which I seem to have little control over. Sex is a part of me I yearn; something I miss. Something I crave.

When I glance back at her she's adjusted her skirt, so she's covered. The lit table lamp casts a warm glow softening her otherwise harsh facial features.

'Shall we go to bed, sweetheart?' I say.

'It's not even ten o'clock yet.'

'Well, we could have a cuddle.'

'I'll follow you up.'

I utter nothing more; afraid she might reconsider. A mess of remnant thoughts fill me. I ease myself from the settee; I coax Caramel away from my feet and she lets out a sharp meow. My back's stiff but I don't refer to it. I don't want to give Sandra any excuse to change her mind.

What I need is to lie on my stomach and do the Superman exercise; arms extended in front of me, arms up, palms down with both feet raised. But even this is near impossible for me to do alone. Sandra has long removed herself from my physio regime.

Upstairs I brush my teeth, insert my catheter; another aspect of my disability I endure though in many ways it has its advantages. I sit on the loo for a few minutes. Do I have the urge to empty my bowels?

In the bedroom, having undressed, I wrestle with the urge to not fold my clothes, to drop them to the floor, but not wanting to annoy Sandra, I arrange them just as she likes me to. I lean back into the pillows and have one more peek at Twitter.

Sandra shuffles to the bathroom; the pipes' usual gurgling echoes through the silence of the empty house. Without Callum our home feels soulless; cold bricks and mortar and the claustrophobia of suburban conformity closes in on me ever tighter. The settledness sits heavily on me… it just happened that way.

#Love is a word people use too easily, be sure of its meaning, the feel of it.
A black and white photo of a couple kissing stares back at me.

The tweet from Maria causes me to stir again. I ♥ it and add:

'Sadly true… but #love can be a wonderful thing with the right person.'

An urge overwhelms me, a burst of endorphins. I want Intimacy, I want sex. Maria makes me feel like this. Makes me want this.

Sandra's plodding draws closer along the landing. I place my phone face down on the bedside table. Our sex is nothing like it should be between two people, but I have resigned myself, over the years, infrequent and routine, is better than nothing and I have always hoped it might lead to more, something more fulfilling and exciting.

The smell of Sandra's last cigarette follows her into the bedroom. I ignore my vibrating phone.

4
Alexander

I grab the car keys and pull on my coat. My shift doesn't start for another hour but I'm keen to get away from the claustrophobia of being at home. Work is my refuge, my sanity. I put in three full days a week and an overnight shift every Thursday and every other weekend.

Danny, the twenty-nine-year-old I supervise, has a mental age of an eight-year-old but he's harmless, and having worked with him for the past ten years, he's comfortable around me and less likely to go off the rails. We have our daily routine and although it's not difficult work the hours, at times, stretch out with the slow pace of his life; nothing is ever done in a hurry.

However, my job suits my capabilities and my physical limitations so I'm not complaining. Working in a busy or stressful role which requires quick thinking and juggling a number of different projects would be difficult for me. I am forgetful, can occasionally get confused and take more time than most to process things. I'm not an Olympic runner or thinker; Danny's stride fits in with my own physical and intellectual pace.

The rain seeps through my coat and trickles down the back of my neck. Big drops smatter my glasses. My walking stick clatters against the door frame as I pull it into the car.

I've left my phone. Damn. A few weeks ago, it wouldn't have bothered me, but now… with Maria…

By the time I fetch it I'm wet through to the skin and exhausted. My lips tremble. My body cannot deal with rushing well, my breaths fast, shallow. A burning sensation fills my lungs.

Fifteen minutes later, I park outside the Highland Hope Centre. I raise my foot off the brake; a stabbing pain shoots up my leg.

It's less dreich here though it's only a few miles from home; the thrashing rain has lessened, replaced by a wet drizzle.

I clock in and let myself into Danny's ground floor, two-bedroom, self-contained flat. The three storey building houses five special needs adults.

'Hello, Danny,' I say, shaking the rain from my hair.

'Hello,' he calls back.

'Hi, Alec,' says Pete, the other carer I share Danny's Care Plan with.

'Having coffee, are we?' I ask, shrugging off my wet coat, propping my cane against the chair. The thick dark roasted coffee aroma hits my nostrils. Danny would drink coffee all day if we let him.

Pete nods in his direction. 'Last one of the day, we agreed didn't we Danny?'

'Last one of the day,' Danny answers, as he gulps the hot

gooey liquid. It reminds me of wet tar.

'Right, the handover paperwork is done. Gosh is it already half two?' Pete files it away and grabs his jacket and satchel. 'Sorry I can't stop and chat, I'm meeting the wife and my stepdaughter, shopping for university,' he shouts over his shoulder. 'Oh, and by the way, great tweeting.'

'Thanks,' I call out. He bangs the front door behind him. He's left his scarf hanging on the back of the chair. My energy is not enough to chase him. 'So Danny, what would you like to do this afternoon? We can still go swimming even with the rain.'

'Last one of the day,' he says.

'Aye, finish it and go pack your swimming bag. And don't forget your goggles and shower gel.'

He goes off and I'm tempted to do the washing up but I'm here to support Danny not do his chores for him. Over the years I've learnt to step away, to stop myself. I sit down at the kitchen table with my tea.

I pull my phone from my coat pocket and my heart races thinking about Maria. What are her eyes like behind her sunglasses? I imagine they're dark to match her black hair and olive, rosy-warm complexion.

I browse my feed and read her tweets.

#Writing is easy. All I have to do is find the wrong words and cross them out.
A manuscript with red corrections all over it and a red pen.

Art enables us to find our true selves & then lose ourselves at the same time.
A woman in a floral summer dress, leaning against a wall full of graffiti, stares ahead of her.

I ♥ them. I squint, trying to read the words of the manuscript. This must be her own work, but the writing is too small. Should I add a comment? I don't rush. What to write? I reread the quote about art and write, 'Love enables to do the same to.' I've left out the word "us" and an "o". I haven't added any hashtags. Urgh.

'Let's get this done up right, shall we and we can head off.' I undo the studs on Danny's bomber jacket and press the first one, going from the bottom up, until it's fastened to the top. It's difficult to do, fiddly, my fingers are big and my small motor skills are clumsy. He smiles at me. His teeth are stained yellow. When did he last visit the dentist? I scribble a note to check his medical file as soon as we're back. I leave it on the table otherwise I will forget. I have a quick root through his bag checking he hasn't missed anything.

Heavy rain clouds move in the same direction as us. I pull my collar around my ears. I'm freezing. My coat is still damp.

Danny loves to sit on the bus's upper deck. I follow him up the narrow stairs, at a much slower pace, leaning onto my walking stick with one hand and the safety handlebar with the other. The bus jolts and I lose my balance for a moment, just managing to stay upright. I feel the pull in my hip.

I'm thankful for the vacant seats up front; Danny's favourite spot. The bus is unusually empty for this time of day and I'm relieved; the rain has kept people at home. Danny doesn't cope well with noise or people around him.

The swimming pool, part of the community leisure complex, is five stops away. I undo my coat; condensation trickles down the windows leaving a pool of water on the floor. The steamy damp fills my nostrils, and my neck is clammy. My hand hurts; I'm clenching my cane.

'We're here. We're here.' Danny jumps: the red brick building looms up ahead of us and he presses the bell at least six times. This is the bus we most often catch, on the same Thursday of every week, and the driver always allows for Danny's behaviour.

Danny gets changed, for the most part unaided, and he folds his clothes and puts them in the locker. He has the same locker every week. It's always available. It's in the last row at floor level and boasts a scuffy dent from a kick. I can't fathom why Danny uses it, but I suppose it's easy for him to recognise it in the rows of identical lockers.

Danny lowers himself into the shallow end, his armbands giant orange octopi. So much for being unencumbered and free. I give him a wave. He adjusts his goggles and pushes himself off the side. He whoops with joy as he jumps up and down; water spraying the old lady close behind him. She tries to move away from the relentless splish-splashes. Danny's excitement gets the better of him; he's oblivious to the shriek of the lifeguard's shrill whistle.

'Danny,' I say, walking towards the pool's edge, 'be careful. You almost drowned the lady with your splashing.' I lean on my walking stick, careful not to slip on the wet tiles.

'And that's one of the most identified with Game of Thrones character,' he says, repeating the phrase he's heard with possibly no clue as to what it means.

He laughs but stops as I give him a stony look. It's enough to calm him.

'Do your laps and if it's stopped raining, we can go for a hot chocolate after.' I mouth an apology to the old lady as she navigates the metal rungs of the step ladder out of the water.

'Oh, don't you worry. Let the wee lad enjoy himself,' she chuckles and disappears towards the changing rooms with surprising nimbleness.

Danny looks a lot younger than twenty-nine; his baby face and slight build lead people to mistake him for a teenager. Part of me envies his energy, his joy; his innate imperfections and childish manner offer him an uncomplicated relationship with the world. I'm old and past my usefulness. I clench the walking stick and my fists turn white. I want to throw it away.

I retreat to the side lines again and Danny swims his lanes calling out *1, 2, 3,* as he completes each one. He does his usual ten laps. It takes him about three minutes to do a lap; our session lasts at least an hour by the time he changes, swims, showers and dresses again.

***

Danny checks his duty rota pinned on the fridge and loads the washing. His mouth has a brown sticky chocolate ring around it; evidence he enjoyed the hot chocolate.

I sit at the kitchen table and go through his care plan folder noting his next dental check-up is not due for another three months. I screw up my note, discarding it in the bin.

The regional manager, my boss, is visiting next week and I want to ensure the file is in order. Pete fails to keep it up to date so I mark in pencil where his initials are required to sign off activities and medication administered.

There's a section for each area of care and development based on Danny's needs and choices. There's a detailed list of the type and level of support we provide him with in relation to his everyday tasks, like domestic duties and budgeting, as well as his social and recreational activities, of which there are only two, swimming on a Thursday and the gym on a Friday. He dislikes change and his routines are set like clockwork, as is Magna Carta.

The supported living is supposed to encourage and motivate the Dannys of this world to increase their independence, confidence, and self-development, as well as keep a level of personal choice and control over their lives and priorities. His parents have a say in the rare occurrence there is ever a dispute or disagreement, but Danny, compared to other disabled and special needs adults my colleagues supervise, is a more capable patient.

'Danny, watch what you're doing.' He overfills the detergent compartment. I tut and signal towards the dustpan and brush. He kneels, making wide sweeping gestures, creating more mess than he does tidying up, but I let him get on with it. 'It's the best you can do, mate.' I hold the top of the bin open for him and he empties the remnant washing powder granules into it.

He presses the on button and the washer-dryer whirrs into action. 'You can watch television for an hour before it's time to prepare dinner.'

I sit in the living room with him but don't pay much attention to what's on, sit with my iPad on my lap.

'And that's the most identified with Game of Thrones character.'

'Very interesting Danny,' I say.

Maria hasn't reacted to my comment. I hesitate for a split second and press send.

Hi there Maria. How's your writing going?

Good thank you. Planning my new story.

Do you have a theme yet?

Different relationships between people.
Why people stay together when they shouldn't.

Interesting topic.
Is it based on your personal experiences?

'Danny, time to get dinner prepared. Turn the television off. What are you cooking?'

'Carrots and broccoli. Fish fingers and boiled potatoes.'

'Righty-ho. Go and get prepping. And don't forget to wash your hands first.'

I bring my attention back to my iPad but there's no reply. Damn. Does she think I'm being weird? I shouldn't have probed about her experiences.

The vegetables are sitting in a pool of water. Danny frowns in concentration chopping the carrots into uneven sized discs and trimming the broccoli. He leaves half the broccoli heads behind with the fat stalks but at least he's preparing the veg on his own. I stand near him. He's not allowed to use a knife without supervision. He splashes cold water over the knife and places it on the drainer.

He lines six fish fingers on the rack and slides it under the grill. He tips waxy new potatoes into a saucepan, scrapes the carrots and broccoli into the same pan and covers them with water. He's forgotten to boil the kettle, but I don't mention it, not wanting to upset him. I know what it's like to be forgetful.

He clutters laying the table.

I pull out my vibrating phone from my pocket.

No, just observations of friends and family who have stayed with their partners despite not getting on and being miserable, though not being with someone can be miserable too.

It upsets me to think of you as being unhappy.

I'm not unhappy, just not in my happy place.
But I have a lot to be grateful for.

If I'm honest I think I'm one of those people.

Unhappy or with someone you're miserable with?

Both maybe. Though I've never admitted it until now.

Why?

I hesitate not sure how much to tell her, how much about my condition. I don't want to frighten her off, yet I want to be honest with her. She's opening up to me and I feel an intimacy between us. A surge of frustration comes at me, and I'm upset at the thought she might pull away from me. What should I do?

I decide to be open, after all, I reason, she will sense it if I hide things and I will lose her trust.

My marriage, my lack of confidence, my health issues.

I'm sorry.

My heart swells at her response. I send her a photo of me, Sandra and Callum; I'm wearing my grey suit at my cousin's wedding.

What a handsome family.
You're tall. Bet you walk fast.

Thank you, you're too kind. I had a playground accident when I was four. walking is difficult, I'm affected from the waist down. but I drive an automatic and have been risk assessed by my employers.

I'm gutted there's no reply. My stomach tightens in knots. I go over different reasons to contact her again but can't find any and there are no new tweets from her for the rest of the evening. My thoughts drive me crazy. Is she married? Is she unhappy in her marriage or unhappy because she's not? She hasn't yet mentioned anyone. I hold onto the hope she's not in a relationship.

5
Alexander

I wake before the alarm on Friday morning. I rub the sleep from my eyes; wait a few seconds to adjust to the hazy morning light. There's little difference between the obscurity outside the window and the darkness of my room. The rhythmic ping-ping of the rain is soothing as it bounces off the pane.

Good morning maria. I woke thinking of you.
And I'm smiling.

The groan of the power shower pounds in my head. I place my towel over the radiator, checking the water is running hot before standing under the spray. The shower at Danny's is perfect for me; I don't have to step up into it which means I don't have to step down out of it which is difficult for me; my balance tips the wrong way.

As the water flows over me, I lose myself in thoughts of Maria, hoping there will be a message back from her when I suddenly panic. I tweeted it instead of sending it as a message. It'll be on show to everyone. Damn it.

The banging on the bathroom door mirrors my own agitation. It's unlike Danny to be out of bed this early. How long ago did he wake up?

'I need the toilet,' he says.

***

In my bedroom, I get dressed; jeans, a clean shirt, which I put on unironed. Sandra isn't around to fuss about the creases. I grab my favourite woollen jumper and slide into my slippers, putting my hand on the wall to keep my balance.

'I don't feel well,' complains Danny, appearing in the kitchen doorway in his underwear.

'Well, I'm not surprised. You'll catch your death. Go and put your clothes on man.' I try not to laugh at the Homer Simpson pants he's got on back to front. 'I'll make tea.'

'Coffee,' he says.

He disappears to his bedroom, and I wait for him to return before saying, 'If you have coffee now you can't have one at the café after the gym.'

He shoves a slice of thick white in the toaster, waits impatiently for it to pop. 'Okay,' he mumbles, munching on his toast, scattering crumbs. The fluorescent light flickers every few seconds, making me nauseous. Despite going to bed ahead of time I feel sleep deprived.

'Did Pete log this in the maintenance book at reception?' He doesn't register what I'm pointing at or saying.

'Right, we'll do it on our way out this afternoon,' I say.

I scribble a reminder to myself. 'Now go and strip your bed and let's get your sheets washed before we head to the supermarket. Then all your laundry's done for this week.'

I pour from the pot, the tea's stewed but still hot. I check my phone. It's 7.13am. Has Maria seen my public message? How embarrassing… again. I guess she can't have missed it. Two people have liked it already. At least I didn't tag her in; no-one will guess who Maria is.

Success comes in cans not can'ts.
Quote chalked on a simple old-fashioned school black board.

My heart drops a little. She has tweeted this morning but not made any contact with me. Maybe she doesn't want to get involved; maybe she hasn't seen my very public message. Or maybe she is teasing me with her tweet. I reread it and I feel like she's talking to me. Yes, that's it. The tweet is meant for me. I imagine her saying, *you can Alexander*. I feel my temperature rise and push away my mug.

I ♥ her tweet and contemplate how to respond.

***

I leave Danny with his assigned personal trainer and wander to the in-house coffee shop and have a green tea which I am enjoying the taste of more and more. Sipping it brings me closer to Maria. I savour each gulp, imagining the taste of it on our lips as we kiss. Am I being a fool? Perhaps she's not thinking about me in this way.

I try to recall her earlier tweet but can't. I go back to my kissing fantasy instead; her lips on mine, her lips brushing my neck, my chest. A hot flush comes over me. Part of me wants to feel every bit of excitement but part of me, the sensible part of me, reminds me I'm at work.

I've always struggled to get my penis to function, understand it's the cerebral palsy, but I haven't always known this. I couldn't enjoy it how most men did, and it wasn't until I was fourteen, I knew something wasn't right.

I was at a house party with school friends. We'd all drank too much; gin, vodka, anything we could find in the drinks cabinet. A group of us disappeared into the back bedroom and dared each other to masturbate, have a wank. The first to come would get a quid off each of the others. There were six of us making the idea of a fiver too tempting to refuse. I masturbated so hard I thought I'd pull my penis off. I came at last, a trickle and everyone fell about in hysterics laughing at me. Hot and bothered and exhausted I dropped into a chair. I zipped up my trousers; my penis red raw.

'It's all the drink I've had,' I said, trying to conceal my poor performance but I laughed just as hard as they did, and I wet myself. The laughing almost burst my ear drums. I sat there in a warm puddle which became cold as they carried on with their jovial, but dirty, talking about their exploits with the willing Jeans, Charlottes and Beverleys of our school.

'Yeah, yeah,' they cajoled but it's genuinely what I thought. Well at least about the ejaculation and lack of erection. The wetting myself was just me. It's what I did for as long as I remember, and my parents didn't punish me for wetting the bed or for having an accident. Mum always carried a spare pair of pants and trousers for me, and it wasn't until I was in my twenties my mishaps embarrassed me.

The following week, at a local youth event in the church hall, Maureen, a lamppost of a girl, in the year above me, with thick-rimmed glasses and glossy long hair, persuaded me to go outside with her. We found an old bunker. I forced the rusty lock open with a rock and we disappeared inside. She kissed me and her horsey teeth grazed mine, but she carried on sticking her tongue into my mouth. I tried to do the same, but our tongues got tangled and jarred. I've never enjoyed kissing because of her.

This was my first experience of sex of being alone with a girl. I was excited by her warm breasts and the feel of her cotton panties as we fumbled around. Her face glistened with sweat and her body throbbed with sex hormones, but I couldn't get an erection. I should have been "rock, solid, hard", words I'd heard other boys use, but nothing... it didn't happen, and she accused me of leading her on and being drunk but I knew I wasn't. Not that night.

After the incident I avoided girls and spent more time listening to all my mates' tales about shagging. What was wrong with me? Was anything wrong at all? I couldn't speak to my parents about it. They always told me I was *special* and *not like those other boys with raging hormones*. But my hormones did rage only my penis didn't come along for the ride.

Instead, I spent a lot of time masturbating in the loo. I tried to get an erection and although I'd eventually ejaculate, I wouldn't come with a normal erection, not like my friends did or the men in the porn magazines we drooled over. I couldn't feel anything down there. Not like I could when I touched my bottom.

My bottom filled with a warm, tingling sensation and I liked it. Once, and only once, my dad hit me with his slipper; the pain, to feel, pleasured me. Years later, I tried to explain to Sandra how the sensation in my bottom excited me, but she wouldn't listen to any of it convinced I'd indulged in watching porn videos. She made me feel disgusting.

My mobile alarm goes off. Danny's session will be finishing in five minutes.

***

Danny flicks through the newspaper. He points at the football pictures with excited *oohs* and *aahs* which I respond to with wow and brilliant. He reads simple words, not whole sentences, and is therefore unable to share details about the actual articles. We're at the coffee shop opposite the bus stop for the gym. He prefers the coffee here; thick, gooey and he enjoys spooning the sugar from the pot on the table. He doesn't like the sachets at gym cafe.

There's no Wi-Fi connection and I'm itching to get back to Danny's. What if she messages and I can't respond? What if she thinks I'm ignoring her?

'Come on Danny, drink up.'

'We just got here.'

'We haven't and anyway you've the laundry to dry and your bed to make-up for tonight.'

'I don't want to.'

'If you don't you'll be sleeping on a bare mattress. It's your choice, but it is Friday.'

He jumps up. 'Friday. Cake, cake, cake,' he says.

***

'We got in just in time,' I say. A clap of thunder strikes overhead. Danny's unperturbed, too busy ticking off his afternoon chores, his eyes flitting back and forth to the plated iced bun on the kitchen counter.

Within minutes he's sprawled out on the couch with the

tray on his lap. He bites into the bun and the thick icing coats his upper lip giving him a white sticky moustache. He's a good man. And the truth is, without him and this job, I'm not sure I'd be worth much to anyone. John and Elizabeth and Callum don't notice I'm different, but I suppose that's part of the problem. I fade into the background; good old Alec doesn't argue, willing to please everyone.

My whole life and everything in it seems to emasculate me; CP has rendered me voiceless. Did I let it do that? Is how I'm feeling my fault? Have I let myself conform to a way of life expected of me? By my parents? Sandra? Callum? The medical professionals?

Sandra's become a nag. Alec do this… Alec do that… Alec when are you going to do this? When are you finishing that? She's like the old gramophone records my grandmother used to have with the arm and needle; jammed, it plays over and over again until the sound grates on your nerves and you want to scream.

I feel myself sinking, like a man in quicksand and I struggle to get comfortable against the sofa cushions, my mind overcrowded with claustrophobic thoughts… my ability to make decisions… ability to take responsibility… ability to accept mistakes… ability to recognise the truth.

I glance at the pile of paperwork I still have to complete before the end of my shift; the tick boxes meant to highlight Danny's abilities and strengths seem to brutally expose my own flaws and failures.

6
Alexander

Having collected the dry cleaning, I wait in the car for the downpour to abate; even with the wipers on double speed my vision is impaired. The rain drops trail down the windscreen like fat beads of mercury. I pull my phone out of my coat pocket. Maria's tweets jump out at me.

Your only limit is you.
A woman with her arms raised in triumph above her head is standing at the top of a mountain looking beyond the valley below.

Just saying… What are you waiting for?
A woman is staring straight into the camera, winking.

All you need is love… and a tiara.
A sparkling jewelled tiara on a pink background.

I send her a quick message making sure it's a direct message this time.

Good afternoon Maria. How are you?

I think about those words on the screen, mocking me, teasing my choices. What have I been waiting for? And have I been waiting for it all my life? I've used my life to offer excuses and build obstacles where possibly no obstacles existed at all, but stepping stones to a different life, had I behaved differently. I wait fifteen minutes. No reply. The disappointment I feel is disproportionately great. I almost cry. I turn the key in the ignition; my escape from reality is receding the closer I get to home.

I swing onto the drive. It's a tight squeeze but I nudge the car back and forth until it's parked, leaving me room to swing my door open. My phone pings. Twitter alert. I put it on silent, in case I forget when I get in, not wanting to arouse Sandra's suspicions.

Hello Alexander. I'm okay thank you.
Hope you are too.

My mood changes in an instant and soars in the most indefinable way. She doesn't mention the tweet on my feed. Perhaps she hasn't seen it. My pulse quickens and a sense of euphoria envelopes me. I imagine myself skipping across the drive, twirling dance steps around my walking stick, singing Zip-a-Dee-Doo-Dah and the image warms me.

Yes. Home from work.
Pouring with rain, grey and miserable here.
How's your writing going?

Okay, thanks. Planning away.

You're dedicated working on a Saturday. I'm off now till Tuesday morning.
Long weekend.

If I don't do it no one will do it for me. Have a good weekend.

True. You too Maria.

'You're home at last. It's almost six o'clock. Your shift finished ages ago.' Sandra peers out into the hallway from her usual spot, slouching in front of the telly; it's all she seems to do since she stopped working on the grounds of stress. A tetchy annoyance grates my skin.

At first, I was supportive. She enjoyed her position as a bookkeeper but after the new senior clerk pulled her up on two mistakes panic attacks set in.

As time went on Sandra dug her heels in; she brushed aside anything I suggested as a way of moving forward and I grew tired of her complaining. In the end she went off sick and stayed off; four months now. It's not healthy for her and not healthy for me either.

Sandra accepts no criticism, constructive or otherwise, and she has always fought against authority. It's as if her strict upbringing, of abiding by the rules, has pushed her to the other extreme where, as an adult, she has to question everything, unless it suits her, and she is gauche in voicing her views.

'I had to collect your dry cleaning, sweetheart or did you forget?'

'Don't be sarcastic, Alec.'

'I'm soaked through. Going to get changed.'

'Don't leave your coat down here, hang it over the bath. I don't want drips all over the carpet.'

'Yes, sweetheart. Has the local paper not been delivered?'

'It was wet, poking half-way out of the letter box in the rain. I threw it away.'

'It would have dried quick enough.'

'It was soaked through…'

Upstairs I forget about reading the local paper which I like to do. I suppose I can check their Twitter news. Twitter. I'm drawn back to Maria's *your only limit is you* tweet. It's a simple statement and it is terrifyingly true. I'd not thought much about limits beyond my CP before now, before Maria.

I hope I didn't scare you off talking about my health. You seem like a good listener.

Scare me? No, should I be scared?

No not at all and recently I realise my disability is a bigger part of me than I admit. It's defined me all my life.

I imagine it has.

And I can't talk to my wife about how I feel.

Why not?

She shies away from those uncomfortable conversations.

Why? You've been married a long time, no?

Can I tell you something about me you may not have worked out?

My heart's racing but it's now or never. If I don't tell her, there's no point in any of this. Whatever this is, I have no idea, but she's got under my skin. I want her to know and hope she will understand.

I already know.
You tweeted instead of messaging me.

Oh, gosh so you noticed. I think I was still asleep.
Sorry. No, I have cerebral palsy. From the waist down.

Don't worry. I've made the same mistake before.

It's a strain. On me. My marriage.

I'm sorry.

It is. Our relations are not good.

Do you mean sex?

I have ED. I can't get an erection.

Well intercourse isn't the only relations you can have Alexander.

A hot spasm twitches in my groin. A bulge of sorts appears in my trousers. I'm ecstatic she hasn't told me to go away and the fact she's talking about relations other than intercourse excites me. Would she be open to a man going down on her?

'Alec! Alec! John and Elizabeth are coming over later. I said we'd do drinks

and nibbles. Hurry up, let's get to the supermarket. What are you doing up there?'

'Coming, sweetheart.'

I change my jeans and put on a pair of purple chinos. Sandra hates them, says I remind her of a grungy student. I want to annoy her.

Maria's responses and our conversation have unlocked new possibilities and ideas inside me. I don't want to be around Sandra, around her ordinariness, her everydayness, her predictableness. I don't want to be around John and Elizabeth either. Their lives are stiflingly suburban and strait-laced. Like me, I realise. Strait-laced too until now, I am changing. Sexual excitement is awakening in me, and I want more of it. Am I having a crush? Like a petulant hormonal teenager, I want more of what was charted as out of bounds... until now. With Maria things might change. A wave of change vibrates around me and in me. It's not just the sex.

It's how I now see my life can change though I'm guilty too of wanting to please Sandra how she needed to be satisfied over the years. I've become less imaginative, less daring in our "love-making".

My laziness now haunts me in the guise of sex on a repeat prescription; sex to a set routine, like the pharmacist who hands me my catheters, and diabetes pills, once a month. I want more than the perfunctory, marital once a month fumbling sex with Sandra who refuses to understand me or satisfy me the way I crave to be.

***

We assemble in the kitchen. I shakily transfer the sausage rolls and mini pizzas from the oven to the plates set out on the counter; the topic of my messages with Maria goes round and round in my head.

'Here, let me,' Sandra says, taking the spatula from me.

'It won't stay on the plate long enough to look pretty,' says John, popping the bottle of champagne he's brought with him. I have no idea what we're celebrating but I join in the merriment and our evening kicks off with a bang. The cork flies off at hurtling speed towards a pink vase, a car-boot find, and smashes it. Champagne spills all over Sandra's just mopped floor and John leaves a trail of spilt nectar across it as he tries to catch the remaining liquid in the glasses.

'My apologies, Sandra,' says John.

'You've done me a favour, always hated it,' I smirk as I reach for the bucket and squeegee mop. He guffaws and steps back from Sandra who's already got the dustpan and brush out to sweep away the rose-coloured fragments.

'For goodness sake, John,' says Elizabeth. 'I'm so sorry Sandra. We'll be sure to replace it.'

'Please don't let her,' I whisper to John and his guffawing turns into a cough. I hand him a semi-filled flute of champagne and push him towards the front room before Sandra sinks into a sulk and ruins the whole evening.

My mood peaks and I'm glad of John's company; his mischievous humour, quite unexpected, is infectious. We push back into each end of the sofa and John stretches out his legs.

'What's happening with you?' he asks, emptying his glass.

'The usual. Work, home. You?'

'Pretty much the same. Life trundles on, right?'

I nod in agreement while inside I'm glowing and filling with everything Maria.

John continues, 'There's minor restructuring going on at the office, job roles changing, but it shouldn't impact on me too much. Haven't told Elizabeth. Don't want her stressing.'

'Have you met my wife, Sergeant Sandra?' I ask, shaking off an image of Maria wrapped naked in my arms.

'What are you saying about me?' Sandra appears carrying the two dishes of food. Elizabeth trails in behind her and proffers each of us a side plate, and a paper napkin folded into a triangle. The image of Maria dissipates. Elizabeth perches, a fat budgerigar, in her cobalt blue blouse, on the edge of the armchair and proceeds to pile four mini pizzas and three sausage rolls onto her plate.

'Just what a lovely host you are,' I say.

'We always enjoy coming over,' says John.

Sandra beams. When did she last smile the same for me? She catches me smiling and her stony expression replaces her smile in an instant. It reminds me of my mother who used to say, *you'll stay like that if the wind changes*. I think to myself it already has. When did that happen? She used to smile a lot more, I'm certain of it. I smile at her and she gives me a feeble smile back.

The women chat about the new hairdressers in town and what a shame it is the pound store is closing its doors. Sandra will be worrying about where to buy her discounted dusters and the potent air fresheners which suffocate the house with rose.

'The council's getting its knickers twisted about that Australian tycoon. Did you read it in the–'

'No politics or golf tonight, John. Let's keep it light, shall we?' Sandra butts in.

'Cigar old chap?' asks John, colouring at her rebuff.

Night is closing in and he's guzzled two glasses of champagne and a tumbler of whisky in less than an hour. It's going to be a long night.

'Don't mind if I do.'

'Not in here,' says Sandra. 'I can't stand the smell of cigar smoke. It gets into all the furniture and hangs onto the curtains.' Her cigarette smoke lingers, clinging onto the soft furnishings and the carpet like a stubborn ghost. She doesn't care. Hypocrite.

'We'll disappear for half an hour.'

John grabs the bottle of whisky and our glasses and follows me to the shed.

I switch on the heater and the light; a naked bulb hangs above us. John sits on the upturned wooden crate, and I slump into the armchair.

He fidgets around in the inner pocket of his jacket, removes two cigars. We light them easily; with the cigars toasted and the tips smouldering the smoke begins to rise and we both clasp our cigars between our lips.

John tops us up and we clink glasses.

'To a life lorth living,' says John.

'I'll drink to that.' I swig back the amber liquid. It burns the back of my throat. Maria fills my head. A thrilling surge stirs my groin. I fidget in panic, but John's too squiffy to pay me any attention.

'To a wife lorth wiving,' he says again.

'Bloody hell, mate. Pace yourself.' I heave myself out of my seat but lose my balance reaching to swipe the bottle from him. I nosedive. Fast. I don't even have time to cushion the brunt of the fall with my hands. I plunge into a pile of old garden tools. A pair of protruding rusty shears nips my forehead.

John's trying to haul me off the floor. I'm too heavy. My

balance is all wrong. I pull away and fall back down with a thud.

Blood gushes over my shirt and this seems to sober up John.

'Ouch.' He presses a greasy cloth to my forehead, and I break into weak laughter.

'You'll be laughing the other fide of your sace when Fandra sees you,' he slurs and raises his glass before taking another swill of whisky.

I get onto my knees and holding onto the table for support collapse into the armchair where I sit panting, breathless from the effort of pulling myself up.

John holds the cloth to my head again, pressing harder. The bleeding won't stop. I tug at the rag; it's turned crimson. I stare down at my palms; they're shaking.

'Sandra. Sandra. Alec's had a wee accident,' he calls, sobering up.

We stumble along the unlit path towards the house. I brace myself for Sandra's quarrelsome temper.

'What's happened?' Her voice has a soft edge to it but when I catch her eye she's fuming. She'll be upset I've ruined her little soiree and I don't blame her.

'I'm okay. Stop fussing.'

'Not sure,' mumbles John. His face seems to pale, and he vaults to the shed yelling, 'The cigars!'

'Don't set my man cave alight,' I call after him, my laughing quieter but uncontrollable, a combination of nerves and amusement.

'It's not funny,' says Sandra. 'You're going to need stitches. Elizabeth, what do you…?'

But Elizabeth's vanished. Her retching from the upstairs loo too loud to ignore; she can't stand the sight of blood. Laughter wells within me again but this time my head aches.

My breaths come shallow, quiet. What a night. I can't wait to tell Maria about it.

7
Alexander

'Finally awake?' A nurse pulls open the flower-patterned curtain around my cubicle. She doesn't look old enough to be out of school uniform. I adjust the slipping gown to cover my shoulder and pull myself into an upright position.

'Good morning,' I say, wincing from the stabbing stitch in my hip. I've slept in an awkward position.

'Can the kitchen staff bring you a wee cup of tea or coffee?'

'Tea please, thanks. White no sugar.'

I check the time. It's 8.07am. My coat is folded in the cubby next to me. Sandra must've put it there. I shake it out, feel both pockets. No glasses, no mobile. A panic rises in me; what if it's in Sandra's hands? What if she's seen Maria's messages? A heat rises in me. I convince myself that's unlikely, why would she and anyway it is password protected.

An overweight woman, an apron stretched round her middle, plonks a cup of milky tea on the bed tray and walks away. My stomach rumbles. Have I missed breakfast? I drink the tepid over-stewed tea in one go. It leaves a metallic taste.

Minutes later, I follow the nurse's directions to the toilets and bathroom holding the threadbare bath towel provided and my clothes. The water in the bath, no shower, is scorching. I manage a wash using the dregs of liquid soap from the dispenser. I don't have a toothbrush and rinse my mouth with water. I catch my steamy reflection in the mirror. I can't go to work patched up like this.

'I understand you had a knock to the head.' The consultant avoids eye contact. I fold yesterday's newspaper; I can't read it without my glasses. His eyes dart across the clipboard he's removed from the foot of the bed, and I nod as he mentions tetanus jab, normal temperature, blood pressure.

***

Sandra drives home and she tries to be sympathetic and kind and I, in turn, try to be patient with her. Her voice grates on my nerves. My mind wanders: what sort of voice does Maria have? In the end Sandra quits talking. I welcome the silence. She's concentrating on the road; it took her seven attempts to pass her test.

At the roundabout she dawdles and the driver behind us honks his horn. She tenses more; she stalls the car not once, but twice. At the traffic lights she's in the wrong lane to turn left and drives back and up again to turn right. By this point she's flustered, and I wait for her to blame me.

After numerous backward and forward jolts and turning of the wheel too far and not far enough, Sandra parks on the road; the tight swing onto our driveway too challenging for her. I find my phone in the kitchen. It's dead. The relief I feel is enormous.

Downstairs, after I shower and change into a pair of jogging bottoms and a T-shirt, Sandra pulls out a chair for me; she has made me a tea and a ham and pickle sandwich. A jolt of guilt stabs me. I turn my fully charged phone on silent.

'Nice shower?'

'Yes, thank you sweetheart.'

'I think she's missed you,' she says as Caramel sidles up and weaves between my legs.

'And you? Did you miss me?' I ask.

'You frightened me, Alec. What were you thinking?'

'I'm sorry. I tripped, lost my balance.'

'John and Elizabeth send their love. I think John's feeling rather sheepish,' she says with a little huff.

'We did get a little adventurous, I suppose.'

'The whisky had nothing to do with it?'

'Maybe a little.'

'You're so silly,' she says. Her face breaks into a grin.

'I know. And I'm sorry. We'll invite them over again soon. For dinner. I'll do my special chicken and mushroom lasagne. Promise.'

She squeezes my arm, and another prick of guilt consumes me. She's not all bad, I concede. I eat my sandwich in a bubble of warmth and comfort, something I haven't felt from Sandra in a long time.

'Do you feel okay?'

'Aye, but couldn't read the paper without my glasses this morning… where's the local one?'

'It's your turn to wash up.' Sergeant Sandra is back and the cosiness between us dissipates into the air which is cold again. That familiar ache for Maria replaces it.

She gets up and disappears into the sitting room, ignoring my question.

I scroll through a mass of tweets, Maria's included. I'm probably reading too much into what she's tweeted, but I want to know everything about her. I want to absorb her into my skin, into my soul. I want her to be a part of me. I reach for my bulge. I've missed her.

Great people do things before they are ready.
A man is stood at the top of a mountain.

Surround yourself with those who make you happy.
A group of women are sitting round a table chatting.

> *Good afternoon, Maria. How are you?*
> *I've read your tweets. You sound smiley.*

> **Hello Alexander. I am thank you. Hope you are too.**

> *I had a little accident but I'm OK.*

> **Oh no. What happened?**

> *Got a little squiffy and banged my head. I was in A&E.*

> **Do you mean drunk? Lol. Oh no!**

> *Yes, a bit merry.*

> **I hope your wife's looking after you.**

> *She is indeed. So, is your writing making you happy?*

It is, yes. Very.

Do you know what would cheer me right now?
Seeing your eyes. I've missed you.

I'm being daring. I like it. I stare at the selfie Maria's sent me. Her eyes, pools of mystery, black, seem to beckon me. Her skin has the same beautiful olive sun-tanned glow of her profile picture and the dark locks of wavy hair framing her round face fall past her shoulders. Her dress skims her left shoulder; I feel a stir at the sight of her bare skin. Is that a tattoo? I want to touch her, feel her and I'm suddenly warm, too warm. I want to feel her softness, drink in her complexion. I imagine us laying together her golden honey skin against mine, white and milky.

You're beautiful. Your eyes are just as I imagined them.

They are, are they?

You've given me a tingle.

Have I? You feeling oozy?

I don't know the word oozy but if it means turned on, then yes, I feel oozy.

Gosh. It doesn't take much does it? Lol.

Not around you, no it doesn't.

Well, I will leave you with your ooziness. I've got to be somewhere in half an hour and it's already 3. I hope you have a good day and get better soon.

A panic-like wave engulfs me; I don't want our conversation to end. Not now, not when she's baffling me with this bombardment of emotions, lust, attraction.

Are you leaving me like this?

Like what?

Your picture, your beautiful eyes and lips have ignited something in me.

I want to kiss those lips. Feel them on mine.

Stop it...

Kiss me.

Persistent, aren't you?
Sending you a kiss... Did you get it?

I am. I did. Those lips on mine. Hot. Wet. My tongue finding yours.

Glad you like my kiss.

My lips move over to your left shoulder. Kissing your soft skin, moving towards your breasts.
Maria, can I carry on? Do you want me to carry on???
I want you. Those eyes. Those lips. Your left shoulder.

Have you done this before Alexander?

No, never. I've played it safe for too long.

My cock twitches with each of her coaxing sexy words, the images she conjures up. I leave my tea. I'm trembling; every breath coming faster with each new message between us. My reaction to her is wonderful. Her reaction to me is wonderful. I'm in another world; something which hasn't happened to me in a long time, if ever. I want her like I imagine an addict craves his fix. I feel my whole body aching for her.

'Alec. The washing up isn't going to get done unless you do it. Your legs are still working even if you have banged your silly head.'

I'm annoyed at the interruption, though Sandra has pampered me with kindness since the accident.

'Yes sweetheart.' I grin at the word coming and in my head I'm cumming. With great effort, I compose myself, will the trembling to stop.

I post a tweet and hope Maria will notice it. It's bold. Not like me. I'm on fire.

Together is where we should be.

A shadowy couple are lying on a bed with silk sheets tangled around them.

'You're shaking,' Sandra says, returning to the kitchen. I prop myself against the sink as it subsides, eventually, but it leaves me weak. I feel a twinge of guilt as Sandra slips off her wedding and engagement rings, snatches the sponge out of my hand saying, 'Go and sit down, Alec.'

Within a few seconds she is splashing in the washing up bowl, the plates and cutlery clink as she stacks them on the draining board. We're rarely in the same room nowadays and when we are we're just two people in the same room; we don't share the space. There's nothing "common" in our being together. I recall the Venn diagrams we used to do at school where the circles overlap but there's no overlap with Sandra. Was there ever?

We met through a Sunday church group when my family moved from a quiet village in the north of Scotland to Inverness. It was how my parents integrated into their new community and the only social activity they engaged in. Sandra's family was there every Sunday too.

After a few months we found ourselves in each other's company after surveying each other from the relative safety of our parents' strictness.

'What's with the limp?' she asked the first time she spoke to me; she an awkward, fifteen-year-old and me four years older.

'I've got cerebral palsy. It affects the joints in my legs, my muscles.'

'And will it get worse? Your limp?'

'Likely. But not for a long time.'

After our first conversation I looked forward to meeting up again and we were given permission to wander off together in the old, rudely fenced cemetery, while our parents attended the after-service tea every fourth Sunday.

Then, for no apparent reason, her family stopped coming to church and after my initial shock I missed her less and less.

A few months later I saw her at the bus stop waiting for the No. 28. Her appearance had changed, especially her make-up. She had always worn too much of it according to her mother, but I always liked it, found myself second guessing what colour eyeshadow would adorn her lids. I liked the green and blue eyeliner with the flaunty flick and her signature red lipstick; a bold Sandra, much more than the other one-dimensional girls who didn't pay me any attention.

'My mum says you'd make a lovely husband.'

'I think you'd make a lovely wife,' I said.

'Your awkwardness has turned into kindness,' she said. 'You've got kind eyes. You'd be a good father.'

Three years later, our first ever sexual encounter, came to pass before we married; blundering hot and frustrating. She was in her early twenties, and I was nearly twenty-four. Her unnatural forthrightness shocked me, but equally excited me.

Sandra didn't seem to mind my inability to get, or hold, a proper erection. I penetrated her once; I mustered all my energy to masturbate myself into an erection and a pitiful trickle of semen dribbled out of me. She pulled me to her, pulled my penis into her and I lay there lost in her softness.

Finding out she was pregnant delighted me. Our wedding was rushed, family and friends, a small reception in the church hall. She chose an ivory satin dress with a high neckline and a matching lace veil. I wore a tartan kilt and frilly shirt, frilled front, frilled cuffs.

In those heady, early months she tried to please me but not with the same passion as the first time. The desire dissipated to the point I doubted her ever being so full of sexual energy. What she did do well was always remain in control. This exacerbated the fact that after that one time I had no control and couldn't bring myself to achieve any point of erection again.

The months and years went by and as if realising her fruitless efforts, she demanded less and less from me; at first a relief, but it emasculated me.

Once Callum was born, she became more controlling. It was as though her existence was based on conforming to being the ideal homemaker and mother. If it wasn't perfect, she fell into dark mood swings that lasted days, ran into weeks, until after almost a year, she found a happier equilibrium within herself and our family.

The two roles offered her something tangible she couldn't fail at. She tried hard at being a mother, though strict and often unbending, and I excelled at being the breadwinner, a doting father. This domestic ideology, this compliance with the outside world, helped us both establish a normality of sorts which we both came to be comfortable with.

'Does it bother you I can't? Not properly?' I asked her after Callum's birth.

'No why should it?' Her voice flat, hopeless, as though all her heart was drenched in unexplained sorrow and, in that moment, I wanted to look after her and love her. We didn't talk about it again.

I hark back now and stumble over the truth; it was a mistake. I shouldn't have let it go so easily. It was as if by doing so, I acknowledged and blamed myself for our lack of effort in the bedroom. It was as if we had both signed our fate of co-dependence. Had I not, we both might not be in this situation now. Sex is sparse and when we do, it's to a repeat prescription, the same timetabled routine.

No kissing, touching, caressing. She doesn't ask if I need to be satisfied or how I can be satisfied. It's as if my erectile dysfunction negates all my sexual desires in her mind. There's a clear lack of communication and communion between us and I'm angry too, guilt-ridden for letting my needs be ignored, to lie unspoken and dormant, for so long. My life is slipping by, like a car in neutral and I can't meander along in this mindless state anymore. I'm desperate and alone. For a split second I ask myself if Sandra is too.

But Maria— this frisson igniting us — is as real for me as if she is standing next to me and it's physical, my bulge is there. I can't ignore it though I've spent much of my life pretending it's not there. She makes me *feel*. The sex online is satisfying beyond belief; my body comes alive, the most alive it's ever felt.

I drink a glass of water with my diabetes pill. Diabetes is an added, though separate, complication to my CP, further exacerbating my erectile dysfunction. But the thought of me lying flaccid against Maria's thigh arouses me again; my bulge fills the space in the front of my trousers. A heat fills me.

'I'll put the kettle on, shall I?' She gives my shoulder a squeeze, a rare sign of affection, before turning her back to me.

Are you OK? Was that OK with me?

Why wouldn't I be? Are you OK?

Kissing you was incredibly exciting. It was all incredibly exciting.

It was for me too.

I tremble again. I'm bursting with happiness. Maria's my happiness. I feel like the luckiest man in the whole world.

'Alec.' Sandra's voice screeches in my ears. 'Did you want a green tea?'

'Yes, sweetheart.' The word sweetheart catches in my throat. I feel like I'm cheating on Maria. How can that be? How can I feel like that? How can she make me feel like that after being married to Sandra for all these years? Is it because the extramarital sex online with Maria compensates for, and surpasses, the strait-laced physical sex seldom had with Sandra? This is the boldest thing I have ever indulged in. I feel invincible.

At night, with Sandra asleep next to me, I put my hand inside my boxer shorts and close my eyes. I conjure up the picture of Maria, recalling every single detail, until something in me stirs and my cock responds. I squeeze it, willing it to stiffen. It doesn't. I imagine Maria on bended knees between my legs. It jerks against my grip. I imagine the top of her head as she bends towards it; the visual blows me away and I perspire. I'm shocked; it's lusty, dirty, not like me at all. The physical signs of my excitement are negligible, but my blood is pumping hard, I throw off my side of the duvet, a sudden heat smothering me. I imagine her thick, pouty lips round me as I hold it and eventually fall asleep.

8
Maria

I've planned a spa hotel break with three friends; the online offer, for the last week of February, with a whopping 60 percent saving on the full price, includes a beauty treatment. I deserve a pampering and look forward to the escape.

Natalie can't wait to organise a sleepover. I don't think there will be much sleeping though and, if her last sleepover is anything to go by, there will be too much take-away food and the awful rap music she listens to, but I'd rather she stay in than go out, get in at goodness knows what time. I just hope they don't neglect Fluffy who loves a cuddle.

In my bedroom, I distract myself, from thoughts of Alexander. I pack my overnight bag: underwear, toiletry bits, nightie, flip flops, a couple of magazines, notebook, and pen. I stash the bag behind my rocking chair, next to the built-in cupboard, and lie on my bed. The heating's clicked off. I wrap my dressing gown tighter.

Monday morning comes round, and the rush-hour traffic invades the relative quiet I enjoyed on Sunday. At eight o'clock on the dot, the drycleaners downstairs turn on their machines and their rhythmic tremor pulsates through the flat. I'm reminded of the time I used to dry clean my business suits every month. The thought prompts me to inspect my unpainted nails and tatty cuticles; the spa break can't come round quick enough.

I browse Twitter; my followers have grown overnight. I'm on 476 followers; determined to make this work, a wind of emotion hits me. I'm grateful for my part-time PR job in an economy which is shrinking fast, and thousands are unemployed. But I still have this dream to write full time, to be a proper writer. Maybe my time will come soon. I hold onto that hope.

I retweet and ♥ a few interesting tweets and add my own. I browse through my Kindle's downloaded images and pick two; the first is a silhouette of a young girl with her hands in the air, a pellucid sky around her, and the second of a woman, her hair in a topknot, her face hidden behind an old leather-bound book. She's sitting outside and the background is blurred but the sun is shining behind her.

Alexander's tweet catches my attention, and a titillating thrill runs through me. I'm surprised at my reaction. The flirting and sexting we've engaged in lacked any seriousness on my part, didn't it? He's tweeted, *I bought this in a charity shop. It's called The Orange Blind.*

I study it, enlarging it on my device. It's a picture of an old-fashioned sitting room or salon… there's a man writing at a small bureau with his back to us… a woman is sitting, stiff and upright on a chaise longue with a bolster cushion bearing a huge tassel at the end of it. She's ready for afternoon tea; the silver tea service is arranged on a low table covered in a white linen cloth; the crockery is white; a crystal chandelier hangs above her alit with candles.

The picture is cold despite the beautiful décor and furnishings. The man has his back to the woman, and she seems lonely despite his presence. A blind, at the room's floor to ceiling sash window, blocks the light making the room dark and gloomy. I add my comment, *Lovely picture Alexander... but sad how disconnected the two people seem with each other.*

I spend the next few minutes panicking, my comment sounds like criticism. I wish I hadn't sent it but recognise I'm trying to maintain a friendly but formal tone when tweeting publicly.

***

Walking home from my local supermarket I try not to fret about the £23.57 I've paid for a basket of groceries. I crave something sweet, something forbidden.

I make a tea and open the chocolate biscuits, Natalie's favourites albeit the cheap supermarket brand. I switch from TV channel to TV channel; blue, yellow, red light flickers, programmes about cookery, sport or pets. I turn on my Kindle instead, a message is waiting. I think about Alexander and a heady distillation of excitement surprises me, an intensifying sizzling lust.

It's a month or so since we "met". Is anything likely to happen in real life? How do online relationships work? I've not done anything like this before, other than the dick pic stuff, but he's still messaging me, and the attention is exhilarating. No strings. Just sex. It's perfect.

At first, I am inquisitive about his situation. What was it like for a man not capable of having sex, making love? I mean how would he keep things "alive"? Stupid question I suppose because there is so much more to sex than making love. I might be the one to cure him, though I don't know much about it. And there's the trust thing. Can I trust him? Is he who he proclaims he is? Would he lie for a few sex messages on Twitter?

I've browsed websites, obsessed with finding out more about erectile dysfunction and whether it can be cured by eating certain foods, watermelon and grape juice and walnuts and kale and even red chilli peppers. I've messaged Alexander and passed it all on and he's grateful for my support. His wife, he says, has never tried to help improve things.

I want to believe that by being turned on by me, my allure will excite him to the point of an erection. I make it my mission and want this for him. I recall all the partners I've had; imagine them not making love to me. Would I feel less loved if they couldn't? Would it make so much of a difference? I recall how sometimes it all went on for too long; found myself willing them to get on with it. I didn't always have the energy or the inclination for all the oohs and ahhs and the prolonged lovemaking from one position to another.

He's persistent and I like being pursued and wooed and desired; hiding behind social media emboldens me more than I'd be in real life. This might be less complicated than real life. He's not going to appear on my doorstep, is he?

Good morning Maria. How are you today?

I'm good thank you. You?

He sends me a poem; red roses whispering passion, white

roses breathing love... his love of words, his poetry, and his intellect, are attractive. I can't ignore him. And I don't want to ignore him though I'd feel uncomfortable if this was happening to Natalie. Social media and dating sites can be grounds for harassment and cyberbullying but this is not what's happening here. I feel excited about life and my new-found friendships.

I'm okay too. You're perceptive.

What makes you say that?

What you said, the two people being disconnected.

Oh right, yes. Don't you think so?

I do. That's how I feel with Sandra most of the time and it's getting increasingly worse.

I'm sorry. What are you going to do about it?

I'm not sure. But meeting you has made me feel alive again.

I don't know what to say... What would your wife say?

I don't know she'd even care. We hardly have anything in common anymore let alone spend time together, you know, proper time together.

I suggest doing more stuff with his wife but deep down I don't want him to be doing anything with his wife. I realise

I want Alexander all to myself. I want him to satisfy me the way he has already.

She's not interested in what I'm interested in and vice versa. It's been like this for a long time.

So what now?

*I don't know. All I know is I want to get to know you...
Properly.*

That might be a bit difficult with you in Inverness
and me in London.

*You make me want to get up early and stay up late... to
talk to you. I want to touch you.*

Really?

*Yes, you do that to me. I want to touch your skin,
Feel your lips on mine, undress you.*

But why?

*You're beautiful, you're intelligent, you're interesting.
You've got come to bed eyes and kissable lips.*

I don't know what to say to you.

*Say I can kiss your lips again, your neck, slip my hands
under your top, Inside your bra. Make you oozy.*

I find myself being drawn to his tone, his words. I don't

tell him to stop. This fantasy, or whatever it is, leaves me wanting more. What we're doing is safe, and risky all at once, and I like it, I like the tension, the secrecy, the danger. Will this continue between us? I admit I want it to. I am flirty in my messages. Where's the harm?

That's a yes then? Feel my fingers, my lips on your breasts, over your belly, between your legs, your secret place.

I lie back on the couch and lose myself in the feelings evoked by him, his words.

Are you OK? Tell me you're OK.

I sit up and try to compose myself but can't. I feel the wetness between my thighs. I've soaked through my knickers; me leggings are wet. A heavy sick sensation spins through me as I shudder with rippling, fizzing pleasure.

I read over our messages and can't believe how he "got" me again. This is the most sexual pleasure I've had in ages and, with no expectations or demands on his part for anything more, it suits me fine. Is craving adoration shallow? Does it matter if I like it too much? Despite my hasty impulse, and my doubts, an inexplicable elation floods through me again.

I'm yearning a physical, emotional, and intellectual connection not satisfied through my friendships. I'm not into casual sex and one-night stands making my willingness to engage in an online sexual thing with a man I barely know scandalous. It's not like me at all. But nothing shocks me anymore. Life has a way of tipping us near the edge again and again. This time I'm in control despite less money, less confidence, and a long-suffering and bruised ego.

Working for JangleJewels is convenient. It's eased me back into work. I have good, solid friends, who have supported me through my worst but there's still a broken piece, a missing piece. I want stimulating conversation; I want a partner who satisfies my mind and my body.

Twitter has presented more than two-way conversations about poetry and writing; I crave the experience now more than ever; to learn new things, to submit to new experiences and I want to feel and touch and taste and smell everything around me. I'm like a butterfly set free after being trapped in a child's nature jar for too long. This online thing with Alexander is an unexpected and welcome part of that; I can talk about my writing with someone who's interested.

My friend Fabio's words come to me, *You're full of wonder. You have this ability to fill everything with magic.* I suppose he's right. I see and feel the wonder, the newness in everyday things around me; how the sun filters in from behind the closed curtains, shadows dance on the pavement, birds flitter from one tree to another, a smooth pebble feels in my hand. Life hasn't eradicated the magic within me, my spirit.

I read through Alexander's messages again and my heart leaps, my senses sharpen. I feel every tingle within every part of me.

Alexander is teasingly erotic, energetic, exotic sensations run through me. I feel unashamed and yet vulnerable all at the same time with him. I want him to think he's in control. It's like I want to help him recompense for what he can't do by letting him control what he can do.

What sort of a woman won't put in the effort to strengthen their sexual relationship with their husband?

Alexander's vision of me evidently exceeds what he sees, and his attention is attractive; he connects with my mind.

His actions are forceful. His passion swells in me and it courses in my veins like sweet nectar fills a honeybee.

Are you OK Maria? Please tell me you are.

I think so.

In a good way or a bad way? You're wonderful. Xx

In a good way. How are you?

If you're OK I'm OK. In fact I'm more than OK. I'm totally ok with you. I feel alive. I feel happy. You make my heart soar. Xx

I do? I'm glad.

You do. And I'm glad too.

I'm all at once tired but full of energy. I zoom in on Alexander's bio pic again. I study his reddish face and mop of carrot hair, a straggly moustache, and a slightly unkempt beard. His pink shirt clashes with his complexion. I'm not a fan of facial hair; it always prickles but he's still attractive. He has these gentle eyes, understanding eyes, yet tense and brilliant, touched by his big smile. I try to recall his height, but I've deleted the photo of him and his family.

I can't deny the connection between us. I try to recapture my earlier mood; carefree, shameless joy. A wave of heady dizziness washes over me and I direct the energy into writing another chapter of my book; a first meeting between a much younger man and an older divorced woman.

My words flow as I free-write, and the eventual closing darkness alerts me to sit straight and stretch; writing for over four hours is draining. I vaguely remember Natalie running in, grabbing her folders for Tuesday's lessons, rummaging in my purse.

'I'm staying over at Yasmine's,' she called, rushing out again.

I recall the crazy rush around of after school ballet and Saturday morning gymnastics and the endless pottery painting parties which filled my calendar week after week. I miss doing stuff with her and I want to make a conscious effort to spend more time with her, another year and she'll be living away at uni.

Nat, it's Mum. You okay? Love you. Within a few minutes of leaving the voicemail a WhatsApp message pings: *Yeah x Love u 2. N x.*

I lie awake in bed. I'm shattered but my mind is racing.

I want you to know how happy you make me. I want to do what we did this afternoon again and again and again. Xx

Are you still awake Alexander?

Yes I am. X

It's almost midnight. Me too.

Do you want me to help you sleep? Shall I kiss you gently on the lips? Will that help? X

Bloody hell Alexander.

How's that going to help me sleep?

Sorry. I thought now that we have this connection. Sorry I got that wrong. Forgive me? Xx

Nothing to forgive.

Good night darling Maria. Xx

I can't sleep at all now. Thoughts of you. Thoughts of what we did.

Thoughts of touching you. X

Stop it!

Hah. You're still awake too. Are you thinking the same things as me? Xx

No.

Yes. I don't know.

All I know is it's time for sleep but keep thinking about you.

I'm glad you're thinking about me. I could help you drift off. Xx

I'm tempted to respond but I'm conscious of making myself too available to him. I'm scared, scared of getting involved, scared of getting hurt, scared of it all, but he's like a drug. I like it. I like him. But I don't want to feel obligated either.

What is this between us? Where's it going to go? With his inability to get an erection it's an ego thing I suppose. I want to reciprocate how he makes me feel; to give and receive love. Will I be the one to give him what he craves; sexual satisfaction and sexual release in a way he has not had from his partners or his wife?

I envisage his wife in the wedding photo he sent me; the word plain comes to mind. I feel kind of bad thinking it because I wouldn't normally judge a person by their appearance but what's struck a chord with me the most is she won't satisfy him. His words. But all the same. I know how that feels too; Natalie's father, in the end, was selfish in life and selfish in love.

I drift off to sleep, that thought the last on my mind, like a leaf floating on the wind in the middle of the night.

9
Alexander

I wait for Maria's response; the minutes flip one by one on the digital clock next to my bed. Sandra is already asleep, her drawn-out snoring another irritation, her back turned to me, a clear no entry.

It's 12.43am; still no answer. A hollow emptiness fills me. I get out of bed and go to the bathroom. I take a catheter from the supplies in the bathroom cabinet, insert it, stand over the toilet. It's painless; I don't feel anything down there though this has its disadvantages. I've long suffered with urine infections and soreness.

It's a mundane straight forward procedure which I'm used to. I remove the tube. Would Maria be repulsed, or would she accept it and smile her beautiful smile at me?

The days of wetting myself seem a long time ago, growing up everyone acknowledged it as something which happened to me. Sandra accepted it as part of me when we first got married, her patience saint-like, but as the years have passed, her tolerance has dwindled. It's another source of agitation for her and increasingly frustrating for me to listen to her uppity sighs and sarcastic swipes.

Into my older adult years, it became evident I had to intervene. It's another symptom of my CP plaguing my daily life, yet I don't speak to anyone about it. Sandra considers it to be a problem I *just have to deal with* and even a stranger, I imagine, would show more empathy. I have those clinical nurse-to-patient conversations at the irregular check-ups, not specifically for my CP, but never an opportunity to say how I feel about it, how it makes me feel less of a man. It's one more thing my penis can't do right. Why do I even have a penis? It causes me so much upset. Well, it caused me so much upset. It twitches in my hand, I pee, pull out the tube, flush the toilet.

Back in bed, Sandra shifts position; she's facing me.

'Are you awake, sweetheart?' I snuggle into her, wrapping my arm around her waist, to channel the familiar tingle Maria ignites in me towards her. I'm being unfair towards Sandra and in the same instant I feel guilty because I want to snuggle with her when I've just had the most intense experience with Maria; who am I cheating on?

'No.'

'Can we have a cuddle?'

'No, I'm sleeping.' She turns away from me again. 'You've got a one-track mind Alec. I'm not here to be at your beck and call when you feel like it.'

'I thought you might like me to… make you happy.'

'And you think that's the only way, do you?' Her words, and her actions, cut like a knife and turning onto my back I feel a pull on my head from the tight scar my butterfly stitches are leaving behind as it heals.

'Good night,' I say, and lie in the dark thinking, thinking, thinking. I slip my hand under the covers, under the waistband of my boxer shorts and fumble with my penis. It comes alive in my hand, with a few minutes concentrated coaxing, although I barely feel my hand on it. I imagine the sensation of Maria's hand around it, clasping it, the inside of my stomach bubbles. It's how she makes me feel – as free as floating bubbles on the air – free to be me, to have my thoughts, to express myself.

***

'Alec, are you getting up?' A gentle prod and, a second later, an impatient shove presses on the small of my back.

'Good morning, sweetheart,' I mumble, wiping the sleep from the corners of my eyes.

'It's gone nine o'clock.'

'And?'

'We can't stay in bed all day. I've a list of chores to be done and we've got church.'

'You go to church. I'll stay and do the chores.'

'No, Alec. We go to church together and you can do the chores when we get back.'

Her words sink in and like an elastic band stretched too far, I snap. I feel stifled, belittled and I lash out, fierce as fire.

'I'm not coming. I've had a tough week at work with all the admin checks and questions from that bigwig who came snooping. And you know what else? I'm not doing the chores. I'm going to do what I've wanted to do for a long time on a Sunday. Enjoy a bit of time on my own, away from your nagging and your demands and your constant reprimands.'

She glares at me, as she leaps out of bed, fighting with

her tangled nightdress. She comes at me. 'How dare you?'

'How dare I? Oh, Sandra, sweetheart, how have I not dared all these years?'

I shrug on my dressing gown, pulling it over me any old how. Trembling, I grab my iPad from the bedside table and stumble from the bedroom leaving her staring after me.

On the upstairs landing, Caramel is already awake. She stretches in her basket, gives me a slow blink, as if winking at me, and meanders in and out of my legs, excited for her breakfast. I ignore her, not in the mood for her affection.

I catheterise, shower, shave. I nick myself; breathe in the comforting smell of antiseptic. I don't rush and try my new nose hair trimmer. My stray nose hairs have not bothered me before but now I'm appraising myself from a different perspective, through the eyes of Maria. How would she react meeting me for the first time? I have found myself browsing men's grooming sites on the internet. I've ordered a moisturiser and beard oil.

Sandra leaves for church, slamming the front door behind her. It's half past ten and I'm ravenous. I cook breakfast; kippers, eggs, baked beans, three pieces of toast. I slurp down two mugs of tea. I relish every morsel. Sandra seems to disapprove of anything which brings me joy, even my choices regarding food, though she'll argue it's because she cares for me, but I know it's about control.

I leave the crockery and the pans soaking in the sink. I'm not going to waste precious alone-time washing up. It will irritate Sandra and I want to be mean. She evokes an unkindness in me these days I haven't expressed or let surface in the past. Not towards her and not towards anyone. I suddenly feel guilty pushing Caramel away.

I home in on Sandra's pot of hand cream on the windowsill. She doesn't use it; it's there to show off the posh brand. I feel a pulse pounding in my neck and in a moment of childish spitefulness I bin it. The clatter startles Caramel; she eyes me with suspicion from her stance, keeping her distance.

My malice reminds me of Sandra and a time John and Elizabeth came over for Sunday lunch. Elizabeth brought a home-made carrot cake decorated with butter icing and miniature carrots made of orange and green stained icing sugar. Sandra, angry at the compliments I'd given Elizabeth, and the fun Callum had pretending to feed the little carrots to his stuffed rabbit, got hold of the whole thing, with the cake board, and dumped it in our wheelie bin after they had left.

I was so dumbfounded at the sheer pettiness of her actions, her petulance. I didn't want to give her the satisfaction of knowing how much she'd angered me, and we never again referred to it. I doubt whether Callum even remembers. My mother always used to say, *no response is a louder response*.

***

Caramel escapes into the garden and I escape to my shed; my own quiet space, where I no longer feel Sandra's presence stifling me. She created an abundance of warmth and safety, like my own mother did for me, but not anymore. Or is it because I'm no longer grateful to her? Through sickness and in health once felt full of possibilities, but now I know otherwise; I've fought this state of loneliness for a long time, unaware of when I began to feel like this but knowing it has to end.

Raising Callum forced me to be responsible for another and I was good at it. I loved him and nurtured him; did everything any parent would do and more; taught him how to skim a stone across the lake, build a fire, knot a tie, read a compass. But he's an adult now, he doesn't need me and I suppose, in turn, Sandra doesn't need me other than to boss about.

The shed is too warm, and the morning light floods through the moss-stained glass panel in the roof and the window smudged with dust from the flower beds. Caramel tight-rope walks along the top of the ageing fence. She leaps onto the corrugated roof of the neighbour's lean-to before disappearing from sight.

I settle back in my armchair, smirking at the two discarded cigars in an old saucer. I struggle to get comfortable against the push of an errant spring digging into my thigh. Ouch.

The row I've had with Sandra invades my thoughts. I picture her at the Sunday service, in her usual pew, third row from the front, singing out of tune. The newer members of the congregation surreptitiously steal glances at her, with looks of disdain, but the older, long-serving parishioners are used to her sharp and out of rhythm hymning. The thought of her irritates me; uptight and constipated. I'm annoyed with myself for letting thoughts of her ruin my time alone. I won't let her impinge on my precious time. I flick on my iPad.

Maria's tweets read as though they are talking to me and me only. I find consolation in this. An escape from my boring world riddled with overbearing rules and expectations.

There's a tweet thanking a list of named followers with an image; the words *tis love that makes the world go round, my baby*, a quote by Charles Dickens, makes my heart beat faster.

Believe in the beauty of your dreams.
A portrait of a woman with her hair tied in a messy bun, strands framing her face, is bent over a book.

If we don't change, we don't grow. If we don't grow, we aren't really living.
A woman with a veil over her face is looking into the distance as she stands barefoot in garden.

You can't start the next chapter of your life if you keep re-reading the last one.
A man and woman are looking into each other's eyes as they hold hands, a table strewn with coffee cups and a sugar shaker.

> *Good morning Maria.*
> *How are you today? Xx*

I sit in anticipation. I imagine her still in bed, sleepy, her long hair splayed across the pillow. I imagine kissing her good morning, bringing her a cup of green tea and drinking it with her while she leans into me, holding my hand.

> **Good morning Alexander.**
> **I'm good thanks, you?**

I'm OK. I'm missing you. Xx

> **You are? How comes?**

Thinking about yesterday. You're wonderful. Xx

> **I am?**

Yes, you are. Xx

> **x**

For the first time she signs off with a kiss. I'm convinced I feel my cock pushing against the fabric of my boxers. My mind's cloudy with delightful thoughts of her and what we did yesterday. Is she thinking about it too?

This is a new experience for me, this online dating thing or whatever it is. I imagine how perfect it would be to with her, touch her for real. Maybe we will meet one day. Maybe this is the start of a new life, where I start living at last after being shrouded in the blasted numbness of CP and catheters and clinic visits.

Is Maria my angel, breathing life into my dull, rather boring existence? Maybe this woman is going to be my new lease of life where I can laugh and talk poetry and visit bookstores and teashops. My mind fills with images of us strolling hand in hand, I haven't done this with Sandra in years, and a honey-like warmth fills me.

What are you doing today? Xx

> Tweeting, writing a new website promotion for the news feed at work. You? x

I'm in my shed reading and thinking about you still. Xx

> It's warm today so it must be nice to be in your shed. x

Yes, it is. Warmer still because I'm hugging you. Kissing you. Xx

> I'm sure you are. X

Yes. I am. Kissing your lips, my hands searching for

your breasts. Sit on my lap, will you? Xx

Alexander... x

My tongue searches yours, plays with it, I stroke your hair, as I kiss you deeper. Your body leans in towards me, you want me as much as I want you. Xx

I pull you closer, you moan my name, I reach under your top, undo your bra. Losing myself in you, xx

Really Alexander? How can you be? You don't know me, don't know anything about me.

I know how you make me feel. I haven't felt like this for years. I haven't lived. You've woken me up. I'm totally lost in you. Xx

But you're married Alexander. You can't get lost in me. This isn't real, not like it should be.

It's real for me.
It's more real and more wonderful than anything I have ever experienced before in my life. You are my lover. Xx

I don't know what to say.

Say you feel the same.

I like talking to you.

Just talking to me? Lol.
What about everything else we do? Everything else we

can still do and share? Xx

You're embarrassing me. Yes everything.

I mean it when I say you're wonderful. Xx

I'm away for a couple of days from tomorrow.

Where are you going? Leaving me already? Xx

Lol. No... I'm going to a spa with friends.

Lucky you. Will you keep in touch? Xx

I don't know what the Wi-Fi connection will be like.

Here's my phone number 07891 564989. You can text me any time you like. Xx

Thank you. x

Do what you feel comfortable with. Xx

I've never done anything like this before... but I'm not uncomfortable Alexander... I don't know what I'm doing to be honest.

I want you to feel the same as me, Maria, my darling. Xx

OK. Gotta go.

Will DM you later. Xx

She doesn't know how she feels about me, or maybe she doesn't want me to know. This worries me, but I push my doubts to the back of my mind. She's not where I am yet but she will be. I'm certain of it. She just can't feel the same as me because she can actually feel. She can ordinarily feel what I cannot feel on any given day, and she evokes a coursing hedonistic pleasure in me.

I delete all our messages. I can't risk it with Sandra using my iPad every now and again. Maria has made me feel worthy in a way Sandra never has. When we first married, I had so many expectations of what being in a loving relationship would be like. I can't risk losing what is a possibility for me.

She doesn't reject with unkind words or shoves or pushes. What would it be like to touch her, satisfy her, fulfil her, and me, at the same time? Would she enjoy what I do, and would she enjoy touching me? Would her skin be soft and silky, would she react to my touch in the same way as I imagine over and over in my head, in our fantasy? Would she touch my bum… or let me touch hers… probe it with my tongue, my fingers?

The thought of her touching me, where I have some sensation, sends sparks of arousal through me; I'm throbbing, twitching, hot, flustered. I close my eyes and think of her touching my anus. A river of electricity passes through me as real as if she is right next to me.

10
Maria

'Glad we're sharing.'

'Like our trip to France, d'you remember?' asks Tina.

'How can I forget? First time we were both away from our parents and we had the best-looking teacher in the whole school with us.'

'Gosh, I'd forgotten about him.'

'No way. How could you? I've still got a photo of the three of us in front of Notre Dame. Me in that awful brown coat and red shoes.' I pretend to swoon, my hands clutching at my chest, and I flop into the high back winged chair but the moment is lost in our sadness of the recent fire there.

Tina shakes out her arms and legs as if dispersing the sad notes and bats her eyelashes mimicking Natalie; Natalie has an Oscar award-winning flutter.

'This room,' I say, 'It's like the pages of a home magazine. I'd love to have this again one day.'

'You're the dreamer out of all of us. You need a knight in shining armour.'

'What I need is to get my story published.'

'But a prince would come in handy, right?'

A smile fills my face.

'Oh my God… you've met someone.'

'No, I haven't,' I say, too quickly.

'You have. You're glowing. Right. Save it for the Jacuzzi. Katia and Elaine will want to hear this.'

***

Condensation runs down the opaque glass walls of the indoor swimming pool and Jacuzzi area. We slip off our robes and slippers.

The Jacuzzi's warm bubbles wash over my shoulders as I sink down into the turquoise lake trying to mask the pump's humming behind me. I re-position myself, the triple jets behind me shoot water, massaging my lower back.

Katia and Elaine stare at me wide-eyed and can't hold back their smiles. Tina reminds me of someone who's suffered a slap in the face with a sopping swimming costume.

'So that's it in a nutshell,' I say.

'That's it? Oh my God Maria. You're having an affair with a married man and you say that's it? That's a huge "it". It's an exciting "it". It's a dangerous "it". But it's not just a "that's it",' says Elaine.

'Good for you,' says Katia.

'Really? I thought you'd be shocked, disappointed even,' I say, fighting the overwhelming emotions strangling me; her cheating husband walked out on their crystal wedding anniversary less than a year ago.

'Nothing shocks me anymore and you deserve this

swoony, crazy, lusty relationship– even if it's with someone you'll likely never meet.'

Her words force me to sit up. She's right. I will never meet Alexander and the thought shakes me. But I don't say that to her, to any of them.

'Thank you for being so gracious about it. I didn't want you thinking badly of me,' I say instead, conscious of steadying my voice.

'It's about time you were daring,' says Elaine. 'You've always been so careful, careful to do the right thing. Set yourself free, let go, free the teenager in you.'

'A nun? I'll never be that saintly,' I say.

'You're quiet, Tina,' says Elaine.

'Sorry. It's a lot to register but I'm glad you're happy. Don't get me wrong, I'm not putting a dampener on this, but isn't this risky? I mean he could be anyone. He could be luring you into anything.'

'Ever the cautious one, Tina. She's having a bit of fun. What harm can it do?' says Elaine.

Tina gives her a look. 'Okay, okay, let me finish. I was going to say since you're having fun then I'm glad for you. But promise you won't give away any personal details. Your safety has to be a priority… and Natalie's. You have to think about her too. Teenagers these days are more vulnerable than we admit.'

'Nah, teenagers are savvier than we give them credit for. They've grown up with all this technology. We haven't,' says Elaine.

'I promise to be careful and never put Natalie in danger.'

'I'm serious, Maria. Not intentionally maybe, but so many women and children, even men, fall for these online predators' traps and games. Safety has to be your main concern.'

'I'm not online as such. I've met him through Twitter. His posts and interactions with other people are on my feed every day.'

'He only shows you what he wants, Maria. Remember that. Be careful.'

'I will. I promise,' I say, adding, 'You're all amazing. I thought you'd be having a go because of his wife. I'm so lucky to have you all. Thank you for being so great about this even if you don't wholeheartedly agree with what I'm doing.'

We all hug and slip and slide against the tiles. The steamy bubbles tickle my nose and I giggle. I giggle until my sides are sore and my eyes are streaming, tears of happiness, of relief. It feels real now I've told them.

The rest of the afternoon is languorous. We spend a little less time together, than we had anticipated, as we each indulge in our treatments at various times. In the conservatory I lounge on the silk chaise longue, flicking through my magazine. I say mine but I took it from the dentist's surgery last week by accident. I stuffed it in my bag and even after realising what I'd done I didn't return it. I can't justify paying £3.95 for a magazine and it was up to date for March.

A headline grabs my attention: Affair Rumours That Ended Their Ten Years of Happily Married. It slaps me round the face and I'm not sure what I feel. Am I worried Alexander's wife will find out? If Alexander isn't why should I be? Do I care? Do I owe her anything?

The article discusses a marriage dogged by repeated rumours of the wife's infidelity. A so-called expert talks about a "conscious uncoupling" where two people decide they'd be better off separated. He explains how the emotional process is a way of viewing divorce as a natural process, a positive one, which grants progression for the two people involved separately. It is a way of choosing not to renew your love for each other but to move on.

I stop and consider how I would have felt had Natalie's father said I don't want to invest in our relationship anymore and I want a life without you. Would that have devastated me less than his gambling and lying? How would I feel if Alexander chose to leave his wife? Would I feel guilty then?

I turn the page not wanting to dwell on the answer, not knowing what the answer might be. The rest of the magazine bursts with articles on everything and anything; The New Belly Botox, Simple Tweaks That'll Shift How You Feel, The Coolest Denim, High Street Hottest and the Horoscopes.

"Life may throw a few lemons at you,
but you will make lemonade, so move forward
and whatever is meant to be in your life will find a way to be."

The word lemons prompts me to check on Natalie. She's not right recently. She's moody, short-tempered. She's up in the night and she's missed a couple of days of school which isn't like her. Perhaps the stress of coursework deadlines is getting to her. I leave a voice mail.

With no internet connection I can't message Alexander and I don't want to text him, not ready to engage in a more personal way of communicating. I close my eyes shutting out the leafy palms and sky-blue ceiling. I imagine him here with me, reading poetry and talking about books and my writing and learning about his favourite authors. Would he be patient and attentive or would he be too keen to have his way with me and leave me? Well maybe not exactly. He seems considerate, unworldly even. I imagine him in Inverness with its towering mountains and glittering lochs, thick woodland, and miles upon miles of golden beaches; the opposite to my traffic-full, noisy North London.

'Hi honey.'

I open my eyes, Tina's standing by my side.

'How was your body wrap?' I ask.

'It was heaven. My skin feels so smooth now. Hubby's in for a treat when I get back tomorrow night.'

'Too much information.'

'You okay? Have you heard from Alexander?'

'No internet connection, so I have no idea.'

'Oh dear but it will be good to have him wondering. Are you missing him?'

'I don't think he's into playing games. He's pretty serious about his feelings and expressing himself.' As I say it I know it to be true. He's genuine and he stimulates me.

'He sounds perfect for you. You've always expressed yourself so well. You're a ball of feelings waiting to spill. How many times did our English teacher say that?'

'I don't remember, but I suppose that's why I'm a writer.'

'Why are you two so serious?' asks Katia.

'Maria. Alexander. Food. I'm getting hungry,' says Tina, pressing down on her rumbling stomach.

Katia shuffles through a folded sheath of papers searching for our dinner reservation time. Tina and I burst out laughing as I annunciate the word hungry.

11
Maria

So good to hear from you. Did you have a wonderful time? Xx

> Not back yet. But managed to get a connection. So relaxing x

I thought you might have forgotten about me. I'm missing you. Xx

> It's only been two days. x

Feels like a lifetime. Feels like you disappeared forever. Xx

> One more night and I'm back home and you can have me for as long as you like. X

'Twas partly love, and partly fear,
And partly 'twas a bashful art,
That I might rather feel, than see,
The swelling of her heart.'

Until then my darling. Xx

I let out a giggle. I have the approval of my friends, and this pushes the adrenaline through me like an aphrodisiac. I check my lippy in the bathroom mirror and before I run out I try Natalie again.

'Just in time,' says Katia. I join my friends a few minutes after eight at a table on the far side of the elegant dining room.

'Finally got through to Nat. She sounded tired but otherwise the flat's still there.'

The room's ceilings are adorned with ornate plasterwork and sparkling chandeliers. Swags and drapes of silk fabric in faded peach and gold frame the tall windows.

A waiter hands us menu cards and disappears only to promptly reappear with a jug of iced water infused with lemon slices and fresh mint leaves.

'She's sensible. Now, about your new man. Just promise to keep us posted if you meet him… or if there's anything uncomfortable about him. You're not on your own,' says Tina.

'Is that why you came down before me? To have a gossip?'

'No, I thought you deserved to pamper yourself in peace. Stop being paranoid,' says Tina.

'And what do you mean by she's sensible? Meaning I'm not?'

'Stop it, Maria. You know that's not what I mean.'

'I'm not planning on going anywhere with him. I don't have the money to dash off to Scotland.'

'He's all the way up there? How's that going to…' Tina gives Elaine a nudge with her elbow, Elaine's voice trails off.

'I just wanted you to know we're all here for you.' Tina squeezes my hand and gives me a tender smile; most often reserved for her eight- and ten-year-old sons.

I smile back at her, annoyed at my own insecurity. This is what Natalie's dad did to me; abandoned me. It's not an easy thing to get over. I thought I was moving on but here I am being pulled back. I want to be honest with them, to tell them about his CP. Will they think it's weird? Will they see past it like I have?

I shake off the negative thoughts and focus on dinner which is both delicious and healthy.

'So, what else is there to know about this guy?' asks Katia, reading my mind.

'Well, he's determined and doesn't give up. He's lived with CP all his life and…' The words leave my mouth before my brain has time to decide yes or no.

'CP? Oh no, how bad? Is he in a wheelchair?' Tina can't hide her dismay.

'He's got a cane. But he's fully functional.'

'Fully functional? How can he be? Doesn't that effect co-ordination and speech?' asks Katia.

'And that he can't you know,' says Elaine.

'I suppose so, yes,' I say, lowering my voice, fanning myself with the menu card.

The waiter hovers, waiting for our order. He scribbles on his pad, retrieves the menu cards, apart from mine, and promptly returns with two bottles of Sauvignon Blanc.

'If you're asking whether he has erectile dysfunction, yes

he does,' I say, conscious of my cheeks burning, resenting their interrogation, and resenting my embarrassment even more. I'm uncomfortable sharing Alexander's intimate details with them. I feel like I'm disrespecting him when he's shared such an intimate aspect of his life with me.

'He can't…'

'No Tina, he can't.'

The girls are asking the same questions I've asked myself over and over and I don't have an answer for them. I don't have an answer apart from I am wanted by him.

'But you've always loved sex,' says Elaine.

'Yes. And I still do.'

'How's it going to work? Have you really thought it through?' asks Tina.

'I have. But it doesn't bother me. Now let's change the subject.'

'Gosh, I don't do it every night but not to see hubby excited. That would be a no-no for me,' says Tina. 'And not to be made love to?' she continues, but finally shuts up realising I've had enough of the inquisition.

The silence around the table is like a high-pitched shriek.

Katia picks up her glass, 'A toast,' she says. 'To new beginnings.'

'To new beginnings,' we reply, raising our glasses.

'And new sexual experiences,' says Tina.

The tinkle of our clinking glasses is drowned by my giggling. Tina joins in and Katia chokes on her glass of wine. Elaine tries her hardest to be serious, opening her mouth to speak, but our infectious laughter pulls her in too. The waiter approaches our table with our starters; none of us thank him, too overcome with hysterics.

My king prawns, in a mango and chilli sauce, are delicious. I struggle to finish my main course; the salmon en croute is heavy on my stomach. I try to pierce the undercooked new potato with my fork, and it flies across the table and into Tina's lap.

'No need to attack me,' she jokes.

'Sorry hun. I've heard of al dente pasta, but undercooked potatoes are a no-no for me.'

'You not enjoying it?' asks Elaine, chewing on a mouthful of rare-cooked lamb.

'I don't have much of an appetite.'

'Oh my God, you're in love,' says Katia.

'No, I'm not,' I say, but the heat of it fills my face.

Just after midnight, Tina swipes the entry card against the door reader. The door clicks, we shuffle inside.

'That was a good evening,' she says, activating the main lights.

'It was,' I say, kicking off my high heels in the dark.

'Why the sigh?'

'Tired, I guess. Do you think the girls are okay about Alexander?'

'They are. We all are. But are you sure you know what you're getting yourself into?'

'No, I don't. I have no idea. But I'm going to go with it. I want to get to know him.'

'You could meet someone in a bar.'

'When was the last time you met someone in a bar?'

'You know what I mean. Someone closer to home. Someone real,' Tina says, removing her make-up with a cleansing wipe, rubbing at the caked mascara on her lashes.

'He is real. He's not a robot.'

'But he can't get it up.'

'If that ever becomes an issue, I'll end it.'

'What if you can't?'

12
Alexander

The door of the shed flings open.

'I've called you three times, Alec.'

'Sorry, sweetheart. I must've dropped off.' I struggle to compose myself, to focus on reality.

'John and Elizabeth are on their way. They're at a loose end so I suggested we all go for Sunday lunch,' she says. 'And the minister asked after you too.'

I don't trust myself to say anything. This is her way of not facing up to our disagreement. With John and Elizabeth present she can avoid further confrontation. She hesitates in the doorway. For a split second I wait for her comment on my nose trim. She doesn't mention it or the washing up.

Her hand cream, back on the windowsill, taunts me.

'For goodness sake. That cream must be expired by now,' I say, discarding it again.

'They don't go out of date.'

'They do. That's why I threw it away in the first place.'

'Alec, what's got into you? It's my cream.'

'It's in the bin and that's where it should stay.'

She tuts, glares at me, but tones it down when I don't look away, daring her to continue.

Upstairs I freshen up. I slap on my new aftershave, put on new socks and underpants; Sandra opened my parcel but hasn't questioned me. Have I scored one over her? My childish immaturity shocks me. I grab my phone. I'm back downstairs wearing a clean shirt, just as our friends hoot outside.

***

'Your head's looking better than the last time,' says John, punching my arm in a show of comradery.

I run my fingers over the scar. 'Seems to be healing fine.'

'A war wound adds a bit of character,' says John.

'Not sure that's how to look at it,' says Sandra, but I ignore her.

Hi. Out for a Sunday roast with friends. Wish you were here. Xx

Our food is served on oval platters with extra gravy on the side. Sandra has ordered scampi and chips.

'Didn't fancy church this morning?' asks Elizabeth.

'I had a few things to do.'

'Oh, I don't know about you but it's always easier to get things done when Elizabeth's out the way,' says John.

'It's better when you're out of my way too. All that mess when you're DIYing. Bits everywhere. Toolbox spilt all over the floor,' says Elizabeth.

'I'm not messy,' I say. Sandra raises her eyebrow in that "really now" expression she uses for sarcastic non-verbal communication. I call it her sarcapression. John and Elizabeth look from one to the other and tuck into their meal. I know what's going through their minds. Or at least I know what's going through John's because he has said it to me often enough over the years; "Why d'you let her treat you that way?"

I don't rise to it. Instead, I read Maria's reply, glad she's back. Three days, with only that one little exchange, were lonely.

I'm holding hands with you under the table.

Under the table eh? Make sure you don't get a hold of something else. Lol. Xx

I've dropped my napkin, how clumsy of me. I'd better get down on my knees to find it... oh, what's this I've found?

I read her message twice. My face reddens, not with embarrassment, but with intrigue, anticipation. My mind is befuddled. The atmosphere changes with Maria in the midst; heat envelopes me. The idea of getting caught must be turning her on. But her motive doesn't dwell on me.

Instead, I imagine doing it right here in the pub, with Sandra here. Of introducing her to John and Elizabeth. 'Shove up everyone. This is Maria. We met online. We regularly satisfy each other. She's an incredibly sexy woman.' John would probably stutter. Elizabeth would turn the same shade as a tarot reader's red tablecloth. Sandra would sit tight-lipped with her legs crossed at the ankles;

her hands clasped together in a prayer-like pose. There'd be little God could do to help her though.

But for now, I'm on the edge of total elation, doing this right under her nose. I push Maria. How far will she go?

Tell me. What have you found? Xx

> *It fits perfectly in my hand. Can you feel me? Right there... and there... doing this... and now this?*

Oh yes. Yes I can. It's wonderful. Don't stop.
My Maria. So bold. So sexy. Xx

'Put that blasted phone away, Alec. So rude.' Sandra works her napkin in her left hand. 'Whatever it is, it's getting you hot and bothered.'

'It's work. I can't ignore it.' I fumble, undoing the second button on my shirt, a trickle of panic – or is it elation? – drips down the back of my neck. I run my hand inside my shirt collar, undo another button.

John jumps in to rescue me. 'Not like the old days, eh? With mobile phones, emails and text messages keep coming 24-7. I'm the same. Just can't get away from the office. There's always something pulling me back in.'

'It's not normally like this but we're short staffed and Pete's away. I can't just let go, Sandra. Danny's my responsibility.' I'm amazed at how easily the lie slips from me, a slithering sneaky snake.

'Not today he's not.' Sandra snatches at my phone but I'm too quick, pull it away. As I do I hit the waitress who's approached the table; the extra Haggis servings fall out of her hands in slow motion. Crash. Smashed plates, food debris all over the tiled floor, a dollop on my shoe. John guffaws: the diners either side of us stare while others stifle their laughter. Elizabeth is out of her seat trying to scoop up the bits with her napkin, which resemble a horror movie victim's exploded brain fragments.

'I do apologise.'

'Accidents happen. No worries. I'll get this cleaned up and get another order to you as soon as I can.'

'Thank you so much,' laughs John, almost choking as he guzzles down his pint.

'There's always a drama with you,' says Sandra.

'I think you'll find that was your fault, no one else's,' says John, winking at her; his words strung together with alcohol.

'Unlike the last accident.' Sandra reddening, leaves the table, taking her cigarettes and lighter with her. Elizabeth calls after her, but Sandra ignores her, she sips her Coke, plays with her food.

'Sandra,' I call.

'Quite delicious,' says John, breaking the silence.

'Never a dull moment with you two,' says Elizabeth. 'You really shouldn't upset her like that.'

John pretends to admonish me, wagging his finger too close to my face. How much has he drunk?

I'm on top of the world despite the obvious sending to Coventry I'm going to get later on. I am sorry for Sandra, for her embarrassment, although I'm equally fed up with her whining.

I push my plate away, my appetite lost. John and Elizabeth finish their lunch, the forced merriment hanging in the air. The waitress clears our plates and Sandra returns bringing with her the stink of her cigarette. We order dessert and coffee.

'How's your old school friend Jenny? You said you were

planning a visit to her,' says Elizabeth.

'She's fine. Getting over that scoundrel of a husband. The divorce is almost finalised. Hoping to visit her in July.'

I perk up and listen. July. July. July. I might just find a way to visit Maria.

'She'd like that, Jenny. How lovely. Will you go Alec?'

'I may go, work commitments permitting. I could catch a train from Birmingham into London. Visit the museums. Let the women do their thing.'

'How thoughtful of you. Accompanying Sandra, giving her space to be with her friend. Isn't that thoughtful John?' John taps his round belly.

His action prompts me to survey my own extended stomach. I inhale in an effort to pull it in tight, but can't hold it for long, relaxing it a few moments later. It bulges. Maybe I will put in a session at the gym with Danny.

'Aww, that's just the sort of man Alec is. Always puts others before himself. I've said it enough times,' says John.

I'm delighted at how it's come together. It's got to work. I can't wait to put the idea to Maria and hope she's as excited by the prospect of meeting as I am.

***

'So embarrassing today. And that aftershave's awful.' Sandra pushes past me as soon as I've opened the front door.

'I'm surprised you even noticed.'

'All to impress your new friends I suppose.'

'What friends? What are you talking about?'

'Whoever it is you spend hours with on your phone,' she says.

I am tweeting Maria; the scowl on Sandra's face is enough to turn the freshest milk. The ashtray next to her is overflowing with two days' worth of cigarette butts. I'm tempted to say something. At some point, I realise with clarity, I turned into a speechless nobody. I shrunk into myself and the real me became invisible; I became non-existent.

'Sandra sweetheart, they can't smell me or see me. But if they could I'm sure they'd be more complimentary than you ever are.'

Feel my lips on you... my mouth clamped round you. Oh, don't you like it?

I'm in a kind of dizzying panic, swamped by the desires Maria evokes in me. I'm invigorated yet depleted all at the same time; there's a wild raging swell of sea in my thumping heart yet my sensible head is telling me to hold onto the familiar rocks, to not leave the safety of the shore, but I can't help myself. The shore is flat; I want peaks and valleys.

We message on and I find myself thinking about the practicalities of being together. Would she be curious as to how my catheter works, come to my clinic appointments? Would she tire of me using my walking stick or frequently needing the toilet? But I try to push my thoughts aside. There will be time enough for us to discuss these.

Now I've found her I can't let her go. She is my conduit to a feeling, living life. I've not dared in my life, always played it safe; the word dare excites me, pulls me in a different direction, a direction I am willing to follow, to drown in.

13
Maria

It's Sunday, usually a lazy day of laundry and tidying but everything is charging at me.

I'm thinking about Alexander; what we're doing and how far I'm pushing him. Our messaging is exhilarating. Once I initiated it, I couldn't stop and he hasn't tried to. He is enjoying the risk just as much as I am. But maybe my naughty messages over-excited him, especially while dining with his friends and his wife. Have I gone too far? Has his wife said anything? Maybe he's not up for this in the same way I thought he was. Why isn't he responding? I will him to answer me. Maybe I should just stick to the conversations about poetry and all the brilliant authors he quotes off-pat. I'm so relieved when he replies.

My wonderful darling I do like it yes. Don't stop. It's the most incredible feeling. You are incredible.

I want you. I need you. Xx
Yes sorry. Sandra's glaring in my direction. I'm home
now. Xx

Oh OK. Shall I stop?

Darling, no. No. Don't stop. I want you so much. Xx

'*The fountains mingle with the river*
And the rivers with the ocean,
The winds of heaven mix for ever
With a sweet emotion;
Nothing in the world is single;
All things by a law divine
In one spirit meet and mingle.
Why not I with thine?'

***

Days later, still thinking about him, the word risk pops into my head but seems at odds with what's happening between us. I'm in London. He's in Inverness and there are a whole lot of mountains and valleys in between. My friends are relieved about this, and I suppose I am too. It is safer though those outwitted by cheats and tricksters will disagree. When he "talks" to me it's as if he's in the room with me; my physical reactions to him are as if he were right here. I like how reality and fantasy merge, create another world between us.

I try to imagine his Scottish accent quoting Wordsworth and Burns and Betjeman; is his voice gentle or grainy or deep? Either way his appreciation of literature is hugely attractive to me. I imagine him reciting poetry to me, reading extracts from his favourite books. He's like no man I've ever met before; even my schoolteachers didn't spout poetry like he does but I suppose I wasn't in awe of all that flowery prose back then.

I've spent a lot of time around literary people before; he's so different to all the men I've dated. I say dated but I've not given it a proper go since Natalie's father, and I finished. But with Alexander there's a "click" between us. I look forward to our messages. It's easy getting to know him from the comfort and safety of my day-to-day life; sat in the office, wrapped in my dressing gown at home, nestled on the sofa... it's liberating not worrying about my clothes, my hair, my make-up, my weight.

A recent news story, about a journalist being duped by a man she almost married, plays on my mind, and obsessed, I go through his Twitter feed scanning for clues as to how he spends his time. There's no new activity since last night.

What if he's used me for sex, virtual sex and now has moved on? It didn't bother me in the past; dick pics and empty words filled time but that was years ago. I was in a bad place. It's different with Alexander; panic descends on me.

Perhaps he's a groomer, looks so ordinary yet is part of a big ring of others who use charisma and charm to ensnare lonely women and cheat them of their savings, strip them of their worth. Lonely... the word rings in my ears. Am I lonely? Perhaps for attention, adoration, amour?

I scour his feed again, for any interaction with other women. I'm spying on him, being paranoid, but I want to be sure of him. I want to be sure of his intentions towards me. It's a long time since I've trusted a man.

There's a comment thread with a historical romance author but I suppose if there was anything going on it wouldn't be on the public feed anyway. Bloody hell. Am I being naïve?

He tweets with another woman I have befriended. I contact her before I change my mind. I wait. Drink tea. File my nails. Stroll around the flat. Tidy and straighten picture frames. Squirt bleach down the toilet bowl. Wait for her reply.

And what about his wife? He's told me about her and though he could be lying his demeanour tells me he's being truthful; I've tested him. I've posed the same questions and he always gives me the same answer. He's either both clever and manipulative or he's telling the truth; I choose to believe the latter.

Finally, she replies. I'm relieved she hasn't had any sexy messages from him.

I get comfortable on the couch. I bunch the throw under my laptop to prop it at the right angle for typing. I should be writing a new chapter but all I'm doing is staring at the screen, my head full of Alexander.

I wish I hadn't deleted his messages in my moment of panic. Not that deleting them would make any difference if anyone wanted to access them, I suppose they would find a way. I make a mental note not to sit through dramas with hackers and stalkers in them. I try recalling his words, his tone, his matter-of-fact way of putting things, his openness; excitement builds in me.

The glare from the screen tires me; I rest my eyes.

A couple of hours later, showered and dressed, I write by hand for an hour or so. When I'm satisfied with my word count, I open a new word document on my laptop and type. I stop for a break, hydrate myself and run to my bedroom for my Kindle, pulling the duvet across my bed. I straighten the lavish fleece blanket, a reminder of my past luxurious life.

Back in the sitting room I check my feed. I ♥ and retweet and post two tweets of my own.

'In a world where everyone wears a mask, show your soul.'
A woman with dark hair is wearing a golden jeweled mask.

'Never settle for being their 2nd-best. Make sure you are their priority.'
A man and a woman hug against the backdrop of an admiral blue night sky scattered with stars.

I read through my poem again. I'm bursting to share it with Alexander. A message sent over an hour ago causes me to curse my Kindle for being slow in updating my notifications.

Good morning my wonderful lover. Did you sleep well? Xx

> Good morning. I did thank you. Hope you did too.

So good to hear from you! I did yes. Going in early for a meeting at 12.30pm. What are you doing today? Xx

> I should be writing but I've written a poem instead about us.

A poet and an author. You're so clever. Can I read it? Xx

> Yes. I can send it to you.

Looking forward to it. I'm full of your wonderfulness this morning. Xx

You are? Why?

Because you're my darling princess and lover. I'm full to the brim. I can't get enough of you. Xx

Oh, OK. So that's a good thing I take it?

It's the best feeling in the world.
You are all I think about. You're my wonderful lover and I want you. I need you Maria. X

Here's the poem I wrote. I hope you like it!
I've called it Wrongly Rightly.
It started with a simple Direct Message
A hello, a polite thank you for following

But now it's something different
It's bigger, happier, impure, unsettling
Simple messages of how are you shift to
I'm thinking of you, you're in my head

I can't concentrate without you
And when we don't talk I feel dead
We laugh, send emoticons of smiles and LOL
Cheeky winks and hearts and musical notes

We're both lost in this virtual fantasy
Together below inky blue skies, stars and quotes
Last thing at night under the duvet so warm
We tease, we kiss, stroke, lightly touch

Bodies writhe and clash, lose all control

Holding onto each other, a desperate clutch
Closer and closer to passionate heights
You push me and push me, then you pause

I can't take the overload anymore
You take all of me, claim me as yours
I bite on my bottom lip to stop the moan
You stroke, you graze, you nip with teeth

Incessant, continuous...we can't get enough
I lie there totally spent, you beneath collapsed
We imagine falling asleep next to each other
Gasping breaths, then gently falling unison

Our limbs entwined, our energy spent
Two foggy minds grappling, whirlwind illusion
Growing lust, frenzied passion takes over
It's in our breath, our touch, our scent

Messages back and forth, now hundreds a day
Mostly words of joy, love, but too of lament
There's no denying a darker side to this
A woman bound to you through marriage

And through our actions, she is pushed aside
Yet we both recklessly her disparage
We know we can't truly be together
You're but a beautiful face on a mobile screen

Images sent, provocative and inviting
Our emotions rising, a wondrous magic between
And though we speak of how it will end

We hang onto each other desperately, tightly

Hearts scarlet elated, love purple bruised
Our bond painful we know... is wrongly rightly.

14
Maria

I send the poem. Is it too much? Is it too serious? Is it too soon? I shouldn't have sent it. It's showing him I'm in deep. I should have posted it publicly, directed it to him; less personal that way; less about him, less about him and me, less about us.

The rest of the day passes by in a hazy, dazy daydream. I write, scan Twitter and post to my Instagram account. I email my website designer with questions, lots of questions: What will my banner look like? Can I have more than one colour band running through each page? Can I change my images once the website is live? Can I add other drop anchors as my writing develops and when my first book is published? There's plenty to do and my mind reflects my laptop; too many tabs open.

By the time Natalie gets home from school my head is heavy, my eyes sore. I haven't cooked dinner.

'I'm not hungry, Mum.' She shrugs off her backpack and pink bomber jacket, dropping them in a heap on the floor at the foot of the sofa. Her trainers follow with a soft thud. The patter of her retreating footsteps is followed by a squeaking of the running tap in the kitchen.

She wanders into the sitting room spilling water over the carpet. 'Be careful, Nat.' I use the shortened form of her name more now she's older.

'I'm so thirsty.'

'Yes, okay, but the carpet's not stain-proof!'

'You never yell at Fluffy when she's pooing all over the place.'

'That's different. And anyway, you shouldn't let her roam in here. That's why her hutch is in the kitchen.'

'Mum, you're so extra. Always moaning.'

'And talking of "extra" her hutch is filthy.'

She tuts and disappears to her room. She'll be glued to her mobile for the rest of the evening; inwardly I'm relieved I won't have to cook. I get up to soak the spills with a tissue and wish I had laminate flooring and soundproof walls; her music fills the flat and I cringe.

I read through my writing; the words pass before me; I don't recognise them as mine. It's as if someone else has written them. It's 6.30pm. I turn off my laptop. I stretch my arms over my head; do a couple of neck rolls one way, then the other. I'm aching. The lumpy, worn-out sofa, I conclude, is not the most comfortable place to sit all day.

I catch the beginning of The One Show, sitting in a kind of stupor, my Kindle poised next to me, waiting for a message from Alexander. The waiting fills me, threatens to burst. What is he thinking? Does he like my poem? As if aware I'm waiting the number 1 appears next to the message icon.

It's not him. It's an automated message from a profile

I've followed earlier on in the day with a request to connect on Facebook too. I cover my face with my hands, annoyed with myself for being disappointed. After all he's not my boyfriend. Alexander has a wife. But my disappointment is short lived.

> *My darling Maria. The poem is beautiful. You're so clever, talented, so creative, I am in awe of you. Xx*

> **Thank you. x**

> *I love that it's about us! Xx*

> **I'm glad. x**

> *I'm just away with Danny for half an hour. He's packing for his weekend visit to his parents. Xx*

'Mum, can we order pizza?'

'Oh, Natalie. Really? Thought you weren't hungry. There's cheesy chicken pasta in the fridge from last night.'

'You know you want pizza too. You do, you do.'

'I don't have the money for pizza.'

'Come on, we can get cosy.' She gives me her fluttery eyelashes and big eyes look. She came to know how to win people over with that trick since a little girl; it still works.

'Oh, okay. Bloody hell. But we might end up eating in the dark with no lights if we carry on spending money on pizza.'

'Thought you said you had an agent for your book,' she calls and returning from the kitchen she hands me a take-away menu, concentrating on her mobile phone screen.

'Who's that?'

'Dad... and before you say anything he's asking whether he can buy me more art stuff... he's got a voucher through the post.'

'That's sounds about right. Texts you when he can avoid spending any of his own money.'

'Don't be like that, Mum. At least he's trying. Isn't that what you want? For him and I to get to know each other better?'

I don't answer her remembering how annoyed I was when he first contacted me wanting to reconnect with her. I couldn't say no. I want her to enjoy a relationship with him, but he just gets on my nerves; even when he's trying.

A part of me feels guilty her dad's not around more but the protective part is glad of the distance between them. Natalie is better off without him and his manipulative ways. His gambling addiction left me no choice but to end it before he swallowed up everything I had worked for. Being the main bread winner for most of the six years of our married life, my good judgement and savvy investments kept us afloat and in the lifestyle, we had both come to depend upon.

But his gambling got worse, his tongue-lashing became more aggressive and targeted towards me. In the end he gambled his car away, leaving him with no means of working anymore. I tried reasoning with him, begged him to seek support.

He looked lost, beaten, yet he had this angry glint in his eye. His last words to me were: *'You made me like this. You're ugly inside and out. You think because you graduated university, you're superior to everyone but you're not. You're the same as every other woman. A bore in bed and a cow!'*

He emptied our joint current account and disappeared. I cried for three days when he left. I hardly ate a thing, hiding in my bedroom. I struggled to look after Natalie. I was like a ball of wool unravelling, becoming more and more tangled as the end winds up a hopeless knotted mess. I lost trust in everything— a sympathetic nod, a gentle word, a kind gesture, a friendly text.

On the fourth day I woke up determined; I had to sell the house, pay off his debts and move on. It was bad timing; Natalie had just started school. I needed a place to live and local was expensive.

An old university friend, who owned a local estate agents, found a buyer for me within two weeks and the flat I'm living in now within three weeks.

When I sold the house, I thought I'd be devastated but I wasn't. It had become a noose around my neck, ploughing money into a place which didn't feel like home anymore. If I let him back, he'll try to do the same again. Though, this time, he has no access, or knowledge of the savings account I opened for Natalie.

She reluctantly gets on with her coursework waiting for the pizza. I think back to how I was at her age. I was geeky at school and didn't shirk my homework or school responsibilities. My mum was especially proud of me, and Dad always gave me money to buy pens and pencils, notepads, and sticky notes. Any spending related to my studies was never questioned.

I'm thankful Natalie doesn't bunk off school and I don't have to deal with complaints from her teachers. And she is conscientious even if she needs the odd prod.

I follow her hand moving across the page; her writing slants to the left; that means she's an introvert. Her ts are crossed with a long line; she's determined and stubborn. That's true; a trait inherited from her dad. I remember doing handwriting analysis tests at school; my writing pointed straight up, logical and practical. How boring. I want to be more than that. I am fed up of being practical. Is ordering pizza bold and unpredictable? Then I remember Alexander. He's my bold, my unpredictable, my out-of-character.

The bell in the hallway chimes its irritating ding-dong, ding-dong-ding. Natalie bundles in seconds later, with extra-large pizza, barbeque ribs and garlic bread.

'Sides as well?'

'Mum, it's the two sides for £2 offer, stop being stingy.'

'Okay, okay. Too late now anyway. Grab two plates and kitchen roll. And a knife and fork too, Nat.'

'Mum, no-one eats pizza with a knife and fork.'

'I do.'

The Fake Britain theme tune comes on. I increase the volume; Natalie's chomping fills the room.

'Take the last two pieces, Nat,' I say, rubbing my tummy. 'I'm stuffed, too many carbs. I need to cut back.'

'You have the last piece of garlic bread.'

I force myself to eat half, leaving the rest. Does Alexander like thin women? I wish I hadn't eaten the bloody pizza.

'Have you finished your homework?'

'Yep.'

She leaves the room, discarded empty cartons and scrunched up napkins strewn over the coffee table. I tut, scooping everything up, but she's oblivious to my irritation holed away in her bedroom. In the kitchen I stuff the rubbish into the bin; Natalie's half-eaten tuna-filled bagel stares back at me.

I snuggle back on the couch, tucking the blanket over my bare feet where I feel the cold the most. I try to concentrate on the TV. I can't. Why did she not eat her lunch?

I get changed into my nightie and survey my nails. The spa manicure lasted well but it is time to redo them. Will

Alexander message me again? I'm tempted to send him a message but hold out. It's silly but I like him chasing me, making the effort.

I browse the internet for information on curing erectile dysfunction and try to imagine what Alexander will be like in real life, lying next to me. Kissing me. Lots of different words jump from the screen at me; struggle, arousal, erection, psychological issues... I don't read anything which is helpful, not to me anyway.

Natalie charges in and launches herself onto the bed.

'For goodness sake, Nat. Be careful. My nail varnish's going to spill everywhere.'

'Sorry. Can I go to Thorpe Park?'

'Not if you waste good food and money.'

'Muuum, stop acting like we're poor.'

'I'm not. I'm being practical and yes. I've signed the permission slip.'

'Dad said he'd pay if you didn't have the money.'

'I can pay it Natalie. I spoke to your Head of Year. I'm paying in two instalments.'

'Alright. Why are you always down on Dad?'

'I don't need his money.'

'I didn't say you did, he's only trying to help, pay towards stuff I need.'

I ignore her, she has a point. 'I put it on your desk.'

'I can't find it.'

I drag myself out of bed. I'm back, waving the permission slip within seconds. 'How blind are you? It was right there.'

'Who's Alexander?'

15
Maria

'Alexander?' My mind races. What did she read? I repeat his name trying to give myself time to put a plausible answer together.

'He's just sent you a message.'

'Oh, right. He's a guy who likes my tweets.'

'Mum, this isn't a tweet. He's messaging you.'

'And so are lots of people.'

'A man you don't know. He says you're wonderful.'

'Well, I am wonderful.'

'Mum! He could be cyber-stalking you.'

'It's hardly stalking.'

'Be serious will you and…' but before she finishes her sentence she's puking in my bin, narrowly missing my suede boots. I try to rub her back, console her, but she pushes me away. 'I'm fine. It's the pizza. I ate too much.'

She retches again and this time she lets me rub her back

in circular motions until she finally stops.

'Piggy,' I tease, but inwardly I'm worried. Her face is red and blotchy and she's shaking. It's not the first time she's retched and blaming the awful school canteen food isn't cutting it with me anymore.

'You sure it's nothing else?'

'Mum don't deflect. We're talking about you and that man.' She wipes her mouth with my face towel. 'You're so naive. You can't just talk to anyone.'

'I know that Nat.'

'Well, don't cry when you get freaked out.'

'I won't. I'm being careful.'

'Dad'll go mad if he finds out.'

'You are joking, right? And how the hell will he find out?'

'I don't know.'

'I do. If you tell him. Natalie, don't you dare. I mean it. Him on my back is the last thing I need right now. I'm just having a bit of fun.'

'Mum why aren't you listening. This is serious.'

'It's just a friendly chat. Don't make it sound sordid… please.'

'You're not getting it.'

'Go on now, and stop being a drama queen.' I grab her and give her a big hug.

'Mum, you're losing the plot.' She pulls away and a whiff of acid fills my nostrils. She slams the door behind her. Her thumping steps bounce down the passage and another boom pierces the air; her bedroom door bangs shut.

I clamber back into bed, pushing my Kindle away. Is she right? Am I being naïve and is this riskier than I care to admit? And should I be worried about her? I think long into the night. I can't sleep. I'm conscious of a tiny pulse racing in my wrist, a reminder of how Alexander makes me feel.

My daughter saw your message. Awkward.

I'm glad you've said daughter and not husband. X

No, thankfully.

Is there a husband, then? X

No, there isn't. Just me.

Sorry. I hope you're not going to block me now or ignore me. Xx

No, I wouldn't do that.

I'm so relieved. How was dinner? Xx

Nothing too elaborate, pan-fried chicken and asparagus with a butter sauce I put together. x

I'm guessing you're a fabulous cook. Xx

Lol. Not really, I like to keep it simple. x

Simple you are not my wonderful, beautiful Maria... I can't imagine anything being simple with you. Xx

Well thank you for the compliment... glad I'm not predictable. x

What am I doing painting this exciting picture of myself and life? This makes me as bad as all those other fakers. My life isn't exciting, I'm not exciting. I'm ordinary and boring and broke. I don't have my nails done regularly or dine in Mayfair like I used to. I'm being a hypocrite when Alexander's honesty and openness is clear. What am I doing?

What's unpredictable… me kissing you, me touching you, me running my hands towards your secret place? Xx

Oh, Alexander.

I can feel you trembling under my touch. Xx

I don't respond to him. I know what he's trying to do, what he is doing to me, and I don't want him to know the impact he's having on me— evoking those real physical reactions from me. I think about him and his story. How can a man with such little sexual experience make me feel this way? Natalie's words invade my thoughts and Tina's words fight for space too. Then I remember it's make-believe… it's only words… the right words… making me feel like this. It's not Alexander. He's not here. He has never touched me like that.

I resist messaging him for fear of being drawn into a night of sex with a stranger. An attractive, intelligent stranger, miles away, in bed with his wife next to him. Natalie's words ring in my ears.

16
Maria

'What aren't you telling me?'

'Mum, nothing. For God's sake stop going on. I was sick. Big deal.'

'But you've been sick a lot lately. I hope you're not taking those stupid pills teenagers rely on.'

'What pills? Bloody hell you really are stupid.'

'Don't talk to me like that.'

'Well stop going on at me.'

'I'm just concerned.'

'Focus on yourself, Mum. You're the one opening up to men you don't know on the internet.'

'For goodness sake. It was one message. I'm connecting with authors, writers…'

'Yeah, what-e-ver.'

'Let's not argue Nat. I hate this.'

'I'm late. I've gotta go.'

'Thought you didn't start till eleven?'

'There you go again. Thinking you know it all. You don't, Mum. I've got coursework to do with Yasmine.'

For you sweet princess. X
"I'm in my bed, you're in yours. One of us is in the wrong place."

I curb my emotions despite the welling anger and frustration, channeling my energy into my writing. I glance at Alexander's message but don't react. I'm not in the mood for his banter. Which isn't fair on him, but I don't care right now. Natalie's on my mind.

I text: *Hope you're feeling better. Love you, x*

She replies with a *X*. At least she hasn't ignored me.

I haven't come this far to have her go off the rails. I can't fail her now. I don't want her father's shortcomings to pave her life with more shit, adding her to the increasing statistics of mentally and emotionally scarred children from failed marriages and broken homes. I've worked too hard and cried too much to get to where I am. She's a young woman with a mind and life of her own. I have to set her free to live her life, but it's been just me and her for so long.

How's your daughter? Has she said anything more? X

She's said plenty but it's okay. Her temper's like that of her father.

Aren't you worried about your husband reading our messages? X

He's not around. I'm divorced. Are you worried

about your wife reading our messages?

No... I'm deleting them as I go along which makes it difficult for me to follow our conversation at times. I forget what's come before if your reply doesn't come through straight away. Xx

Oh okay. x

I'm so relieved you're not with anyone. Xx

Why? What difference would it make? x

I want you to myself. I'm selfish and greedy. But only with you. Xx

I want to explode. Xx

Sounds good to me. I wish I could make you explode. Maybe one day.

"Maybe one day" dangles in my mind, swaying back and forth like a swing in the wind. Where will Alexander lead me?

His persistence, and his words, fire me up with ease; suggestive, playful, in tune with me. It's as if he feels a sexual tension in me that demands to be freed, satiated. I like it and I'm not fighting it. I'm embracing it despite Natalie's reservations.

As Nelson said of Malta...
"sleeping or waking Malta is always in my thoughts..."
and in my case, it's you who's always in my thoughts. Xx

I giggle. I have no idea where the quote is from but love what his message implies. I like how he's uninhibited for a man who says he's had little sexual experience or pleasure and this knowledge comforts me. I don't want to be involved with a "big I am" or a "woman magnet". I like the flirty Alexander… it's a total contrast to his more serious side.

He doesn't think of me inadequate. I am in control and have more experience than he has hinted at, giving me a rush of superiority, though I wouldn't reveal my thoughts to him.

He's sent me a picture of his "bulge" under his jeans, and I shudder with pleasure at the thought of arousing him from hundreds of miles away.

'What are you smiling at on your own?'

'A poem… a romantic one,' I say.

'Not that guy then?'

'Nat, leave it, okay?' I sound like a petulant child and rein it in asking, 'How's your day been anyway?'

'The same as always. What's for dinner?'

'Hot dogs okay?'

'Yeah. I'm starving.'

I'm relieved she's hungry and wish I had planned a more substantial meal. But it's too late now and I don't want to fuss, risk annoying her.

Maybe this is how daughter-mother relationships work… up and down… back and forth. The door of the bathroom slams shut. Why is she being sick again?

17
Maria

I struggle to settle into my tasks and my to-do list stares back at me. Work is bitty. Nothing seems to be gelling and my boss, Leo Souter, is in a foul mood. I try not to get too involved when he's like this but it's hard not to be affected. I go home and moan at Natalie and she moans back, and we end up having a row. I ask myself if it's worth it but the overdue council tax bill is a reminder it is.

JangleJewels, a women's British jewellery brand, has expanded organically over a decade. My PR job keeps me away from my writing and home life two days a week and I enjoy it. I develop promotional campaigns, I plan and travel to exhibitions, co-ordinate and showcase our collections and do lots of useful networking.

But recently Leo is not 100 percent focused on the business how he should be. He's easily distracted. Instead of focusing on one thing at a time and making sure everything is in place and running smoothly, he jumps from one idea to another. He has no stickability.

Flexibility and multi-tasking are not the same as hopping from one project to the other and getting nothing done. He's always busy but, in my opinion, the least productive. I should talk to him; give him the benefit of my experience but I risk him getting all uppity.

I draft an email campaign for the newest piece in our new collection to send to our key influencers; connections made at an event in Birmingham last year.

The interest, initially slow, has generated thirty active leads. The problem with moving forward is Leo has no set budget for this part of the business. Anyone who is business savvy knows that to grow and expand you have to invest in PR as an ongoing expense. I hope we continue working with the new accounts. Who knows what they may bring in over time? This could be Leo's big break… and mine. A pay rise would be great.

I push back my desk chair and stretch my arms out in front of me and out to the side. My eyes are tired from staring at the computer screen all morning. The clock has stopped working. I make a note to buy a battery from the local shop; like that for weeks it's irritating the hell out of me now.

The kitchenette, a small space between the shop and the office/showroom, is situated behind the retail premises. The showroom doubles as a workshop where Leo works on his latest ideas. The shop is styled and decorated beautifully; a top-end boutique. He sells his own JangleJewels pieces and stocks a select number of other independent brands to balance the price range and also offers a bespoke design service.

I flick on the kettle, empty a soup sachet into a mug, cream of vegetable with croutons.

'Do you fancy a tea or coffee Leo?' I call out to him on the shop floor.

'No, thanks. I'm ordering a cappuccino from the cafe. Earl Grey for you?'

I'm relieved he's calm after all the effing and blinding this morning.

'Ooh, yes please.'

'... with a drop of milk, no sugar please mate.' He's placing the order by phone.

I swallow the last dregs of my soup when Leo bursts into the office, kicking the door with his rubber-soled brogues.

'Special delivery.' He plonks the take-away cup on my desk, walks out again.

I check all three work email feeds; mainly spam. I glance at my Kindle's Twitter message box.

> *I don't want to do this but I think we should stop before it goes too far. Xx*

I don't take the message in. I reread it.

> **Are you saying it's over?**

> *I feel like a first-class shit because I'm hurting you and what I'm doing is wrong even though it's so exciting. Sorry, truly sorry. Xx*

> **I don't think I can let go of you. Can we just talk from now on?**

> *I feel like a total bastard.*

> **Are you sorry cos you don't want this anymore or**

sorry that you've messed me around or sorry you've done this behind your wife's back?
I don't want you saying things you don't mean to me.
Better it's over now than later, but I'll miss this, us, you.

You will never understand what you've done to me, made me feel. You're so special. Xx

I'm not special... you just want me to be.

You've spoken to me even in your last few sentences, in a way I never have before, with such beauty and tenderness. Xx

So, is this it? I'm crying.

Can we be friends? I'm sorry to have made you cry. Xx

I'm inexplicably stupidly devastated. Through my tears, I scan the internet and send him a picture with the words, *I've lost somebody who wasn't even mine.*

Time drags and at five o'clock I call goodbye to Leo.

'You're not going, are you? I've got things to hand over. Another half an hour or so?'

'Leo, You've had all day to talk to me. I can't stay.'

'Half an hour. I promise.'

'It's not the half an hour. I've been here all day. You've had your friends in and out all afternoon and now that it's time to go you're asking me to give you extra time? That's not fair... and it's not professional.'

'I'm sorry, what did you say?'

'It's not professional. It's not the way to make JangleJewels successful.'

'Well, excuse me but don't you think you're talking out of turn here. You're working for me remember.'

'Then behave like a boss should. Put the business first.'

'I don't…'

'No, you don't. I'll see you tomorrow. Have a good evening.'

I'm out the door, fighting another onslaught of tears before he can reply. I sprint to my car and throw myself into the driver's seat. Fat droplets plop onto the front of my top falling faster than I wipe them away. I scrabble around in my handbag for a tissue, find a used one and blow my nose. I rev the car and reverse, barely glancing left or right.

At the traffic lights I cry again, the tears free fall. I wallow in the weight of grief swallowing me up and I don't care. I am disproportionately shattered at the thought of not having Alexander in my life… in my virtual life anymore. I've shared so much of myself with him, physically and emotionally, and now he's ending it. Whatever "it" was. I am inconsolable and even my head can't talk my heart round. What am I going to do? And what if I lose my job?

18
Maria

At home, Fabio's already let himself in; his work boots are parked outside my flat door. He's managing a building project a few miles away. He's my oldest and bestest friends, we've known each other since junior school, and he's been my rock since my divorce. He's stood by me and Natalie despite having had a good friendship with my ex.

When Natalie was younger, he would arrive before work to walk her to school which allowed me to get to work on time. I used to fancy him like mad before he came out and he knows it. We still laugh about my swooning around him but now we are like siblings; there for each other.

'Hi darling,' he moves in close, planting a kiss on my cheek, Fluffy snuggled in his arms.

I give Fluffy a tickle under the chin. 'God I'm glad to be home. What a day.'

'Don't tell me, Leo.' He rolls his eyes.

'Yeah, mainly. He was in such a foul mood, sapped all my usual bounce. What time did you get here?'

'Thought you'd be used to him by now. Go and get comfy. Dinner's already prepared. I'll bring your tea in. Forget work. Forget Leo and relax.' His attentiveness exacerbates my guilt. What am I doing? Why am I even upset about Alexander? I've got my best friend here who has never let me down.

I kick off my shoes, tossing them into the corner of the sitting room and slump into the sofa, my arms curled around my knees, my bag next to me.

Fabio hands me a cuppa and a biscuit.

'Don't cry. It's not worth it darling. Forget work. You're not paid enough to be stressed like this. Why d'you think I don't get involved… in anything.'

'Your boss loves you. You'll never be without a job.'

'I'm all for open relationships. But don't tell Natalie I said that.' I give him a weak smile; he's changing the subject. 'You're just a pervert.'

His long curls fall across his forehead. 'Least I'm a happy one,' he says.

'Dinner smells nice,' I say, the guilt gnawing at me from the inside.

'Monkfish skewers with courgettes, mushrooms and red peppers and spicy couscous.'

'Wow, my own master chef. Will you be wearing an apron… and nothing underneath?'

'Darling, if it means putting a smile back on your face then yes.' His comment brings a bout of fresh tears.

He gives me a hug and leaves. He knows when I need space and I love him all the more for it. If he wasn't gay, he'd be my husband.

My phone buzzes. Leo says he's sorry, he's sent a kissy

gif with the words sorry floating in and out of the screen. I smile. At least my job's safe.

I remove my Kindle from my bag; nothing from Alexander. I browse Twitter and ♥ a handful of tweets without even thinking about what I'm doing. Why can't Alexander make me feel better? But I suppose he doesn't know me or what I'm going through… Fabio's cooking dinner for me. He's the one who helps me through the lows.

I sip my tea. Is Alexander as lost as me? Is he distraught our relationship has ended? I should be commending him, for doing the right thing by his wife, and I suppose by me too, but there's a hole in me which he had filled with his attention and silly messages and although I hate to admit it, I miss the ego boost they gave me. I was a teenager again having her first crush.

Fabio's made a great effort with dinner, but my appetite is zero. We eat together in front of the TV. I eat three cubes of the monkfish and half the vegetables; I push around the couscous with my fork. I enquire about his day; barely engaging. He scoops my leftovers onto his plate and finishes the lot. We are both expanding round our middles.

'We'll finish the current job in time to start the next one on schedule so it's going well. The building trade is roaring, so interior design is where it's at.' He chews on his last mouthful.

'Bet you're relieved.'

'Yeah, I am. Who would have thought I'd be heading up my own design team with the country's biggest builder of domestic housing?'

'Me! I always knew you'd go far. Now I think I'm going to have an early night. D'you mind?'

'I should get going too.'

'Leave the dishes. I'll sort them in the morning,' I say.

'I'll say good night my darling. Fluffy's not in her hutch by the way.'

'Sorry Fab. Let's meet over the weekend if you're free. Natalie's at a sixth form revision weekend in St Albans the whole of Saturday and Sunday.'

'Ha. I'm hardly going to say no to a whole weekend with you am I darling? See you Saturday and send my love to Natalie. And don't forget Fluffy.'

I have a shower, top up bunny's water and food. I'm relieved Natalie's spending the night at a friend's. I message Alexander with a quote.

> *"To wander is to be alive."*
> *Roman Payne*
>
> *Are you OK Alexander?*

I try to read a brilliant book on the craft of writing, which would normally have me scribbling notes, but my tears blur my vision. My sobs fill the silence of the flat. I keep checking my Kindle; I'm like a child with an itch. Finally, a message.

> *Hi Maria. I've had the most stressful evening. Our neighbour's son (17) took an overdose, fortunately not enough to end his life. Was at the hospital. Home now, but shattered.*
> *How are you? Xx*

His message is heartbreaking but selfishly I only focus on myself and my feelings of rejection. I respond on auto-pilot writing whatever seems appropriate but without the empathy I should have. I'm too engulfed in my own relief at receiving his message although I am hurting.

> *Also was wondering about you and how you are. Your message, does it mean it's OK to wander? Am I looking for excuses or justifications, so confused, but too tired to think tonight. Thank you for being kind. Xx*

I want to hug Natalie and wanting to feel her close, make sure she's okay, text her a *X*.

Alexander's next message, selfishly, is the one I'd hoped for. I'm on his mind, he's concerned about me. I am touched by his words and can't stem my tears.

> I was just saying that's all.
> But I think we should leave it. I feel so alone but I'm all cried out now, tomorrow's another day.

I read my message out loud; I don't mean it. It's what I think he wants to hear. Can I trust myself not to cross the line again?

> *Sorry to have hurt you so much. No more I promise. Xx*

> I have to accept at least half the blame... I walked into "you" with my heart open and my eyes shut.

> *And I was doing the same thing walking the other way. X*

> I wonder what lesson this has taught us?

I send him another image with the words, *There's you, there's me, and there's the craving in between.* I attach a message to it but the tears streaming down my face make it difficult for me to tap out the message through the blur.

> *And that's where the craving should stay from now on...*

> *If you're OK with that you can be my "boy" friend... nothing more.*

I am at work tomorrow night, can I talk with you then. It's hard trying to put the craving away altogether. Xx

> *We can work on that. Hundreds of conflicting emotions.*

Me too. Goodnight. Xx

19
Maria

I wake as if a heavy rain cloud is hammering down on my head. I don't receive Alexander's usual good morning message or any others from him. He retweets two of my tweets and likes all of them. He makes no comment. Each time I think I'm containing my feelings they find a hole to seep through. I'm like a colander trying to hold onto my spilling emotions. I remember reading a quote on Twitter about how even the mightiest of fires eventually becomes ashes and I cry all over again.

I make a cuppa and wallow in the quiet; no Natalie mooching around, although she would have still been in bed. How she sleeps for as long as she does is beyond me.

I flip open the bread bin and turn my nose up at the two crusts. The thought of eating nauseates me. Is Alexander carrying on as normal or is he missing me like I'm missing him?

The easy banter of the two morning TV presenters washes over me. Subconsciously, I'm delaying getting ready for work. I can't face Leo after our altercation last night.

I yawn fighting the hammering exhaustion bearing down on me from the lack of sleep; I tossed and fidgeted all night. Natalie was up at midnight. She's not sleeping well, she's become uncommunicative. Teenagers!

Three text messages from Fabio; he hopes I have a better day at work, he hopes Leo behaves himself and he can't wait for the weekend. His texts accentuate the fact Alexander hasn't texted or messaged.

I shower and leave my face make-up free, not caring about the dark circles under my eyes. Changing my mind, I rub in a sheen of tinted moisturiser and drive to work. Even the music on the radio doesn't cheer me up, each tune reminding me of Alexander; *I'm in love with the shape of you... I love you dangerously...* one song transitions into the next.

Leo doesn't come to work. I'm relieved. I can't face another day like yesterday. His moods are so unprofessional, but what would he know? He's never worked for anyone other than himself. I think what a shame he won't heed my advice or listen to anyone else. The business could be phenomenal... with the right leadership to match his creative vision the company could easily compete with those popular high street chains.

There's a list of suppliers he wants me to contact for their business terms, two piles of samples to be posted to fashion accessory and jewellery bloggers and three blog ideas he wants me to ghost write.

I work through the list systematically and finish this week's blog post raving about how accessories and jewellery are what put the wow into an ordinary outfit. I send this month's invoices to the retailers stocking our brand.

By late afternoon I'm shattered. I haven't had any lunch either. I wish I didn't have the meeting tonight. Just as I'm about to shut down the office computer an email alert pings.

It's confirmation of a huge order; the one I'd chased for weeks. My excitement pushes to the top of the Richter scale. I text Leo, forgetting our disagreement, and lock the office.

A chill greets me outside; yet despite the cold I'm hot, elated with the news. My poncho flaps in the wind and I laugh out loud. Suddenly my energy is brimming.

The meeting at the UKFT offices, UK Fashion and Textile Association, goes well. I hope to sign up for full annual membership; the benefits presented outweigh anything we can do in isolation and the backing of a reputable government association will give Leo a competitive edge. I forget Alexander for a couple of hours.

I want the company to succeed, though Alexander distracted me for a while. I want it to be a success just as much for my own sake as for Leo's, even if he is a plonker. Too many big multi-nationals are flooding the high street and JangleJewels offers uniqueness.

'Hi Nat. It's me.'

'Hi Mum.'

'I've only just finished my meeting so won't be home before... ten,' I say, checking

my watch. It's past eight already.

'Meeting? You sound too happy to have been at a meeting.'

'It was good, and I got a confirmed order at work this afternoon. The one I've been chasing.'

'That's brilliant.'

'Thank you, my darling.'

'See you later. Love you.'

'Love you too.'

We always report in on each other; a rule I set when she was old enough to go anywhere without me and we both respect it.

An overpowering tiredness, and hunger, engulfs me and I dive into the first open coffee shop I stumble across.

Hi Maria, I hope your meeting goes well. I'm at work this evening and all night if you want to get in touch later. Xx

Thank you Alexander. It went well. Just finished. How are you? x

Empty. X

Why?

Everything. What happened yesterday, you – me. Our neighbour's son. I was tired last night because I'd spent a long time on my feet. I was sore and kept waking up. Sorry, you don't need this. Glad your meeting went well. The UKFT one. X

Sorry, how are you? X

Yes, it was... It's tragic. How's he today? Have you heard anything?
I haven't been brilliant. Feel like I'm looking down on myself and I'm milky transparent. Like this isn't me. I wrote another poem.

***

'I'm home,' I call out.

I navigate a scattered trail of Natalie's belongings and hang up a heavy coat, its pockets jangling with keys. Whose is that? I push her trainers together. In the kitchen, I swallow a couple of paracetamol. Take-away cartons crowd the worktop, and four empty bottles of ginger ale are poking from the bin. Where did she get the money to order food? And when did she start drinking ginger ale? She must be better. I have a quick tidy up and tip the leftovers onto a plate, setting the three-minute auto timer on the microwave.

I tap on Natalie's bedroom door, 'Nat?' A shuffling and a muffled giggle filter through the closed door. Impatient, I push open the door. 'Hi girls. You okay?'

'Uh, yeah Mum. This is Tom. Tom this is my mum, Maria.'

For a split second I'm gob smacked but find my voice, plaster a smile on my face. 'Nice to meet you, Tom.' I glare at Natalie, refocus. 'You ordered Chinese?'

'Yeah. Tom ordered.'

'Didn't fancy the leftovers?' I try to hold back on the sarcasm, but I fail; it drips like tar. 'What time are you getting picked up?'

'I'll get an Uber.'

'Right, okay. Nice to meet you, Tom. Night night Nat.'

The sweet aroma of ginger and lemongrass bursts from the microwave when I ping the door open. I take a forkful and blow through rounded lips to cool the food scalding my tongue. I discard the plate. My appetite vanished.

Natalie's got a boyfriend, and she didn't tell me. But maybe it's my fault, so engrossed with Alexander, I wrongly assumed the friend would be female. The name Tom is vaguely familiar. Why?

Her bedroom was the disorganised mess it always was. A

pair of tights, a scrunched-up T-shirt hung dispiritedly over the edge of the open drawers of her dressing table. Her hair straighteners lay on the floor on a stack of books. Typical teenager; unlike tidy me. Did Natalie's bed look different? Did it look like the messy bed of lovers? I feel sick.

I get changed and tiptoe to the bathroom for a wash. My tiredness calls for a good night's sleep and yet I want so much more. I think about Alexander and his messages and how he said he's sorry. I think about Natalie in her bedroom with Tom.

I was far older when I had my first proper sexual encounter with a boy. I say proper encounter because I don't count the time a guy molested me in a park when I was twelve. I wasn't scared though. It left me with a strange sensation. My brother came along on his chopper and frightened the pervert away before anything more sinister could happen and I suppose it would have. But the incident excited me more than scared me. It was my first sexual experience. The feeling it provoked in me played on my mind and I tried to recall it many times over those first few months and still years later. The stranger wasn't old, twenty something. It wasn't until I recognised the feeling again, with my first boyfriend poking around in my knickers, I realised I had enjoyed it, longed for it.

Duncan. Duncan Tom Benedict; that's why Tom rings a bell. We were paired up to do a uni presentation on statistical analysis of the export market in the UK. We got sent packing from the library at eleven and we shared a bag of chips on the way back to mine.

In my room, we kissed and ended up in my single bed trying not to wake the mousey girl next door who complained anonymously about every bit of noise in my block; but we all knew it was her.

From that moment on Duncan and I became boyfriend

and girlfriend until I caught him, off his head, masturbating over a porn mag in the shared bathroom on my floor. That was it, over as quickly as it started, seven and a half weeks after we first kissed. I had to retake my statistics module twice before I finally scraped a pass. I hope Tom doesn't let Natalie down.

I take a quick shower, the water only just warm, and slip into my pyjamas. I snuggle into my dressing gown, remembering my sheer disappointment at not being enough for Duncan despite all we did together. Even with the heavy duvet wrapped around me I shiver. It's chilly but not worth flicking the heating on; it's past eleven.

Alexander fills my mind. I hesitate a second; I'm laying myself bare, making myself vulnerable, but want him to know how I feel, but fear it's already too late. I send the poem.

Here it is. Lost in the Depths of You.

Watery blues, liquid azures
Waves wading passion over us
Frothy, licking love no longer secures
Refracting light through clouds cirrus

Holding onto each other's desperate touch
Pulling current close and then apart
A connection one last time too much
Effervescence illuminates the heart

A pain, mind's eye rejection
I see the sky reflected in your eyes
Diving, tossing a watery reflection
A blue canvas, heart-felt sighs

Kissing seashells toss on glass waves
Lavender, turquoise and colours in between
Shimmering frothy emotion raves
Cerulean sea storm our hearts have seen

Translucent light, briny waters
Still shining a breathless spirit inside
But in us our soul's disappear into quarters
Thick tears, wet eyelashes abide

White crest, salty droplet tossed fears
Drawing breath, a sea storm mosaic of blue
Kicking in the wrong direction, wet tears
Love gone, lost in the bluest depths of you.

The poem is beautiful but heartbreaking. Xx

Are you still empty?

Drained might be a better description, last night was emotional. Xx

It's not the answer I'm hoping for. He has let me down. He hasn't related the "empty" to being lost without me, our relationship. I'm tired and fed up.

Natalie's giggly goodnight to Tom interrupts my thoughts. For goodness' sake. Talk about the long goodbye. Finally, she tiptoes back to her room, and I wait a few minutes, muster the energy to go to her room.

'So, you and Tom…'

'What Mum?'

'How come he came round?' I try to sound casual, but my voice has a steely edge to it.

'Why shouldn't he?'

'I'm not saying he shouldn't just that it would have been nice to know.'

'Mum, you weren't here. How could I ask you? And what's the big deal? It's not like you caught us in bed.'

'I should bloody well hope not. How long have you two dated?'

'We're not dating. We're seeing each other.'

'Isn't that the same thing?'

'No, it means we're seeing each other, free to date other people if we want.'

'And are you?

'What?'

'Dating other people?'

'No, I'm not. But Tom might be.' I move away from the bedroom door and sit on the edge of her bed. I spy a silvery piece of silver foil glinting in her bedroom bin amongst the chocolate wrappers. I'm too scared to look again, not ready to face whatever it is. Is it a condom packet? Is she sleeping with him? Panic envelopes me.

'And if he is wouldn't that upset you?' I utter the words, reddening, and I try not to sound judgmental; guilty about Alexander, and me and his wife.

'No. We've agreed so it's okay. You're so old-fashioned Mum and yet you're flirting with men you haven't even met.' Her sarcasm stings.

'This isn't about me.'

'Well, it is when you're doing worse.'

'Natalie! Don't speak to me like that.'

'Mum, you're tired.'

'Of course, I'm tired. I'm trying to hold things together and you're being ungrateful.' 'You're always so emotional. I'm going to bed.'

Wanting to avoid any further confrontation I leave it. I can talk to her tomorrow. It's late, almost eleven. I yawn. Natalie is growing up too fast, I'm not sure I can handle any more complications.

***

The following morning, groggy from a sleepless, I wander tidying up. The flat's a mess and after a load of washing, hoovering and dusting, I go for a brisk walk to the Co-op. I want to cook a nice meal for Natalie. I want things to be right between us. In the end, she doesn't come home. When she finally replies to my messages, her text confirms she is staying at Yasmine's.

Settled in bed, it's almost eleven at night. I give in and message Alexander. Part of me is bored; part of me is missing him. I don't sign off with a kiss; I hope he notices. I hope it stings.

> *Hello.*

> *Hello. Thinking about us.*
> *How did we go so quickly from occasionally "liking"*
> *And DMs to this all encompassing thing between us?*

> *What triggered it all? X*

> *How did we get so inside each other? X*

> *I don't know, my heart is aching. Sorry. I can't talk about this Alexander. I'm crying again.*

I didn't mean to hurt you, I didn't mean to make you cry.

But I did and I'm sorry. X

Can you forgive me? X

> There's nothing to forgive. I need to mend myself and only I can do that, the way only you can heal your hurt Alexander, only you know how.

I have the same feelings as you, I might be a man, but I have feelings and was running down the same road as you, hand in hand. Xx

Just reminded me of the lines in the Merchant of Venice, Shylock saying if you cut me do I not bleed? Sorry. X

> I understand but you let go of my hand. I wanted to hold on, to feel your hand in mine, to feel your pulse in unison with mine.

I let go because deep down I thought it was what you wanted. The right thing. Was I wrong? Should I have held tighter? X

> It's happened now and we can't go back. I don't know why but I'm an absolute mess and yes you should have held tighter but I also know you are holding onto Sandra. x

Being torn apart. Xx

You shouldn't have given up on me. You should have let me love you.

I tried to use that word the other night, I longed to use the word love. Xx

But you still let me go.

I still feel for you what i felt yesterday and the yesterday before. Friends? Xx

Friends. Mirrors lie all the time... I'm not real and you're not real.

Maybe you're Brian a long-distance lorry driver from Basingstoke. Xx

You've made me laugh. Goodnight Alexander.

Goodnight wonderful Maria. Xx

I sit in my bed and cry like I've lost the love of my life. Abandoned... again. Rejected... again. My tears fall; for me and for my little girl who's no longer a child but a young woman with a life I know little about and even less control over. Why does life have to be so hard?

20
Maria

I've splurged, bought crumpets, real butter and a small triangle of camembert, Fabio's favourites. They are not Fortnum & Mason, but the local supermarket hasn't let me down. He loves the cheese melted over the buttered crumpet which suits his personality to a tee. He's kind and generous, he's funny and he's squidgy and cuddly and his curls always entice me to twirl them around my fingers.

We sit in front of the television; a Saturday morning cookery show with perfectly made-up presenters and a spotless kitchen taunt me. Fabio talks with his mouth full; I catch a glimpse of the creamy camembert coating his tongue. It's his most annoying bad habit but I don't say anything. I make a mental note to wipe down the inside of the microwave.

'So, what's been happening? The other night was more than Leo being a plonker,' he says, putting on his serious voice and, turning to face me, he folds one leg under him.

'It's nothing.' I fidget with my hands and melt into him at the same time. 'Okay, okay... You're right, as usual. I met a guy online but it's over.'

'A one-night wonder was it?' He winks at me with mischief.

'Yeah, kind of.'

'You can talk to me about anything.' His serious tone returns, and I owe him the truth. He's my forever-by-my-side best friend.

'It was amazing. It was like a magical fairytale for a few weeks.'

'Weeks?'

'Yes... don't look at me like that.'

'And you didn't say anything?'

'I'm telling you now,' I say, in my cutesy voice.

'And?'

'I fell for him... and I thought he fell for me.'

'Why's it over?'

'Well, I'm assuming it had something to do with his wife,' I say, ignoring his shocked expression.

'Not again, Maria. Why do you go for the same old sleazebags?' He reaches for me but I push him away.

'That's not fair. The last two lied about being single. And I was in a different place. I was playing it safe.'

'And the dick pics?'

'None. I promise. This guy's not sleazy. He was thoughtful and made me feel good about myself... we had a connection... sexually and intellectually. I really liked him.'

'Is there a pattern here? Safer with married men? Do you think they can't hurt you? Because they can you know... I should know.'

'So, you know how it can happen.'

'Come on…'

'It didn't seem to matter because he's miles away and this was just an online thing. I didn't intend to get involved, to feel like this. I liked his intellect. I liked the non-committal fun and the permission to just be naughty with him with no strings.'

'And Natalie?'

'It's got nothing to do with her. This won't hurt her. She's got her own life without me. I'm telling you it felt different. No naked videos or drunken sex messages.'

'And now that it's over?'

'I'm trying to forget about him, and I refuse to spend our weekend together talking about Alexander.'

'Ooh, Alexander, is it? Nice name.'

'Yes, and it's not is, it's was. Past tense.'

I eat the rest of my breakfast, my movements mechanical like a clockwork instrument.

'I think I fell for him. I didn't mean to, but it became something more.'

'Are you mad at me?' he asks, breaking the silence hanging between us.

'No. This felt different, and I suppose I hoped it might lead to a more serious relationship. He was so sensual, saw beauty in me. We boiled over together. It felt like he put me first, couldn't live without me.'

'Blimey, boiling over is an understatement. What was he meant to do with his wife?' I burst out laughing and grab the cushion tucked under my knee and hurl it at him. He catches it and tosses it back playfully. 'Seriously, what are you going to do?'

'Nothing. I can't do anything. If he doesn't play ball, I have no choice but to leave it and hide until I'm over him.'

'That bad?'

'Yeah... that bad. He got to me.'

'I think he'll be back.'

'No... I don't know. I thought I could cure him of all his troubles... with his wife, his erectile dysfunction, his lack of confidence...'

'He can't get it up?'

'He's got a less severe form of Cerebral Palsy... it affects him from the waist down.'

'And where would you go with that? I mean you've always enjoyed sex. Be realistic Maria.'

'There's sex and there's sex... I don't know.'

'He doesn't sound like he had much going for him.'

'He did... he read poetry and literature and quoted stuff I've never read in my life. I liked that about him. I liked his romantic side, his wordy side.'

'Well, compared to most of your exes who couldn't even speak proper, I bet that was just marvelous darling.'

'Ha-ha, you're so funny.'

'But seriously. I mean if it did work out and you did get together, how would you cope with a man who couldn't give you a good seeing to, without sounding crude?'

'I don't know. And it wasn't the sex stuff that attracted me initially. It was his mind, his love of literature. It was the romance.'

'Literature my darling won't get you far... he's not your Mark Darcy. And what about Natalie?'

'She's another story altogether. She's not herself recently. She's distracted, withdrawn, rude.'

'She's a good kid, needs stability, a father figure.'

'He is a father. He has a son. He knows how to be a father figure.'

'You know what I mean.'

'Well, she doesn't have to even know about him.'

'Oh that's great after the moan you had not knowing about Tom.'

'That's different.'

'It's the damn same. You're in denial. I'm telling you it's great and dandy while it's online but if you meet? If it does develop? What will you do?'

'She's got you. You're her surrogate dad.'

'I will always be here for her but come on. Stop it. I'm being serious.'

'It didn't get as far as that so it's irrelevant. Still enough about me. What about you and your open relationship with Mattie?'

'You going to read it?' he asks, catching me sneaking a peek at my Kindle but I turn it face down.

'Maybe.'

'I'll put the kettle on unless you want more crumpets?'

'No thanks, Fabio. I'm all crumpeted out. And you're not going to get out of telling me by stuffing yourself with more comfort food.'

I wait for him to disappear, glancing at Alexander's message, my fingers twitch to respond. I miss him; I got used to him filling the empty hours at home, he was my company.

How are you Maria? I can't stop thinking about you. Xx

My heart leaps, expands and squashes against my chest. I dance my fingers over the screen like a pirouetting ballerina. I'm not surprised at my reaction; Fabio's words go round in my head. What impact would his CP have on me? What would it be like for real? Would I be satisfied being the woman who never made love with her partner?

But his message excites me, pushing the thoughts away.

How can I go from despair to total elation in the space of a few seconds? What am I doing? Why do I want the contact with him?

'Was it him?' Fabio asks, back with another three buttered crumpets.

'Yes, it was if you must know.'

'What did Twitter Daddy say? He wants to get back with you, doesn't he?'

'No, he's just asking how I am.'

'Everyone knows that's code for I want you back.'

'Stop it, Fabio. This is a mess. How could I have got so drawn into this… this messy relationship?'

'Because he made you feel special, desirable… gave you attention, chased you.'

'Am I that shallow?'

'Look at me and Mattie.'

'But you know what you mean to each other. You're not vulnerable.'

'Neither are you… you're just a bit naïve at times. And you're still hurting from the break-up of your marriage… it hit you hard… you can't deny that.'

'Yes, but it's not an affair. He wasn't going to run away with me,' I say.

'Richard Gere and Julia Roberts in *Pretty Woman* never thought they'd fall in love either…' he says. 'Maybe deep down that's what you were hoping for.'

'It was all to do with letting him in… it was about trust.'

'Trust means so many things.'

'It means so much… trust is a big word.'

My words sit on my chest precariously like a fat pigeon on a delicate branch; trust is a big word.

'Trust gelled us. We opened up about things we have not so easily discussed or admitted even to ourselves,' I say.

'Me and my craving to be loved again, my writing to be taken seriously, him to be seen as a man with sexual desires despite CP.'

'Heavy but I understand where you're coming from. So do you trust him?'

'I've had no reason not to trust him until now, until he dropped me. And in a way I understand why he has. What was this between us anyway?'

'Are you going to answer him?'

'I want to but I'm not sure I'm ready to get drawn back in… his persistence is attractive though. I enjoy the thrill of being chased, him wanting what I give him. And I want to please him. I willingly did stuff with him, liked being who he imagined me to be.'

'Bloody hell. You're right into him, aren't you?'

'I don't know what I am. It hurts as if it is real. Our messages to each other are so comfortable, unpretentious, unguarded. I'm me, a braver me.'

'You can be you with me as well,' says Fabio, looking a little bruised.

'I know, but I mean in a boyfriend-girlfriend kind of way, talking about stuff… doing stuff…'

'You mean "mess-sex-ting", if there is such a word.'

'Yes, ha-ha. But no… it's more than the sex thing.'

'You do what's right for you for now, don't overthink things. Stay in control and you'll be fine. You're low without this guy in your life, so go with it. But don't give him your bloody address.'

'Bloody hell, really? I thought you were anti all this, especially since being my stop-gap boyfriend for so long.'

'I want you to be happy but promise me one thing.'

'What?'

'Don't message him back today. Let him wait. Let him

realise what he's lost.'

***

The yearning for Alexander subsides, or at least I push it deep inside where I can ignore it; ignore it for now. I focus on Fabio. We dress up, hit the local bars and plod most of the way home at one in the morning. Sober-ish. I sing, *When will I see you again,* into my can of coke at the top of my voice and Fabio stuffs his face with a shish kebab smothered in Jamaican hot sauce.

'You're not going to see him again, Maria, because you haven't even seen him to start with,' he laughs, choking on his mouthful and spitting half-chewed lamb onto the pavement.

'Here.' I proffer my drink, pulling a face of utter disgust. 'And have the rest. I don't want it back with all your kebabby saliva all over it.' He tries to swipe me round the head with the can, but I duck giggling.

'Too slow,' I tease, as he chomps another bite of the filled wrap and finally home, I hand him Natalie's duvet and a spare pillow. I open a bottle of red wine and we sit snuggled for another hour or so until I lose focus, my eyelids too heavy to keep open.

'Sofa's all yours,' I say, giving him a hug. 'My bed's calling.'

He pours the last of the wine out and knocks it back in one. 'Thanks. We've had a laugh. Glad you're happier.'

'It's been great. I hope the study weekend's been worth it for Natalie too.'

'That school's working them so hard… we didn't have study weekends.'

'You wouldn't have gone even if we did,' I tease.

172

'And don't you dare message that Alexander bloke.'

In my bedroom I unplug my Kindle, annoyed I'd left it charging all evening, sucking up all that electricity. Natalie pops into my head and I shiver involuntarily. I don't recall signing anything for a weekend study session.

Twitter connects. Three direct messages, sent hours ago, catch my eye. I drop my make-up wipe onto my lap, abandoning my cleansing routine.

Maria please tell me you're OK. I think I've made a terrible mistake.

I'm missing you so much. Xx

Maria I want to speak to you. I'm lost without you and I want you back in my life, how we were. Xx

I will wait to hear from you. I'm not giving up on us. You were right. I should never have let go. Xx

He wants me back. He's made a mistake. Fabio was right. I try to stay calm resisting the urge to tell Fabio, and a warm glow fills me. I recall Alexander's recital of Burns, *my love is like a red, red rose that's newly sprung in June.* I'm no longer tired and dance around my bedroom undressing seductively, imagining Alexander with me. I pull my leggings and my top off so I'm just in my underwear. I slowly, teasingly, undo my bra, spilling out as I hold the bra up against me. In my mind's eye, Alexander touches me, wants me.

I flop onto the bed, finding my pyjama top from under my pillow I slip it on. It stretches across me, the top riding up over my belly, breaking the spell. I battle with my conflicting emotions, should I play it cool or run back into his arms? After tapping out and deleting two different messages I simply send him a *x*. It's 2.24am.

I keep checking for a reply. Still nothing at 3.07am. My mind fades in and out of the here and now with the warmth of my memories. My soul lights up at all the possibilities yet to come. My vibrations are speaking to the universe around me. *There's still hope*, I hear them whisper, and I know it to be true.

***

I squint against a thin light filtering into my room. My head is heavy, like it's stuffed with cotton wool balls. I reach for my Kindle. It's 6.06am– no messages. Stuff him! I'm setting myself up for a tug of hearts but can't help myself. My throat scratches like sandpaper, I can't swallow. A metallic taste coats my tongue. I tiptoe down the hall to the kitchen for a glass of water.

Back in bed I snuggle under the duvet. I close my eyes to Alexander's bearded face and his ruddy red cheeks. I imagine his big hands all over me, touching me the way his messages described many times over. I shudder and it's not the chill in the early morning air.

I go over and over what we've "done" together. Words pulsate in my head like a merry-go-round. Alexander's words, Fabio's words, my words… they all crisscross like a Sunday newspaper puzzle, and I realise I'm crying. Tears soak my pillow.

There's a gentle tapping on my door. 'Come in,' I croak, drying my eyes.

'Thought I heard you. Good morning.'

'Gosh you're up early. Did I wake you?'

'You okay?' Fabio asks.

'No, I'm not. I'm such a stupid cow. I've let this man get to me and now I'm totally discombobulated.'

'Now in English please,' he says, shoving me over and climbing into my bed.

'Stop it. You know... off balance, confused.'

'He will be back, but when he is, you choose whether you want him to be.'

'There's more to be said, to be discovered. I'm on the outside of the circle and I don't like it.'

'Sometimes it's better to be left there,' he says gently. 'So you didn't hear from him?'

'Yes, I did. I just sent him a kiss.'

'A kiss, eh? He's sure to reply to that... I imagine your kisses are irresistible,' he teases me.

'Stop it. Now what shall we do today?' I ask sniffling.

'I suggest I cook a big breakfast. We might as well use all the supplies I've bought. Snuggle in front of the TV for a movie binge? What d'you reckon?'

'You've hit the Sunday vibes spot on. I love you Fabio.'

'Not as much as I love you,' he says. He leans in and squeezes me tight, and we hold onto each other like that for what seems like a long time.

21
Alexander

It's an unusually hot day for Inverness. I persuade Danny to go for a roam along the beach, instead of swimming, his usual activity for today. I can't face the stuffy changing rooms and steamy pool; condensation running down the tinted glass wall and the unbearable sweaty stench mixed in with chlorine which lingers on my skin and in my hair.

The promise of a cup of coffee on me, not paid from his weekly allowance, swings it. We hit a tailback behind a crawling lorry; traffic accumulates along the dual carriageway. I lower my window hoping the fresh air will calm the twist of agitation in my stomach. With effort I loosen my hands from around the steering wheel, but my bulging knuckles only tighten their grip again. The rest of the journey is slow and painful until the truck pulls over into a layby two miles from the secluded beach; after that it's forty miles per hour all the way.

'No swimming today,' says Danny, for what must be the twelfth time since we got into the car.

'Danny, that's enough. Stop repeating yourself.'

By the time we arrive my nerves are as taut as the stretched elastic band on a child's bow and arrow kit.

I carefully ease the car door open; stretching my back and rolling my neck, for a few moments, to release the tension in my shoulders. I haul myself from the car and gingerly get to my feet. I look out across to the lighthouse. A beacon of hope, white, shining.

Danny scrambles down the sloping path. I struggle on the rocky decline, relying heavily on my walking stick for extra support. My mood jars with the percussion of waves singing to me.

He removes his shoes and socks and stuffs them in his rucksack. He scampers along the beach ahead of me, screaming, *no swimming today* and waving his arms around. His rucksack dangles over his shoulder.

He's oblivious to the elderly couple toddling along arm in arm, evidently enjoying the serenity, until now. He comes to an abrupt stop and leans forward, hands on his knees, puffing out his exhaustion, gasping for breath.

Overhead a squabble of seagulls glides and soars, drifting on the air current. The flash of white against the china-blue sky is truly magnificent and the birds seem to float on the unseen thermals. Their sudden squawking fills the air; seeking their next snack. Are they expressing their happiness or hunger? Either way they are mirroring my own feelings towards Maria. An urgent hunger for happiness torments me.

I can't run after Danny and don't even try to. Instead, I wander along as slow as a much older person, lost in my thoughts. Each step sinks uncomfortably into the soft loose sand and I struggle to gain a foothold; my left foot turns habitually inwards. I drag my foot along to where the incoming waves have solidified the beach; it's easier for me to walk where my feet aren't sinking, than on the powdery dry grains. My walking stick gives me extra stability as it digs into the squelching sand, yet I want to toss it away. My frustration gnaws at me. Danny can never live independently but if I had to, I could live without Sandra's overbearing mollycoddling.

The warmth of the sun, and the sound of the breaking tide, imitates the aura of a romantic setting and I shake off my exasperation. I miss Maria. I shouldn't be thinking about her but can't help it. I shade my eyes from the sun's momentary glare and imagine my bare feet moving in unison with hers as she leans into me, our pace in harmony with each other's, her steps slowing to fall in time with mine.

A Golden Retriever races ahead of its owner and splashes into the rolling surf, spilling onto the sandy beach, bringing with it tangled twists of seaweed and loose debris from the seabed. The dog barks and wags its tail from side to side, a glistening glaze of saltwater clings to the hound's golden fur.

The owner increases his pace and breaks into a sprint towards him.

'Here Bailey. Here boy.'

The dog stops instantly, shakes off the excess water, sending droplets into the air, regarding his owner; the jiggle of a treat bag sends the canine scurrying back, with twitching ears and a wet soggy face, towards the man.

'There's a good boy, come on Bailey.' His owner kneels in front of his doggy companion and dries him in a huge, faded orange towel and its hue transports me back to a holiday we took many years ago. Callum had an orange hooded robe;

he dribbled his ice cream down it, the sun melting it quicker than he licked it. Sandra fussed over the stains worrying they wouldn't clean and her complaining spoilt the rest of the day for me. I doubt either of them remembers.

The white crested waves are coming in faster, the tide creeping in, the wind heightening. In the far distance I spot a pod of five or six bottlenose dolphins. The sight is compelling. They ride on the swells and tidal swings; their movements seem whimsically impetuous, their boisterous forms sleek and smooth.

My mind wanders to another dimension; Maria wet from the spray, turning towards me, her arousal pushing against her T-shirt. I want to feel her sexual tension and that familiar sensation around my bulge fills me; God, her illusion fills every pause between my breaths, melts into and fills every crevice. I tremble.

I snatch a piece of driftwood, careful not to lose my balance, and write MARIA in the sand. Her name etched on the beach fills me with a sense of fulfilled promises and like the endless ocean in front of me, I hold onto the hope "we" can be forever. The "we", bigger than the both of us, doesn't frighten me. It shocks me and I fight the short swells of nausea pummeling me. My face drains of colour.

'You okay?' asks Danny, in a rare show of unprompted awareness.

I nod, not trusting myself to speak, trying to compose myself. He saunters off towards a mass of boulders and driftwood; he picks his way, like a mischievous imp, sinking into the wet sand and jumping over mounds of pebbles, some crusty with limpets and slippery seaweed, reminding me of happier long-ago days.

I snap a photo of my sand art with my mobile and send it to Maria. I'm being a daft old romantic. I can't believe we have reconciled… can't believe I almost lost her with my overthinking and cowardice and misplaced loyalty when she has brought me so much joy these last few months.

The guilt I carried about cheating online with her behind Sandra's back was short lived and did not outweigh the emptiness I felt without our daily interaction. My physical well-being suffered equally with my mental and emotional balance; I became moody, withdrawn, snappy one moment and brooding the next.

Within seconds, the onrush of waves washes away half the letters and only the M is visible in the midst of the foaming yellow sand. A glint catches my eye. I spy a piece of sea glass; no bigger than a ten pence piece its edges smoothed by the sea's tugging and dragging. I bend down, again with difficulty, but grab it before the tide steals it away; ultramarine and heart-shaped, a rare jewel.

I place it in my jacket pocket and push down an uncontrollable urge to cry. I shiver against the late afternoon breeze. I came so close to losing Maria. How easy it would be for her to sever communication with me at any moment and my heart constricts in my chest. Lying in bed next to Sandra night after night with no intimacy, not even a gentle touch or kind word, shakes me to the core.

I can't handle losing Maria again when I have only just found her. When I have only just began to feel alive again, giving me more than the humdrum of work to surface for in the mornings. The light creeps in; brighter than ever before.

My phone beeps.

Oh wow! Where are you?

I'm at the beach called Fortrose and Chanonry Point with Danny.

180

I wish you were here with me. Xx

Has he not asked who Maria is?

No. He's in a world of his own. Xx

Are you having a nice time?

I'd have a much better time if you were here with me. Xx

Well imagine me close, splashing you with the water, getting you wet. X

We'd have to sneak off somewhere to get out of our wet clothes, dry each other off. We'd have to think of how to keep each other warm. Xx

'How do I love thee? Let me count the ways' My darling. XX

We would.

Her message conjures up a kaleidoscope of images. I taste her on my lips, I imagine her in front of me naked, an open flower. I reach into my pocket and finger the sea glass, warm in my hand.

'Can we have a cup of coffee?' asks Danny, pulling me back abruptly into the present moment. Maria's image dwindles and disappears, fading hues in an optical illusion.

'We could, aye.'

'No swimming today, no swimming today...'

His whoops of joy startle a dosing baby, wrapped in layers of crocheted blankets in a rainbow of colours. The mother leans over the buggy, rubs his chest, gently shushing him, easing him back into a lulled sleep. I mouth an apology to her.

We amble back, retracing our steps. The path's slipping pebbles threaten to topple me. I pull up the collar of my shirt against the growing chill coming off the spin of the sea breeze, but it sneaks under it, slides over my neck and shoulders. I shiver against the cold.

Danny sits on a boulder to put on his shoes and socks. The socks are inside out but I don't bother highlighting this.

I glance one last time at the beach, and the solid lighthouse, and a tremor of longing washes over me as I think of Maria and her name written in the sand, now disappeared, but the image etched in my heart and locked in my photo album marked "M" on my phone.

Danny insists we sit and have our drinks there instead of taking them away. I sit down on the worn bench, my patience ebbing. The corrugated iron, make-shift coffee den is draughty and the weakening afternoon gold struggles to warm us as it slithers through the thin net curtains.

I'm not usually short with Danny but I'm finding it hard to be here after my messaging with Maria. I don't want to be here, and I don't want to be at home either. Sandra's mood has lingered for two days and no matter what I do or say it's the wrong thing; her words cruel. Against the backdrop of my increasing friendship with Maria, with her kind and thoughtful words and understanding, Sandra's words seem all the more spiteful and mean.

I long to be with my new love. I dream of her in my waking hours and in my hours of broken sleep where half-awake I can feel her beside me; her hand in mine, her legs intertwined with mine, her head snuggled in the crook of my arm. In that blissful place, between sleep and full wakefulness, I have reached out to her only to suffer a sharp poke or shove bringing me back into the thick of reality; Sandra is sleeping next to me and not Maria.

I long to share my happiness. Talking about Maria may help me contain my emotions. Telling Callum might be a good idea; we've always shared a special closeness. He often chastises Sandra for talking badly to me or belittling me. But how would I explain it?

Deep down I am convinced Callum would condone my friendship and newfound relationship, understand why I am so preoccupied with the realms of this online simulated affair. I could speak to John but dwell on how he's known Sandra since childhood, may choose to be loyal to her, may not see fit to withhold such a revelation from her.

If he were to tell Sandra, I don't know what would happen. Would she declare her undying love for me, or would she roll away and leave me to it, taking most of my dad's inheritance with her? She's certainly made a big show of her new dishwasher and washing machine. Or would she feel betrayed I sought another woman to give me what she doesn't? Would she harbour any guilt?

Callum has said on more than one occasion, *if my wife spoke to me like that, I'd be outta here. You're lucky Dad's still around.*

Your dad's not going anywhere are always her words. Does she believe no one will want me? Does she believe I've got it too good where I am? If I'm honest with myself I have to admit she's tolerated a lot over the years; the wetting myself, my inability to manage finances and stick to a budget, the endless hospital appointments, and check-ups, but I've been a good husband, hardworking, loving, when she lets me, and I've never strayed... not until now.

'Bloody hell, Danny. How much sugar have you put

in your coffee? Pete will kill me. You'll be up all night.' He smirks and grabs another sachet. 'No, you don't laddy boy.' He's too quick and snatching it from me he pours more into his foam cup. His defiance grates on my nerves when usually I'd be amused. 'Hurry up. Let's get going, it's almost five o'clock.'

Having a coffee with Danny then I'm home for the next three days. Oh the joys. Xx

Lol. Don't you like being at home?

Sometimes I feel like I go to work for a break. I can get things done and be myself without the constant have you done this and have you done that from Sandra. Xx

Oh dear, you can always say no. Try it and see what happens.

I do sometimes aye but the backlash goes on for days so it's easier to do as I'm told. Xx

Hide in your shed... with me!

Oh darling, my wonderful Maria. You don't know how I would love to be with you, close, together. We could read poetry and you could share your writing with me. I'd love to hear your voice. Xx

'The curtain white in folds,
She walks two steps and turns,
The curtain still, the light
Staggers in her eyes.

The lamps are golden.
Afternoon leans, silently.
She dances in my life.
The white day burns.'

That's beautiful. Thank you.

It's by Harold Pinter… it reminds me of you. I absolutely
love the line she dances in my life. Xx

22
Alexander

No sooner have I stepped into the hallway Sandra's high pitch whines from the kitchen.

'Why are you so late? Why haven't you answered my calls?'

'I went to the beach with Danny,' I call back to her, swallowing in an effort to quash the intense urge to shout, 'Shut up.' I sit on the stairs, toe off my shoes, and enter the kitchen, a forced smile on my face. Sandra's best crockery and party food is piled by the sink.

'I was worried, thinking all sorts.'

'I'm here now so stop fretting, Sandra. I'm hardly a child.' My nerves tighten. 'What's all this for?'

'John and Elizabeth were having friends over for drinks tonight but they're in the dark, a power failure, so we're hosting them here. It's Alastair and Abigail, the couple we met at theirs two Christmases ago.' So, this is why she was worrying; it had little to do with my welfare.

'Here?'

'Yes, are you not listening?'

'Oh righty-ho.' Am I relieved I won't be spending all night in front of the TV with Sighing Sandra or agitated at having my home invaded by people I'm going to have to make polite conversation with all night? I'm being grumpy and I don't like it. My mood seems to exacerbate the onslaught of aches and pains consuming every part of me.

'What time will they all be here?'

'Eight-ish.'

'I'm going for a shower and change. My hair's full of salt.'

***

I linger in the shower, enjoying the water's hot spray on me... the steam rising around me brings on the desire to be with Maria. My loins tense, my cock stands to semi-hard attention. I imagine Maria in the shower with me, a tingling sensation prickles its way through me from head to foot and back again.

I'm in love. I must be. This is bigger than my physical twitches and my yearning to be with her; it's about wanting to hear her voice, knowing where she is, what she's doing, learning more about her writing, her hopes, her dreams. I want to share it all with her in a way I haven't with Sandra. I get the urge to message her. Tell her how I feel. The overwhelming realisation is too much, and a gasp escapes me. My outstretched arm knocks the soap off the holder.

I stretch for the soap clogging the plughole. I lose my balance and grab onto the shower tower for support. It rips out of the wall. Gushing water spurts from the pipe. The shower head dislodges and snakes itself around my feet. Instead of panicking a huge belly laugh rises within me, and I can't stop laughing. Sandra is going to kill me, but I don't care.

I fight with the spray and turn the shower off, stemming the water from the broken pipe by stuffing a flannel down it. I'll have to turn the mains off.

Sandra's voice travels up the staircase. 'How long are you going to be?'

'Two minutes. I've had a wee accident. Need to get to the main water valve,' I say and opening the bathroom door I leave watery footprints all over the floor.

'No. No. You're such a clumsy fool.' She stares from the door, her eyes bulging at the pools of water. She tut-tuts as if telling off a child.

I quell the titter threatening to explode again.

***

'Good to see you again.' I force myself to say almost an hour later when our guests trail through the front door.

'You're a life saver, Sandra,' says Elizabeth, air kissing Sandra's flushed face before slipping off her jacket.

'Welcome Alastair and Abigail.'

'Hello Alexander,' says Abigail. 'You've lost weight since we last saw you. It suits you.'

Sandra hangs their coats and jackets on Dad's coat stand. She jolts her head to the side, urging me to get everyone a drink. She ushers them into the sitting room. My phone vibrates in my trouser pocket.

> *Well, you can imagine me there next to you, although I imagine you're at home by now. X*

Yes, I am. But I can still imagine. Got friends over for drinks but would much rather be with you. Xx

Ooh, are you going to get squiffy? Don't bang your head again. Lol.

Will save getting squiffy with you! I wish you were here… I could slip my hand under your skirt. Xx

Stop it. You're going to get me oozy. x

Am I? I'd better carry on. Xx

xxxxxxxxxxxxx

When she responds with a line of kisses it means she's turned on despite her protests; those little crosses are our code, my green light to carry on and to bring her to a climax. I've often wondered whether when she tells me she's cum she has come for real or whether she's cum in her imagination.

'Sorry about all this. Elizabeth may have laid it on a bit thick to your Sandra and here we are. D'you want a hand, mate?'

'Not a problem, John. Good to have you here. Better than a night in front of the TV on our own.' I slip the phone back into my pocket.

'Work?' he asks.

'No… no… blasted insurance… PPI message…' I trail off, conscious I'm waffling.

'Such a nuisance. Call all hours of the day.'

'Aye, aye.'

'Are you bringing those drinks in?' Sandra bustles into the kitchen, her ample bosom bulging against the fabric of her blouse. When did she get so big? I hadn't noticed, but how would I when we barely spend any time together let alone naked. The word naked pushes my mind back to Maria. I have to connect with her. I imagine her waiting for me. I can't disappoint her.

'D'you mind excusing me, John?'

Touching, licking, pulling at your panties, my lips on yours and then... Xx

I sit on the toilet, the lid down. I'm shaking at the thought of her having an orgasm, surrendering to me. I know I love her, I'm sure of it. I have to meet her. I have to know her like this. Know the reality of her next to me, lying with me, being in my arms. The reality of us being together, in the same place, at the same time comes at me with great force. I want to be with her, with every fibre in my body. I'm tingling in places I knew nothing about until I connected with her, and I won't let her go. I'm in too deep.

CP has held me back long enough and I'm not going to sink under each day anymore. I've let it and my relationship with Sandra thwart all I ever wanted to experience, and now I feel like a man. I can bring sexual satisfaction to a woman not as a matter of course but because she wants me to, gains pleasure from what I can offer her. As I imagine her in front of me, I experience sensations like never before, never thought I was capable of and it's beautiful, not dirty or perverted. This is my life. This is the life of a man who has CP and erectile dysfunction, yet I can feel. I can imagine and I can satisfy a woman.

What I imagine is as real to me as being with her, more real than lying with my own wife who in comparison has become a cardboard cut-out and it's not enough anymore.

It was never enough but I didn't know anything different. But now I'm alive. I have found myself when I hadn't even realised until now, I was even lost. I never knew how wonderful a sexual relationship could be, never experienced this level of heightened pleasure, mutual satisfaction.

I've gawked at porn over the years, but porn is not the same. Those images and films didn't stir anything in me; I felt revulsion, acutely aware of my own inadequacies in the bedroom and as a man. But this bond with Maria is real. She stirs my blood. Conscious of how long I've disappeared, I flush the toilet to cover my tracks and adjusting the front of my trousers I head back to our guests.

The usual conversation topics fill the hours until the evening's glow eventually fades into night. Every chance I get I message Maria. I want her to know she is in my thoughts, that I want her like I've never wanted anyone before. I'm not going to let her go. She hasn't told me much about her past relationships other than she's divorced but I get the impression she has suffered, not merely emotionally but physically. I feel her anxiety and all I want to do is wrap her in my arms, tell her it's safe to be with me. I will take care of her.

'Alec, John's buying an electric car. What d'you say?'

'Say about what?'

'An electric car, us buying one too,' says Sandra.

'Aye, we could have a think about it.' I'm not concentrating. I don't want to buy a new car. I don't want her to have a new car. I can't get Maria out of my head. She's in every thought, every waking moment, and every moment in between.

'You look a bit flushed, mate. Too much whisky, eh?' says Alastair.

'No, can never have too much whisky,' says John,

refreshing our glasses with a glint in his eye. I take another swig and the ice tinkles against the glass. Sandra's best crystal.

My gaze settles on the greasy sausage rolls, dried up cheesy pizza bites and the soggy vegetable spring rolls. Nausea engulfs me and I swallow the bile rising in my throat.

'You don't look well,' says John.

'He's not eating properly. And he's even going to the gym. Mid-life crisis or whatever they call it nowadays,' says Sandra.

'Nothing wrong with nurturing ourselves,' says John. 'Still life in us yet, eh?'

'Actually, can you all excuse me? I feel a bit sick.'

'Not the company I hope,' jokes John.

'No, no. I think Sandra may be right. I've overdone it. I'm so sorry. But you carry on without me. Lovely to see you Abigail and Alastair. See you soon John. Good night, Elizabeth.'

John eyeballs me. 'Oh, sorry mate… should we go?'

'No, no. He's after a bit of attention. Honestly, he's like a child.' Sandra's words wound me and, as I head to our bedroom, she complains, 'He's drank too much as usual. You'll be joining him next if you carry on John.'

> *I've given myself up to you, held nothing back.*
> *What a beautiful mess we're in. X*

Upstairs I stretch across my cold marital bed, guilt consuming me for a split second. My remorse is swallowed by Maria's uninhibited abandonment to me. In that moment I want to scream but a sensation in my bowels forces me to the toilet and I'm angry at my body and its inability to control natural forces and motions. I huff and puff with frustration. Tears crumple my eyes.

Back in the bedroom I urgently continue messaging her despite it being after ten o'clock. I'm a man obsessed. Wild. Daring.

How wonderful my darling. I want you to be all mine. I love you. Xx

Are you having a good night?

I love you. Did you hear me? Do you understand what I'm saying to you? I have fallen in love with you. Xx

You have fallen in love with the thought of me, of what we do together, but it's not real. This isn't real. You're in lust with me. X

I read her message, frustrated she thinks what I feel isn't love, isn't real. It is real to me, and I start to panic. Am I being ridiculous? Am I fooling myself? Perhaps she's right and this is all an illusion, a game of lust and wants tangled up in a myriad of moments, of getting carried away.

I know what I feel. I know it's because of you. Don't tell me it's lust. I've never felt this way. I want you, it's more than what we do. I'm alive with you. I know I love you. Xx

I'm glad. X

How do you feel? Do you feel the same way? Xx

I'm so happy. X

How you react to me tells me you feel the same. But I won't press you. Xx

I cut our conversation short to get changed. Weary footsteps fill the downstairs hallway and cheerful goodbyes sit congruent with my own feelings. Sandra laughs and the lightness seems out of place, alien to me. The latch clicks behind them, Sandra locks the front door.

The evening has collapsed into a starry night. I haven't drawn the bedroom curtains, which will annoy Sandra. I take a peek, standing back slightly, out of view. The four shadowy silhouettes of our friends hug and kiss before disappearing in opposite directions to their cars.

In the curtain-less window of the unkempt, run-down house across the road, a light shines and I imagine the young NHS couple lying together. Polite, they always seem to be holding hands, or kissing when I pass them in the street. They always seem affectionate and tonight it bothers me. I want to be the other half of a loving couple. I want to have what they have.

I should go downstairs, help with the clearing up, but can't face Sandra; I don't have the energy.

Maria has stirred me from a deep sleep where I was only half alive. Where I couldn't feel, I can feel; I am a sensual man. She is the flame igniting me. Where will this online affair lead to? If it will lead anywhere at all I don't know. All I care about is being with Maria in every way I can, in virtual reality or in the real world. I don't care much which it is. Either way I am the happiest I've felt for years, if not my whole life.

'Did you have a nice evening?' I ask Sandra when she

appears almost an hour later, after midnight.

'I did. We all did. What's wrong with you?'

'Nothing a good night's sleep won't put right,' I lie.

'Really?'

'I wouldn't mind a bit of a cuddle, sweetheart.' But the words stick in my throat and the battle between guilt and conflict rages within me; I'm lying to myself. How can I carry on like this and for how long?

'Come here you soppy sod,' she says, and we do our thing, like robots. The romance, the flirting, the teasing, the swelling… there's nothing. She gasps. It's over in minutes; the sex between us hollow, one-sided.

It's grey and soundless when it should be rockets and Catherine wheels, sparklers, and fountains. Instead of a firework display it's a slow-burning rubbish heap at the bottom of the garden, all smoke, and no bang.

She falls asleep within seconds. I lie awake, hating myself for putting my marriage at risk, hating myself for the years and years of pretending.

23
Maria

'Hello.'

'Hello my darling.'

'I can't believe we're talking to each other,' I whisper, twiddling my necklace, leaning back into my pillows with a soft sigh. I stifle a giggle, I'm getting hot. I imagine Natalie warning me with *SULA*, Sweaty Upper Lip Alert, in the superior tone she has adopted with me the last few weeks.

'Aye, but we had to properly before meeting up, don't you think?' he says back down the line.

'Yes, I know that. Sorry, I'm so nervous.' I'm breathing hard. Meeting up, his words fill my head. I sit up. My upper lip sweating again.

'Don't be my darling. It's me. It's so good to hear your voice.'

'You too.'

'So, how are you?'

'I'm… I don't know. This makes you real.'

'Aye, it's doing the same for me too, you know, aye,' he says. I adore his Scottish accent and I'm swooning despite the nerves.

'I know. Gosh how did we get to this point Alexander? It feels like we're on the brink of no return.'

'Now that's a good question but I do rather think it's our sexy messages, don't you?'

'Well, yes. I know. But it was something else that started all this, something more.'

'It was?' he asks with a ping of incredulity in his voice.

'Yes, I mean, that was it to start with but then I kept coming back for you and your CP. I wanted to know what made you tick. And I love how you spout poetry and read literature.'

'It was? So, what we do doesn't make you want me more?'

'Yes, it does. But it wasn't about that to start with, but I do like all of that. It was more about whether I could help you, support you through your problems with your wife. Or at least that's what I told myself. Maybe that was just a way of justifying our relationship, easing my conscience. I know that sounds ridiculous with what's happened, but this isn't like me. I don't do this.'

'Ditto. I've never done anything like this either. But I can't ignore what I feel for you. Ignore how you make me feel.'

'And how is that?' I ask the question but in my head I'm all over the place, our conversation surreal.

'Like I can be anyone I want to be and do anything I choose. I feel free. Free and weightless and I'm so in love with you,' he says.

'Where's your wife?' I ask, but not caring. I don't want to

waste time talking about her.

'Downstairs, making breakfast I think.'

'Are you excited about meeting me?' I ask.

'Are you excited about meeting me?'

'Alexander, if anything happens between us this goes from being an online thing to being a real affair. Can you cope with that? The guilt?'

'Guilt? No. You're too beautiful and too wonderful to feel guilty about. I feel nothing but elation and desire and I want to hold you.'

'And you will,' I say, in a kind of sexy voice which doesn't sound like me at all. I'm still playing a game, hiding behind the telephone. Teasing him, imagining I'm a beautiful seductress when in reality my hair is greasy, and I haven't brushed my teeth yet.

'Sandra doesn't come into this. This is between you and me. This is about our world, us. I will answer any questions you have but I won't volunteer information about her. I have no relationship with her. We're strangers. I've connected with you more than I ever have with her. You're interested in me... you ask questions, you've researched my CP and tried to understand it. She pays no attention to me... and I don't give her any attention either.'

'That makes me sad,' I say. 'We all have parts of us that scare us, Alexander. But we have to see, we have to look.' This is a big mess and it's only going to get bigger and messier. I try to slow the palpitations.

'Don't be sad. It's nothing new, nothing to do with you. It was here all along. Like this for a long time. You've just made me realise how much living I still have to do and want to do. I realise how hard it's been.'

'Oh, Alexander.' A strangled mumble escapes me. The tears come and the more they fall the more I'm sniffling.

'Don't cry my darling. I don't want you to cry because of me. I want to make you happy.'

'You do, Alexander, you do… this is all just…' I wipe my eyes and a smear of stubborn black mascara stains the back of my hand. I spring off the bed and check my face in the mirror above my chest of drawers. I'm so knackered. He won't fancy me when he meets me.

'Maria… you there?' Panic fills his dulcet tone, the tiny pause of hesitation falls between us, and a stab of guilt comes at me like the blade of a knife. 'When I come to London, I promise there'll be no expectations on my part. I won't force anything onto you. You can choose how it all plays out between us… okay my darling? Please promise me you won't change your mind.'

I'm certain the dynamics of meeting will change what we have and what after? I don't want to lose what we have but I don't say that to him. I want to hang onto our illicit virtual rendezvous and yet I want to make him real, feel him, feel him touching me.

'Yes… okay. I'm sorry. It's all so big, isn't it? After all these months of messaging.'

'Nothing is too big for us my Maria. Nothing.'

'We'll meet as arranged and go from there.' I sound more assertive than I feel; what if he doesn't like me? What if my words and our exchanges don't match the reality of who I am… or who he is?

'We will. And I promise you I am just ordinary Alexander from Inverness.'

***

'Can you strip your bed? I want to stick your sheets in the wash,' I insist, searching for an outlet to channel my nervous energy, my high.

'I'm late for my sociology catch-up class,' Natalie yells.

'Catch up? Are you falling behind?'

But she's gone and the vibrations from the slamming door shudder through the flat. Silence.

Grudgingly I go to her room and throw open the curtains. It must be at least three weeks since she changed her bed linen. I wish she would do more to help me or at least show some appreciation.

I fold her clothes, strewn over her bed, and pick up her dirty underwear. I put the lid back on her face cream and zip her make-up bag, noticing the film of dust on her dressing table.

I untangle her duvet and pull off the sheets, rolling the linen up into a ball. I shake off her pillowcase. A small, spring-bound notebook falls onto the bare mattress. I recognise it for what it is straight away. I don't recall her writing in a diary.

The curiosity in me wants to read what she's written, especially with the growing and undeniable rift between us. I'm curious whether she has written anything about us in it, about Tom; she doesn't talk to me about him. She's always fobbing me off with, *Oh, you're so embarrassing* and *Yasmine's mum doesn't hassle her all the time*. How did we drift so far apart?

I pull back the purple cover and after a moment's hesitation I turn over the first two pages; slightly waxy, ruled with the faintest blue lines. Her handwriting is easy to skim read, her letters fat and round, entries about school and parties. There's a page full of how she fancies Tom, argues with Yasmine, a poem called happy-ness. There's a concert ticket stub and a make-up discount voucher, the use by date expired.

With no real intention of reading any more, I am about to close the book, place it back under her pillow, when an impulse push me to turn over one more page. I home in on three entries in a messier script. The writing is not like hers.

June 1st
"I think I'm in love, love, love. In love with Tom. Tom my utterly perfect love. Or at least I think I am. Yasmine says I'm behaving like some Shakespearean damsel. She's always spouting some quote or other. Not eating or eating too much is what love does to you because love is the food of love, or something like that. Yasmine doesn't know about love. She leads them on and all she's ever done is lipsed a guy. I ate crap today - chips, popcorn, garlic bread. If I'm not careful Tom'll notice how much rubbish, I eat and how fat I'm getting if he doesn't notice my smelly breath first. He's such a good kisser. My bra's chafing. Or maybe it's Mum's cheapo washing powder. I need a new one, something black, more sexy..."

June 3rd
"I had such a shitty sleep, weird dreams, running, stopping. A nightmare I suppose. I think I was being chased. Probably Mrs. P chasing my sociology coursework. LOL! Mum'll go mad if she calls home to tell her. I'm knackered and I've been in and out the loo. Drinking like mad. I've been so thirsty. Yasmine joked I was pregnant, and I panicked a bit especially after me and Tom doing it twice while Mum was at work..."

A stab of disappointment comes at me. Pregnant? How could she be so deceitful? I feel suddenly inadequate. What sort of a mother wouldn't realise her daughter's sleeping with her boyfriend? She's seventeen. Younger than I was.

"... I googled symptoms of pregnancy but being thirsty wasn't one of them. Oh and Tom told me he loves me. Like really loved me. He kind of went gooey and all soppy and I laughed. Then I stopped. He was so serious. We just cuddled all afternoon instead of going to the boring careers talk. We stayed squashed in my bed. I might ask Dad if he'll buy me a double bed. Mum'll hit the roof, but I don't care. She's always on at me about something."

I reread the bit about "doing it twice" and a sadness replaces the disappointment. She didn't tell me. She didn't tell me she did it a first time let alone twice again. When did she stop being my little girl? When did she become so secretive? I can't help but smile at the double bed entry though and it takes the sting out of the word pregnant. She's too sensible. I put the diary back and the next week is fraught with anguish.

What the hell am I supposed to do? Reveal I have read her diary and I risk losing her trust completely. She hasn't asked about the diary, whether I saw it when I changed her linen. She must know I washed her sheets even though I hauled them to the dry cleaners and made her bed up again before she was home. I throw myself to the mercy of Alexander. We talk about honesty and being open. Our late-night conversations are becoming more frequent.

'Sometimes you just have to go with your gut. Don't rush in. Let your thoughts settle into you. You'll know what to do when the time's right,' he says gently.

'But I need to advise her. Tell her I'm here and I understand.'

'She knows that. She knows that because you're the only parent she's really ever had caring for her.'

Two weeks later, Natalie, in a particularly foul mood, leaves for school without breakfast. She slams the door so hard the intercom falls off its holder. I instantly head for her bedroom. I can't help myself. Her diary is still there.

June 14th
"I called Tom crying down the phone, almost shouting at him. I don't know what to feel or how to feel. Am I supposed to be happy? How long have I even been bloody pregnant?"

The words swim in front of my eyes. The word pregnant seems to flash on and off the page. Pregnant? No… no… no. I slump onto her bed. Natalie cannot be pregnant. What about her exams? What about university?

I read on, ignoring the teary ticklish sensation behind my eyes.

"I can't work it out and all the leaflets are crap."

Stop panicking. Stay in control. She might not be pregnant. Is that what she's saying?

"So many things are running through my mind that at school today I could hardly breathe, I felt dizzy and ran out of sociology, told Mrs P to shut up. Mrs. P hates me even more now. But I don't care. Tom came and found me, and I told him, just told him straight. He was shocked but said everything was going to be okay, he'd stand by me whatever happened. I need to do a test. Yasmine is more suspicious than ever, but I've fobbed her off for now. I need to sort this out. What am I going to tell Mum?"

I finish reading, struggling through my crumpled tears. Stupid, stupid girl. When, in the past, she's always proven to be so sensible, so mature.

I put back the diary, smooth out her duvet.

Drinking a mug of chamomile, feeling calmer, I wonder how I will be able to support her to have the baby. Having the baby will be the most amazing experience of her life but is she emotionally mature enough to cope with it? Do I even know her anymore? Or will I let my own dismal, heartbreaking experience of being abandoned cloud my judgement? Either way it's too late. She is pregnant. What am I going to say to her?

My own pregnancy had been hard. The initial joy of being pregnant quickly fell away, replaced by a constant gnawing anxiety. Pre-eclampsia in my third trimester kept me a lonely prisoner in my own home, reading online articles on what could go wrong and why while real life continued without me.

Colleagues stopped calling, friends fell back into their own routines and lives. I wallowed silently, and tearfully, on my own. I didn't voice my concerns to anyone, not even Natalie's dad who wanted nothing to do with check-ups or appointments or scans, or me. The excuses, plausible to begin with, took on a twisted, almost, cruel turn as time continued.

'I don't want to hurt you,' he said, refusing to sleep with me. And as time went on, 'Do you honestly think you're attractive with that whale-sized belly?'

It was a lonely time. I hid my real feelings from him, and my family and friends, behind the driving and motivating belief he'd be besotted with his son or daughter the moment their little eyes opened and curled their tiny finger around his. But it didn't happen like that. He distanced himself from

Natalie insisting her bond with me was more important.

'Isn't that what new mums are always hoping for?' he repeated.

And then he distanced himself so far to the bookies and casinos until he left me. Stranded. Alone. A single parent in my mid-twenties.

I scan the pages for more entries, all the while listening for the bang of the flat door. Natalie used to come home for lunch on a Wednesday knowing I wasn't at work, but she has not done that for weeks now. What are the chances she will walk through the door today and catch me?

If I don't read the diary now I won't ever again. The guilt is enormous but the pain I feel for Natalie is even bigger. My little girl going through all this on her own. I'm sad and angry and furious. I want to sweep her into my arms and tell her everything will be okay. That I can make it better. But can I? This mess won't get better. I know how the repercussions will ripple for a long time to come, whatever her decision.

I spot another entry and read through it frantically taking in Natalie's scribbled words. Her writing is legible, evidence of the turmoil within her and I think about her in bed writing the words. It's hard to read anymore; two smudges mark the middle of the page, probably her tears.

I sob. I stop. I sob again. My emotions weeble-wobble from one extreme to the other; part of me wants to shout at her while the other wants to hold her. But I know that things won't be okay for a long time, not for her, or Tom or me. Not now and suddenly I want to talk to Alexander. Tell him what I've discovered. I want him to assure me and tell me it's all going to be okay. He doesn't pick up.

I frantically message Natalie telling her to come home. Her reply is evasive. I push her for a time and finally she replies, Bloody hell Mum. C u @ home @ 4. X.

Okay. Right. Let me figure what I'm going to say to her. How I'm going to explain reading her diary. My heart's beating like a base drum; I will it to slow down, breathing in through my nose and out through my mouth like my midwife showed me all those years ago.

Only four minutes have passed since Natalie messaged. Suddenly I'm nauseous. Will I make it to the bathroom? I launch myself over the toilet bowl. I miss the toilet; puke splatters the front of the pedestal and drips onto the mat. My face prickles. I steady myself against the sink and splash my face with water. I have to get a grip; getting emotional will not help the situation. I will myself to calm down. My phone buzzes.

'Hello. You called me?'

'Hello. Yes. Can you talk?'

'Yes, I'm in the car. You okay?'

'I'm whispering because Natalie will be home any minute.'

'Oh, okay. Bit risky, isn't it?'

'I just discovered something, and I had to talk to you. Hear your voice.'

'What is it my darling?'

'She's pregnant Alexander. She's had sex, slept with her boyfriend. I didn't even know. I'm so upset. I don't know what to do. How to handle this.'

'My darling Maria, you'll deal with it like you've dealt with everything before, but you won't have to do it alone. I'm here for you. Tell me what you want me to do.'

Fabio said the same and though I'm disappearing into an emotional melting pot I smile my tears away knowing I'm not alone. 'Gosh, you're amazing.'

'What now?' he asks.

'I don't know. I just needed to speak to you. Hear your voice.'

And the longer we talk the safer I feel, the safest I've felt in a long time.

I eventually hang up, conscious of the time and go over and over my telephone call with him; the situation with Natalie seems less overwhelming. I'm not alone. I have this man by me; a man who listens, and believes in me, and listens to my worries and I am reassured of his love and support. I snuggle into the sofa and fall into an exhausted sleep.

Natalie's key clicks in the lock. Finally. I sit up, stretch. The door bangs behind her; she always kicks it shut with her foot. She's home at last.

'What's the emergency?' She throws her satchel down and stands at the end of the sofa, one hand holding a can of lemonade, the other fiddling with her earring.

'I need to speak to you.'

'What now?'

'Come and sit with me,' I say, pulling her by the arm to sit next to me.

'Mum, what is it? You're acting weird.'

'Nat, please…'

'Why are you sleeping in the middle of the day?' It's not that man on Twitter, is it?'

'It's not about him. It's about you. I know you're pregnant.'

24
Alexander

I'm glad to be away from the confines of the house; Sandra's mood, like a ferocious storm, threatens to drown me.

I've booked my train tickets to London from Birmingham. Sandra criticises my joy surrounding the trip and scoffs at the tickets for an exhibition at the British Library. She has no idea my enthusiasm has everything to do with finally holding Maria in my arms, smelling her scent, touching her soft skin.

I tuck my tickets into my wallet knowing they are my pass to a different realm, at least for three days and I cannot will the time to go faster. I volunteer for two extra night shifts at work, rescuing me from Sandra's sulkiness, affording me more time and space to just be.

At work Danny is in an equally sullen mood. His monthly subscription magazine arrived torn and dog-eared. I promise to Sellotape the pages and flatten the bent corners.

I suggest spending the afternoon at Fortrose and Chanonry Beach Point. I can breathe there – inhale the sea air – and exhale the dusty cobwebs clogging my lungs. With the promise of a coffee, with cream and chocolate sprinkles, Danny's mood lifts and he disappears for his jacket.

'You're wrapped up way too much,' I say when he appears a few minutes later.

'It will be windy,' he says, stuffing his gloves into his rucksack.

'Right, maybe you've a point.'

***

The breeze coming off the rough sea is less blustery than I'd anticipated and it's what I yearn, the excited whisper of a lover. I stretch out my free hand like a starfish and feel the world wrap around my fingers. The sand is sludgy. The searing sunlight renders Danny's cheeks rosy, pink as he chases a lone seagull pecking at the wet sand.

I amble along the edge of the beach, the foamy waves slurping and gurgling at the smooth pebbles and the ocean's soft green merges into an almost invisible seam on the distant horizon. The waves lose their momentum and lick the shore. My steps are tentative in the shifting, wet sand, my shoes sticking. Danny zigzags over the crevices and trapped pools of water, landing in more puddles than he avoids and complains about his wet socks.

The tide is low and in the distance the hook-shaped dorsal fins of two bottlenose dolphins appear above the water. They bow and turn majestically, their acrobatic maneuvers a wonderful sight. As they fall back into the water their loud slaps dance on the wind. I call to Danny, knowing how much he likes them, but my voice carries in the opposite direction.

The nip in the air pinches my face. I'm strangely numb, trying to unravel my soupy muddied life, Sandra, Maria. The mere thought of Maria however brings a smile to my lips and an involuntary shiver strums my spine.

I trundle along, my feet sinking deeper into the oozy sand, trying to keep up with Danny. I wish I didn't rely on my walking stick. Despite the daily concoction of tablets, my life is still hindered by CP, its toll on my energies. An anger rises within me, and I want to blame my CP for everything… for the mess at home, for feelings I've pushed deep inside for too long, for words unsaid over the years, for the things I know I want to do with Maria but can't. Frustration wells in my eyes and I stop to wipe away the tears. I want to be the man I am online with Maria; fierce and strong, full of fire burning with an uncontrollable passion.

Danny is running back towards me with an outstretched hand, and I'm snapped back to the present. I spot the stump of a protruding rock before he does. I warn him. He trips. It's too late. He falls, his face meets the rock and a dull thud rings in my ears. A gull squawks, fighting the wind overhead. Waves are pulled in against the shore.

'Damn!' I navigate the beach as fast as I can. A flash of me tumbling over a jagged boulder, when I was a teen, clouds my mind. He's already sitting up by the time I reach him. His face is bloody but on closer observation I thank God it's only a scratch along his cheek and the top of his nose.

'You can have this for your girlfriend,' he says, holding a pebble in his open palm. My heart stops for a second. Does he know?

'Thank you, but we need to get you cleaned up, laddy boy. You're lucky you didn't smash your face in landing how you did.' I'm shaking. I throw myself unthinkingly onto the beach next to him.

'You won't get up again,' laughs Danny as I dab at his face and nose with my clean hankie.

I'm about to tell him off for being cheeky when I start laughing too. He's right. To get up I will have to maneuvre myself onto my hands and knees, then get onto my knees and from there push myself up using my walking stick for support. Not an easy feat and exhausting.

I laugh and he laughs with me and before we know it, we're leaning into each other chuckling without a care. Two silly fools covered in wet sand and the wind blowing in our faces.

'Are you happy Danny?' I ask. I disentangle myself from the uncomfortable position I have folded myself into. My legs have too much tone, increased muscle tone; my bilateral spasticity pulls in the muscles together making them stiff.

'I am when I'm with you. You're like me.'

His words surprise me, but I know what he means. We are both the same as everyone else on the inside, but people only notice what's on the outside. People treat us like we are made up wholly of our differences despite my optimism they won't. It is a sad thing being an invalid. I mean, how can it be anything else? The quote from Shakespeare's *The Merchant of Venice* comes to me, "If you prick us do we not bleed? If you tickle us do we not laugh?"

'Being different is not easy,' I say, pushing back the lump forming in the back of my throat. 'Come on, we'll get your special coffee take-away and you can drink it at home. Your face requires some first aid box attention.'

Back at the house, I closely survey Danny's face... it's a superficial scratch and will undoubtedly disappear within a couple of days and though inflamed he doesn't complain. His nose might be bruised for a few days, but it's not broken. I wash the cut with a little cooled boiled water from the kettle and smear it with antiseptic cream from the first aid kit. Guilt consumes me. I should have focused on him more. Damn it. Damn it all. I record the accident in his folder, date and initial it, my writing shaky, illegible.

Danny disappears to his bedroom, muttering something about his magazines. He leaves his door ajar; he makes appreciation noises with each slurp of his coffee. He hasn't complained once about his fall and so I am sure he will forget it by next weekend when he visits his parents.

He is easily able to occupy himself. He likes a vast range of topics and even has a number of puzzle magazines which I enjoy helping him with. His concentration isn't great but if there's one thing, I can say about him it's he's resilient and determined; rarely gives up on anything. He inspires me; keeps me holding onto my dreams. There was a tweet quoting the beautiful Audrey Hepburn – "Nothing is impossible, the word itself says I'm possible" – and away from Sandra that's true for me too.

He's got piles of magazines strewn all over his bedroom carpet – *Match, Top Gear, All About Space, Sky at Night, World Soccer* – and no matter how many times I tidy them they always finish up in the same mishmash which makes stepping over them, navigating the room, a challenge for me.

The magazine catches under my foot and I slide across the room. There's only one thing I can do; allow myself to fall onto Danny's bed and in that moment, I know this is what I must do with my life; do away with the predictable, the mundane, and hurl myself into the unknown. A weight lifts like a fog from Ben Nevis's winter peaks.

Pete lets himself in just before five o'clock. He calls a quiet hello from the hallway into the sitting room and comes straight into the kitchen. I recount Danny's accident.

'Are you listening to me? Danny can't have a shower tonight or tomorrow morning. He'll have to keep the scratch dry for a couple of days.'

'Yes, right. Sorry I'm in a pickle.'

'Oh, you okay?'

'I'm in a bit of a mess.'

'What kind of mess? Is everything okay at home?'

'Aye, home's fine. It's money.'

'Credit cards again?' I ask.

'No, not this time. I've borrowed money from somewhere I had no right to.'

'Wife's new shoe fund?' I say, smirking.

'I wish it was. I've been… syphoning money from the church funds.' He swallows, his face beams red. 'And the minister's asked me for the books. There's a new, more qualified member of the congregation who's offered to audit them.'

'You've what? Stealing from the church?'

'Oh gosh, don't say it like that.'

'How would you say it then?' I ask.

'It was a few pounds to start with and then…'

'And then?'

'I became reckless. I got away with it. I indulged in the temptation to be wild. I borrowed more and more. Something boring Pete wouldn't possibly dare do.'

His words hang in the air for a few seconds, and I get hot. Isn't this exactly what I've done? With Maria? But worse because I'm cheating on my wife? Lying to her by omission, by not being honest?

'However you dress it up you've taken money without permission… you had no right,' I say, guilty of hiding behind my own hypocrisy.

'I've been under a lot of pressure… to pay for the

new carpets, the MOT for the car, university bits for my stepdaughter. It started off with the odd £50.00 here and there. I replaced it each time but lost control... what will I say to everyone?'

'How much do you owe?'

'A lot and I tell you what when the wife finds out she'll show me the door.'

'She's the least of your worries. You could be done for theft. Pete. This is serious. You could even lose your job here.'

'Don't say that. It won't come to that. I have to make back the money... and fast.'

'You can have a bet and win that in one go,' says Danny, loitering in the kitchen doorway, fingering the luminous yellow plaster on his face.

We look at each other and back to Danny.

'There's my answer. My only answer,' says Pete. 'Genius.'

'Danny, get back to your magazines,' I say and then lowering my voice, 'For goodness sake man, that's not an answer. That's hanging yourself for sure. You'll have to come clean. Be honest about it and hope the Minister doesn't report it to the police.'

'I can't. I'm not giving up. It's a long shot for sure but it's worth the risk.'

'I know about shame and believe me when I say it fades. People forget to look for it or even mention it,' I say.

'What have you got to be ashamed of?'

'More than I care to admit, but it's okay. I've got used to it and you will too. It might not be that bad. You could offer to help around the church or keep the cemetery tidy for a few months... pay off your debt that way. Or apply for a 0 percent credit card.'

'I've maxed out my cards. Doubt I'd get accepted for

another.'

'What about a loan?'

'No Danny's right. A bet might be my only solution.'

'You're not dragging Danny into this. He's in our care. We are meant to be teaching him good morals,' I say, clenching and unclenching my fist by my side. 'Don't involve him in any way. And you're not thinking straight.'

'He won't be.'

'You mind he isn't. How much do you owe?' I flip open my wallet and hand him three crisp twenty-pound notes straight from the cashpoint.

'I wish that would cover it. Multiply it by ten and some more.'

'How much?' I ask again.

'Nine hundred pounds and eighty-nine pence to be exact.'

25
Alexander

Pete strolls in, turns on the television.

'You're early,' I say.

'I know you're not behind me on this, but I've placed that bet. I promise if I don't get the money together by the end of the week, I'll come clean.'

'You're not serious.'

'Come on…'

'So, you're here to watch the match? And with Danny here?'

'He won't even know what's going on.'

'That makes it far worse in my eyes.'

In the end, with a forced comradery, Danny, Pete and I wait for the start of the game. Sandra is no less pleased than I am when I tell her I'm working later than expected because of a staffing hic-cup. I can't leave Danny, alone in Pete's care, though I sympathise with Pete's dilemma.

Pete perches on the arm of the sofa, his hands clenched in an almost prayer-like pose between his knees, as if about to take a sky dive. I slouch back into the single seater. Danny is munching on his favourite sweet-salty popcorn seemingly oblivious.

'This is a blasted slow game,' says Pete.

It's a few minutes into the match. He thumps his fist into his thigh. My walking stick, leaning on the back of the sofa, crashes to the floor. I jump.

'Full of missed opportunities and short passes.' Danny repeats the commentator's remarks.

Before long I too am caught up in the lively commentary despite a heaviness sitting on my chest. I'm shocked to be so; dare I say it? Excited. Pete is a thief and I'm toying with reporting his deceit to our boss yet can't bring myself to do it. He has promised his tea-leafing has not extended to work though expenses on his shift are not always recorded on Danny's daily spending sheet. I push my suspicions to the back of my mind.

'Ooh! Ahh!' Danny bursts again, 'Full of missed opportunities and short passes.'

Pete's mood darkens. 'There's a total lack of communication between those Queen of the South players. What are they getting paid all that money for, for Christ's sake?'

He disappears to the toilet for the second time. 'This isn't going to work,' he rants, walking back into the room, the fans roar and then imitate Pete's groaning when the referee disallows a clear penalty. Pete pulls and twiddles his ears until they are red.

'There's still the second half,' I say too enthusiastically.

The next forty minutes are strained; no second goal, the minutes tick by on the referee's watch.

'It looks like the possible final outcome will be an equalizer.' The commentator's voice is full of commiseration.

Three minutes stoppage time is added. Pete storms to the kitchen ranting, 'It's the end for me. I'm such an idiot.'

I can't help but agree with him.

The commentators drone on, 'Celtic's pushing for an equaliser as we go into the last three minutes of added time.' And then, 'Celtic have a corner... the goalkeeper's come up for the corner. Urgh, the ball's been whipped in, towards the near post... oh, and it's headed away by the Queen of The South defender straight into Stephen Dobbie's path. He's running... he's running... there's no stopping him. Where's the goalkeeper? And it's in... straight into the back of the empty net.'

'Pete. They've won. Dobbie's done it. He's bloody done it. 2-0,' I shout.

Pete runs back in. 'Yes. Yes, Danny boy I don't believe it. We've done it.'

Danny screams and jumps, upturning the bowl of popcorn kernels and they scatter like celebratory confetti into the air. He leaps so high he taps the ceiling with his outstretched arm. He slurps on his pint of orange and lemonade, our usual rules about manners forgotten.

'Calm down, Danny. You're going to choke,' I warn.

The fans are going mad and Danny high fives us in turn, a rare show of physical contact. Pete's red face a picture of sheer relief. He hugs me and pulling me in tighter I hug him back. He dances round the room hurling victory punches in the air.

'And that's one of the most identified with Game of Thrones character,' Danny says. Pete and I look at each other. I start laughing shaking my head in disbelief.

Pete's phone interrupts our celebrations and we force

ourselves to quieten down when he mouths, *shush, it's the wife*. He keeps a straight face talking to her and manages to sound bored which unnerves me. He's good at masking his feelings, reality. What else is he hiding?

'Oh mate, I'm so relieved. Danny, you can have all the coffee you want next week,' says Pete, reaching to ruffle Danny's hair. Danny ducks away, dodging him.

'Can you stay here while I go and cash out?'

'Yes, go on. You're bloody lucky this time.'

'I've learnt my lesson. I'll never get into this situation ever again for as long as I live. I just lost ten years of my life.'

'And one more thing,' I say to him, my voice as serious as I can make it.

'What's that?'

'No coffee for Danny just before any of my night shifts.'

26
Maria

I'm drawn to Natalie's diary like a drug addict after their next fix. Adrenaline pumps in my veins, I pull it from inside the pillowcase. I'm jumpy but the desire to know what's happening compels me on. I shudder at how disgustingly dishonest and invasive I'm being. I justify my actions with "it's because I want to support her" yet I know it's wrong.

July 10th
"For the whole of this past month, we didn't know what to do. Our lives, school, everything will change if we have the baby. It's definitely a baby. I did two tests at the clinic. The nurse went on about only one, but I told her I wasn't going anywhere until she did another. We don't have our own place, and we can't even take care of ourselves properly let alone a baby. Mum does everything for me. She can't afford to pay for a baby. She's so upset with me. Going on about university and

making your dreams come true. And I'm so tired all the time and don't want to be around mum. I've disappointed her."

July 12th
"Today Tom and I walked to the park during lunch time and talked about how we would try to figure it out if we did have the baby. He looked like shit. I felt like shit and felt so sick. I said I'd move mountains, but now I think I just said that because it felt like the right thing to say and not really the right thing for me. I'm so scared and I'm already exhausted without the baby. I can't imagine how it will be if we keep it. Part of me knows it's a girl too and I'm already calling her Katy or Molly or Mara. Tom seems more sure and talked about how we will grow with the baby and be great parents. But I'm not sure. My mind's a mess. Mrs. P keeps giving me strange looks. Yasmine says she's a lesbian and fancies me. I'm laughing. I'm actually thinking that would be less complicated. At least, I could walk away. Be in control."

July 15th
"We've been back and forth about keeping the baby so much that I feel like I'm stuck in a washing cycle, drowning, and can't sleep, thinking about it all the time. Some days we say we will, and then we go right back to the 'but should we?' To whoever has gone through this, it's the hardest decision I have had to make in my life so far. I want to give her or him the best life and right now... I can't. I feel sad/empty/hollow/ drained/fed up/angry/scared/confused. I feel horrible and cruel and selfish. I hate myself. But I know what I need to do. Tom agrees. How am I going to tell Mum? I need to tell her. Make her understand."

A blinding headache comes at me. I find my migraine

tablets, pop two from the blister into my mouth and swallow; they're sugar-coated. I flick on the kettle. It's almost eleven o'clock. I should be at work; the massive order has come through and though there's not much for me to do now other than support Leo who's flapping around, I feel bad not being at the office.

Natalie, in grey jogging bottoms and an oversized sweatshirt, is leaning on the kitchen counter, her arms stiffly folded, a steely stare daring me to argue with her. When did she become so aggressive, so guarded? I bite down on my lip. I don't want to think about what I've read – again. I can't give myself away.

Eventually she breaks the silence. 'Mum, I'm not going to have the baby. But it's my decision not yours.'

'And Tom?' I ask, trying to steady my voice as an emotion, unlike the relief I thought it would be, overwhelms me.

'He's coming over now and—'

The intercom buzzes.

Tom bundles in with a woman in tow. She seems awkward, shy.

She is introduced as Tom's mum and by the time I process that, it's too late for me to ask her name. I study her trying to figure whether she knew they had slept together, whether Tom had told her. Or did he hide it too? And for how long?

We sit facing each other in the sitting room. My gaze flits from Tom to his mum; he is a male version of her.

Natalie fiddles with the strands of hair poking from her bun with one hand while her other hand rests limply in her lap. I want to run my fingers over the soft hairs at the nape of her neck, feel her soft skin. I notice the ends of the strands shining golden against her natural dark hair which has grown through about four inches. She'll be asking for money to have it coloured again, but the thought comforts me. She still relies on me. I'm still her mum, the one she can come to… in the end.

Tom is wearing jeans. Expensive jeans. His hoodie is black with a designer brand name emblazoned in red across the front. He bites at each nail, in turn, making me cringe. He's sitting on the arm of the sofa, and I'm tempted to tell him to sit properly but restrain myself. And it doesn't seem important in view of why we are meeting. Why do I even care where he's sitting?

Natalie breaks the silence. 'So, Tom and I have decided we're not having the baby.'

'I think that's…' I can't channel my thoughts or emotions. My words are a whisper; hang unsaid, an errant streak of cloud, a loose bit of cotton. I will Tom's mum to say something. She doesn't. She simply nods her head ever so slightly, barely noticeable.

Is she heartbroken like I am, like Natalie is? I know Natalie is because I have secretly read her words. A heat flushes my cheeks. Her confidence and trust in me is shattered. She may never forgive me. I'm embarrassed by my invasion of her most private thoughts and my face becomes hotter. What would Tom's mum think of such a blatant breach of trust?

'I've already made the call…' I listen to her choice of words and want to cry. Taken. Care. Of.

'Are you both sure?' I ask. Claustrophobia seems to strangle me.

'It's what you all wanted deep down. Don't make this any harder. My mind's made up. So is Tom's.'

'Sorry, I never imagined having to deal with anything like this. I'm trying but I'm sure it's difficult for Tom's mum as well.'

'You and me both, Mum.'

'It's what we both want,' Tom mumbles, resuming biting his fingernails.

'I've got an appointment next Monday week,' Natalie says, tipping her chin up in defiance.

My heart is breaking as I listen to how she's talking; detached, cold, as if she's talking about another person, another person's baby.

'Tom?' I ask, looking for reassurance of a joint decision, support for Natalie.

His fingers are red raw from all the biting. 'Yeah, fine by me.'

'Fine by you? Is that all you've got to bloody say? Fine by you? You should've taken more care. But I suppose this doesn't affect your body, your future chances to have children again. So selfish.'

'That's not what I meant,' he says, tears streaking his pale face. He wipes them with the pads of his fingers, blinking hard in an effort to stop himself from crying but the wet drops fall onto the front of his hoodie turning the red letters a deeper shade.

'This involves two people, and I don't think you should be yelling at my Tom like that,' his mum says, her voice shaking. She reaches to hug him only to be shunned. I witness the hurt etched across her features.

I storm to the kitchen. I want to shake him but he's young and naïve and has probably only ever slept with Natalie. He hardly seems a player. He's too timid and quiet. What a bloody mess. There's nowhere to go. Nowhere to hide. For any of us.

A blast of cold air, from the open window, slices the little warmth there is in half. I tear open a packet of custard creams, resisted for a week, and stuff three into my mouth one after the other. I make myself a strong tea, slopping the tea bag into the bin, too upset to worry about saving it to reuse later. I miss and it sits on the rim, dripping down the side of it... a black stain... grief and regret snaking its way down the side like a poisonous snake.

Has Natalie slept with anyone else? I shiver against the realisation I don't know the answer to that question and my hand shoots up to stifle a gasp.

'Can I help?' Tom's mum asks. I compose myself and proffering the packet of biscuits I promptly burst into tears.

'Hey, I've cried for days. Thought I'd never stop.' She rests her hand on my arm; she is wearing a sapphire engagement ring and diamond studded wedding band. The sparkling rings make me feel worse; worse for not having Alexander here to console me.

He's so far away. I yearn to talk to him. He has a way of making everything seem like it's resolving the way it was always meant to. He'd probably quote a Wordsworth or Emerson poem, make me smile through my tears, comfort me with his understanding.

'Sorry. I thought I had it all under control. You know the swinging emotions, the ups and downs of yes and no, the custard cream bingeing,' I say, trying to soften the mood which threatens to suffocate me.

'It's a shock for all of us. But they're good kids. Natalie's sensible.' I realise I don't know if she is, not anymore. 'They both are. But the decision has to be theirs. All we can do is be here for them in whatever way they wish us to be.'

She gives me an awkward hug and I pull away, my smile tense. I grab another mug from the shelf above the sink.

'I know,' I say, nodding towards the tea and coffee jars. She points to the coffee.

I follow her back into the sitting room. Our mugs rattle on the metal tray I'm carrying.

'This is hard on all of us, Natalie the most. Let's not fall out. This cannot be undone but we can try to make it as smooth and as least painful as possible. It's an emotional time,' I say, sniffling, avoiding eye contact with Natalie for fear of crying all over again, for fear of seeing something else in her I haven't seen before.

'Mum, I'm sorry,' says Tom and he grabs his mum's hand squeezing it tightly. In that moment I know he's in pain too and regret my earlier outburst.

'We will make this okay again,' I say. Tears stream down my face, all self-control dissolved. I swallow them and taste their saltiness. In this bitter-sweet moment I desperately want a hug from Alexander. I'm missing him. His visit to London can't come soon enough. I write a poem and call it The First Time I Saw You.

The first time I saw you was before you saw me
Walking towards me, consciously unaware I was there
I observed you whole, your walk, your look, your stare…

Like an outlined drawing I could now fill in the blanks
The gait of your step, the movement of your swagger
How tall you were and the way you held your head

I averted my eyes to avoid you yet noticing me
I wanted that moment of recognition just right to be
One of held locked gaze, not a crumpled weight

Colours of want and pages of love swept through me
Long felt caresses, silver-edged dreams almost a reality
Melting deep within me, sensations infused me abound

Then you caught my eye, and smiled an open song

A collision of desire and brushstroke this is for real
You took me in your arms and wrapped me in scarlet lust

Our hearts tender, entwined threads of silk in fine gold
A sip of eternity as our lips for the first time touched
Creamy beads I felt release as I breathed a heart's wisp

And you held me there for seconds but of all eternity
Lost in your strength, a wrap of comfort, love's creation
Inside the fluttering white wings of angels dusted my heart.

27
Maria

I reach Euston with fifteen minutes to spare. I tug at my bag; the weight of it is cutting into my shoulder.

I check the arrivals board. I check my watch; out of habit more than anything else despite knowing it's seven minutes fast. I dash into a shop, top up my mascara in front of a tiny acrylic mirror. I layer it on thickly; the globully liquid extending my lashes.

Taking a seat in the row of metal chairs facing the exit to Platform 4, I fidget against the uncomfortable seat. From here I am likely to see him before he sees me, and this reassures me; gives me an advantage.

I flick through the interview I have prepared. Who am I kidding? I know this meeting is more than just about the answers to these questions for a possible future novel. But it gives a more legitimate reason for meeting up, calms me.

He warmed to the idea of being the subject of my writing

when I suggested it. Whether I actually write the story is another thing and if I don't find him attractive, or don't want to do what we've done online, at least we will have that to focus on.

The nerves shake me again, threatening to send me disappearing in the opposite direction. Suddenly, conscious of being too exposed I finger the braided spaghetti straps of my cornflower blue summer dress. Perhaps I should have worn my leggings and a T-shirt. My straps keep falling from my shoulders with every movement, the frilled scooped neck too revealing. I slip on my lace cardi, pulling it to cover my cleavage. It appears bumpy over the frill. I'm instantly smothered in an unbearable frustration. I shimmy it off, my temperature rising with each waiting second.

My phone vibrates in my hand. 'Hello. Checking up on me?' I giggle.

'Yes, actually and don't tell me I can't,' Fabio says down the phone. 'Where are you?'

'At Euston. Waiting. So glad to hear your voice. Nervous as hell.'

'He'll be nervous too, remember. Just don't forget to walk slowly and don't trip over his cane.'

'Gosh you're mean d'you know that?'

'Just lightening the mood, "my wonderful Maria",' he teases.

'You are unbelievable.'

'No, you're unbelievable. And don't you forget it.'

'Gotta go, love you.'

'Love you more. I'll be checking in on you, don't you dare ignore me.'

'Bye and have fun with Mattie.' I end our call.

Two message alerts pop up: one from Tina and one from Katia.

> *Pls b careful. Make sure u r in a public place at all times. I hope it goes well. Love u lots*

and

> *Hello Maria. Just wanted to say have the most amazing time. Life's too short 2 have frown lines at our age. Lol. Mwah xxx Can't wait to hear all about it. Xx*

Their messages panic me all the more. This is happening for real. I text Alexander, simultaneously a message comes in from him.

> *Train delayed so I'm arriving at 2.56. I just want to be there NOW. Xxx*

> *I'm sitting outside The Body Shop.*

> *I will find you. Xxx*

I cross my legs, uncross them, tuck my dress's frilled hem under me. A mingling of laughter and chatter blasts at me. I recognise the vivid musical sounds of Italian. A meandering throng of people emerge from platform 6. Two minutes and his train will arrive. I flush red, the tops of my cheeks burn. This is all going to turn real. How will he view me in real life as opposed to words on a screen? I can no longer hide, and a bubbling anticipation builds in me.

I twist my rings back and forth and twiddle with the silver butterfly hanging round my neck. I still have time to leave… no tense hellos or fake kisses. But that isn't my style; not after coming all this way, after waiting all these months to meet him.

Tourists and travellers march past me in a blur; oversized cases on wheels squeak by, bulky backpacks push past and knock unsuspecting ditherers and plastic bags weighted down with shopping threaten to split open and fill the concourse. Children cling onto their parents' hands and elderly people shuffle along. Commuters impatiently weave around them, rushing to their next destination.

From the corner of my eye, I catch a glimpse of a striped shirt and a pair of pale cream trousers. This is him. He's not even three feet away from me. He's so good-looking.

Two lines from the poem I wrote a few days ago, in anticipation of our first meeting, pop into my head:

...The gait of your step, the movement of your swagger
How tall you were and the way you held your head...

He spots me and I stand up and walk towards him, stopping a foot or so in front of him. He almost lunges towards me, and his arm goes around me. He's a big man, heavy boned. I hug him back automatically. I have anticipated this moment a thousand times and it is so natural when all along I expected it would be awkward. He pulls back from me and gives me a peck on the lips, a fleeting, warm wet kiss. My lips tingle.

I can't think straight; the faint smell of sandalwood and musk warms my senses. My mind jumps ahead, two hours, three hours. Can I deliver what we have done together for real? After our first meeting?

He takes my hand; his big, fat fingers wrap around mine. Instantly and strangely, I am cocooned in safety and love and a kind of angelic protectiveness. His hands are soft.

'Hello,' he says. 'It's lovely to meet you after all this time.' His smile is wide, defiant almost.

'Hello,' I say, the nerves falling away momentarily. I'm

lightheaded with the thrill of finally meeting him; does he feel the same about me?

As we walk in the direction of the station's exit I glance a peek at his legs, not sure what I expect. They appear thin and slight under his trousers in contrast to his upper body which appears strong. I home in on the cane, shocked because I hadn't made the connection between that and how he walks, a strange gait, a limp. I'm so naïve. He drags his foot along at an odd angle... but isn't that what CP spastic in both legs means? I avert my eyes, and, in a panic, I ask if I can help him with his suitcase. He declines and a stab of guilt punches me in the chest. I fall in line with his slow steps and hope I'm not being patronising.

***

At Alexander's suggestion we head towards a bar with a tiny, paved patio; high tables and bar stools line one side and a few striped deckchairs overlook a square of lawn stretching beyond a low brick wall.

I pull myself onto a stool, relieved to be free of the weight of my bag. Alexander sits opposite me. He wriggles his shoulders and straightens his spine which I imagine is difficult since it curves inwards. I read about scoliosis and how people with CP suffer from the sideways twist in their lower back. Conscious he has clocked me looking I turn away and focus on a patch of grass beyond the deck chairs; the spray of an automatic watering system gleams across it catching the lemony sunlight.

'Here we are,' he says.

'Are you okay sitting up here?' I ask him, hoping my effort to stem the flow of adrenaline isn't obvious now I'm sitting opposite him.

'Aye I'm okay for a short while.'

'How was your trip down?'

'First class was very comfortable.'

'Sounds lovely.'

'It didn't bring me to you any quicker though.' His words surprise me, embarrassment blushes my cheeks.

'So, you like London?'

'I'd forgotten how cacophonous it is, but I like London, aye. And I like it better with you.'

'The opposite to Inverness I imagine.'

The fishtail wrinkles around his eyes smile at me. 'You'll have to visit me and find out for yourself,' he says.

'Are you sure you're okay up here?' I ask again.

'I can't sit up here for hours. But I'm okay for now, you know. The sitting down will give my lungs a chance to recover. I get out of breath with the sheer exertion of walking, especially the amount I've done today.'

'We could sit in the deck chairs if you—'

'No, I'm fine. They'd be harder for me to get in and out of, no arms to lean on, push myself off from when I get up. You'd have to heave me out and that wouldn't be easy with my weight.'

'Me too, to be honest,' I say, taking a slurp of my vodka and lemonade as soon as the barman places the glass in front of me.

'The most impossible things ever…'

'Almost forgot. I bought you a present. I know it's late but happy belated birthday Alexander.'

He surveys the package, wrapped in purple tissue paper, and tied with a silver bow, which I pull from my bag. He fiddles around with the knotted ribbon, discarding it on the table. His hands shake a little; does this have anything to do with his CP or is it nerves? He pulls back the soft layers and examines the book: *London*'s *Historic Railway Stations* by John Betjeman.

'It's beautiful and so thoughtful. Thank you.'

'I thought you'd like it. I got it second-hand. You're always quoting him, thought it would be a nice reminder, hopefully, of your train journey to meet me.'

'My sweet Maria. You're wonderful. Truly wonderful.'

'I've written a little message too.' I turn back the title page and his hand grazes mine ever so lightly. I tremble, the swell of a summer heat – or is it something more? – hugging me by surprise.

He puts on his glasses, reads the inscription out loud. I blush as his voice, though soft, carries on the drifting air and a man and woman speak to each other in hushed tones. He runs his thick fingers over my handwriting. 'Your writing's beautiful. The writing of a writer.' His voice is barely audible. Full of emotion, it catches in his throat.

'Thank you,' I say and after a moment's hesitation I ask, 'So what do you want to do? Anything in particular?'

'There's so much I want to do. With you it all seems possible.'

'Well, London's never short of things to do,' I say, fighting the thrill his words evoke in me.

Hesitating he says, 'Sometimes it's not the CP holding me back. It's the mindset of those around me, those who believe they know what I can and can't do. What I'm capable of. Sometimes it's my own mindset. But with you, I don't know. You're different. Me being here with you is different… it's vague as a dream.'

'Like a dream, eh? Well, I wouldn't know.'

'I'd like to know more about you now that we're here, together. You're not wearing a wedding ring, so you're not married?'

'You're not wearing one... but you are...' I say, noticing the pale dent of a tell-tell sign in his ring finger. 'Sorry. I was. A long time ago. It was messy.'

'And now?'

'I'm here with you. I don't want to hide anything from you Alexander. It's strange being here, I feel like I know you, but I don't.'

'So far I think you're doing great.'

'We're doing great,' I say, biting my bottom lip. Bloody hell. Am I being patronising? Alexander prises my fingers away from my glass, brings them to his lips and kisses them. The heat rises in me again. Excitement, embarrassment, ecstasy, all rush at me.

'Am I how you imagined me?'

His question catches me unawares. 'Well, I suppose so, yes. Your eyes are bluer than I thought and you're taller.' I don't mention that despite his uneven teeth and looking older than I expected he is incredibly good-looking and sexy.

'Cheers to that,' he says, chinking his glass against mine.

'And cheers to me understanding your accent. It's so much easier to catch what you're saying face-to-face.'

'Cheers to my accent,' he laughs, locking his blue eyes with mine.

I ruffle my hair in an effort to cool down. The back of my neck is clammy and my dress sticks to me, a bead of sweat trickles down my cleavage, I quickly wipe it away with my fingers. I imagine I'm not as perfectly made up as I was an hour ago; my make-up seems to be slipping off my face with the heat.

'You must know London well living here,' he says.

'I don't come into central London often. You probably know it better than I do.'

'I suppose living here you don't see it as the beautiful city it is.'

'But today I can see it through your eyes,' I say.

'And how's your writing coming along?' He changes the subject, seemingly keen to get me talking about my work. I like how his face lights up when our eyes meet, and a swell of happiness fills me.

'It's coming—' I laugh. 'I mean it's coming along. You know what I mean. Oh gosh, I'm getting tongue tied now.' I sip my drink to conceal my clumsiness. It goes down the wrong way. I splutter and cough.

Alexander pushes his stool back. His cane clangs to the ground. He's beside me, patting me gently on the back but it's no use. I'm choking and my eyes are streaming. I'm conscious of creating a scene. Eventually the coughing stops.

'You're beautiful even with smudged eyes,' he says.

I dab at my eyes. 'Ha, ha,' I say, still rubbing the coal-black mascara and smearing the pads of my fingers onto a napkin.

'And going back to what you said, about coming... I know what you mean,' he says.

But does he?

'I'm halfway through,' I continue, 'but my plot has got kind of stuck. So, I've focused on writing poetry. Our interview might kick start it again, push it in a different direction.'

'Your poems are good. You're so talented. I'd love to read more if you have any.'

'Natalie thinks I'm mad. Doing all this writing...'

'I'm sure she doesn't.'

'I haven't always been this together, you know.'

'I know,' he says, stroking my hand.

236

'You do?'

'I do because you're going to tell me,' he says and, in that moment, I find strength.

'I don't know where to start.'

'Just start,' he says gently.

'Well, I'm divorced. Natalie's father left me, walked out on us and it knocked my confidence. It was a shock.'

'I know how that feels,' he says, nodding.

'He had a great job, well paid, as a logistics manager. I had my job as an events manager.'

'Sounds like you both had busy jobs.'

'Yeah, we did and falling pregnant didn't fit in with his five-year life plan and, being the control freak he was, he couldn't adapt. When Natalie came along, and I took maternity leave, he couldn't adjust to anything... the new lifestyle, less money, less time alone, more expenses.'

'Having a baby is hard work,' he says, taking my hand in his but I pull away, unsure.

'Not for him. He had nothing to do with her. He just spent more and more time away from us until he went to work one Monday morning and disappeared leaving me with huge debts.

'I'm so sorry Maria.'

'The only consolation was an account solely in my name. He couldn't touch it. That Monday was the last time I saw him, and the last time Natalie saw him until ten years later on her 13th birthday, four years ago. He tracked us down demanding to be a part of her life.'

'And how did you feel seeing him again? That must've been hard.'

'Facing him again, after all the embarrassment, disappointment, and humiliation, shook me. It forced all the old feelings, I'd kept buried, to spill out,' I say, fighting the tears. 'In the end I couldn't cope with the added pressure. But Natalie loves him.'

He swigs his pint and strokes my hand again and this time I don't pull away. 'Oh, my darling Maria, you've been hurt, I can see that. I won't do the same. I promise.'

'I miss having a relationship. I've not had anyone serious since Natalie's father. Partly because I've focused on work and Natalie, partly because I couldn't be bothered with the whole dating scene and partly because the men I meet aren't interested in the things I am.'

'Until now?' he asks.

'Until now,' I say, surprised at how true this is.

The minutes pass between us and we don't speak. It's as if none of us wants to break the spell between us; it's like magic. His hand rests on mine, he plays with my fingers.

He eventually edges off his stool and stands up. 'My back's aching. I need to stretch a bit, sit in a comfy chair. Do you want another drink, or shall we head to the hotel?'

'Not unless you want one.'

'Let's get going. It's probably about the right time to check in,' he says, glancing at his watch.

He hails a black cab. I lean back into the taxi's leather seat and Alexander rests his hand on mine ever so lightly.

'There's something I want to tell you… but I hope it's not too presumptuous of me.' I listen wide eyed and, can't hold back. I scream.

The taxi driver eyes me in his rearview mirror. 'Good news?' he asks.

'The best!' I sink into Alexander. My heart dances in my chest and I realise the soundtrack of my life can be anything I dare it to be.

28
Maria

'Why don't you sit here while I get checked in,' Alexander says.

A young porter, in a grey uniform and shiny black shoes, marches past and smiles at me. I smile back; I can't stop smiling. Alexander's announcement has me reeling. I might get a book deal. I'm here with my fantasy man. Everything is going to be alright.

I text Fabio a smiley face and a ♥ and forward the same message to Elaine, Tina, and Katia.

'So, all checked in,' Alexander says. 'And this is a room key for you... in case I lose mine, which there's a chance I just might.'

'Oh, okay,' I say, taking it from him.

'If it's alright with you, and if you want to, you can come up with me now. We can have tea and sit and talk... ask me those interview questions you've prepared.'

'Yes, okay,' I say relieved he's mentioned the interview.

'You sure?'

'Yes, I'm sure… promise. The thought of a publisher wanting to read my book has totally wowed me. So, you might just have to put up with my big smile all day.'

'Then we have to celebrate, don't we?'

'Tell me more. Why haven't you told me before?'

'I wanted you to meet me because you wanted to not because you thought there was a book deal in it.'

'I'm not like that but I can see what you mean. Well, now you know. I've met you because I want to. I want to know you.'

'And the publisher?'

'The sweetest icing on the cake. We've a lot to celebrate,' I say.

I walk alongside him, past concierge, the young porter's eyes following me. Is he thinking what is this woman doing with this man? I look younger than Alexander, probably by ten years or more, my usual light bounce in contrast with Alexander's shuffling pace. I consciously slow in time with him, but it doesn't bother me having to do that. Would it bother me to do this all the time? I don't know. But for now, for today, I'm in no hurry. I have all the time in the world to be with him if I want to be if I choose to be.

The lift is tiny, barely enough room for the two of us and his luggage. We stand so close I can smell the alcohol from his warm breath on the side of my face. A heat rises in me and a kind of claustrophobia bears down on me. His fingers find mine and he plays with mine, sending a surge of energy through me. I don't look at him though I sense him looking at me.

The corridors are narrow, nothing plush or fancy, basic compared to the radiance and luxury of the foyer and public areas glimpsed downstairs. The carpet muffles our footsteps, barely audible over the swish of my dress. We walk to room 231. I strut ahead of him, in my red wedge sandals, giving the impression I'm more confident than I am.

Alexander scans the door entry pad with his key card.

'Not lost it yet?' I tease.

The door clicks open in unison with the flash of a green light. Green for go. It winks at me, giving me permission to enter.

I hold Alexander's gaze for a split second before pushing the door open. I want to be in control. Sex is power; I've learnt over the years. A woman can manipulate a man with her sexual prowess, her sensuality, her abandonment in bed. A part of me clicks shut; I don't want to be like this with Alexander.

I put my bag on the dressing table and lower myself into the tub chair next to it. He lifts his suitcase onto the bed. It hisses as he unzips it and imagine the flies on his trousers coming down. The thought shocks me. He unpacks. I don't say a word; too afraid my voice will give away my emotions.

Taking the tub chair mirroring mine, he toes off his shoes. His feet are bare.

'Come here, I want to kiss you,' he says, breaking the silence.

'You want to kiss me?'

'I want to kiss you.'

I get up and, holding onto the arms of his seat, I lean in, move closer. He kisses me, a kiss on the lips, once, twice, three times. We French kiss for a few seconds more. A frothy, sexy dance of wet tongues and saliva until I pull away, biting on my bottom lip, my heart racing, the room suddenly oppressively hot. Gosh, he's sexy. I try not to stare at him, and my girly-giggle surprises me. Where did it come from?

'How I've longed to do that. To kiss those lips. To hear you laugh.'

'Yeah?'

'Oh yeah,' he says, pulling at me again but I slip from his grasp not quite trusting myself, not quite trusting him, and sink back into my seat. The kiss is powerful, sensual, manipulative.

I'm suddenly aware of the dampness between my legs; passion building in me, aware he's staring. I delve into my bag to retrieve my notebook and pen.

A tap at the door shocks me.

'It's room service. I took the liberty of ordering tea when I checked in.'

29
Alexander

She closes her notebook, marking the page with a ribbon marker. Her coloured tabs a reflection of her orderly mind. I try to be organised, but my mind gets jumbled. I forget things, and when I'm in a hurry, things get mixed up even more.

'If I think of anything else, and I'm sure I will, we can have another chat, later, or tomorrow,' she says.

'So, you want to meet again tomorrow? You're not put off by me?'

'Yes, don't you?'

'Oh Maria. *Ever let the Fancy roam, Pleasure never is at home: At a touch sweet Pleasure melteth…*'

'That's beautiful…'

'*…Like to bubbles when rain pelteth; Then let winged Fancy wander Through the thought still spread beyond her; Open wide the mind's cage door…* Our secrets. Mine and yours.'

'Oh wow. You're amazing to remember such poetry. Who's it by?'

'It's Keats. To Fancy…'

'I'll have to google it. It's beautiful. And your answers are safe with me. Nobody will know I've interviewed you. Not unless you want me to reveal my sources.'

'Our secret is the most incredible secret. My heart soars with it. Once consciously uninvited… now slowly unravelling…'

'It does, does it?'

'Can I have another kiss first?' My phone vibrates. I hesitate.

'Everything okay?'

'Aye, it's Sandra making sure I've arrived safely.'

'Okay,' she says as her fingers twiddle with her necklace.

'Don't worry. It's okay,' I say, and I respond to Sandra's message.

'Well Foyles is open till nine. We said we'd go so let's go.'

Is that hurt in her eyes or is it jealousy?

'My legs might not carry me. I'll hail a taxi, if that's okay with you,' I say, struggling to slip my leather loafers back on.

***

The pavement glints. We push our way through the throng of Japanese tourists crowding the entrance; their blurred faces wet from the drizzly summer rain and their heads shielded with a mishmash of Burberry umbrellas and floppy hats. It seems the designer brand is their hallmark.

'So, this is Foyles?' I say once inside.

'I hope you like it. I love it here… the space, the openness, the light and the millions of books. And who knows, my own book might be on these shelves one day. Alexander, I'm so excited.'

'That would be wonderful my darling,' I say, absorbing her delight.

'One day… now where d'you want to start?'

'Anywhere as long as I'm next to you.'

'Ooh, you romantic you.' She seems to have relaxed now we are out of the hotel room. She's like the wind that bears sweet music. I can't stop breathing her in. I fight the urge to keep touching her but know, deep down, all I want to do is hold her in my arms and stare into those beautiful dark pools of her soul.

'Poetry?' I ask. Stay focused on the here and now, I tell myself.

'First floor I do believe,' she says, squinting over at the floor planner on the concrete pillar. 'Yep, I'm right, you impressed?'

'I am my darling Maria. I'm impressed with you. With all of you my darling,' I say. I reach for her, and her fingers slip lightly through my hold before she turns away and heads toward the lift. I instinctively follow her. I would find the stairs a trial. Does she remember me telling her this?

In the poetry section we read words of love and heartache, and hopes and tomorrows, to each other. My body heat seems to seep through my damp jacket; my glasses steam up. I lean in towards her and I reach for a book on the higher shelf. I recognise my own renewed boldness and I flirt outrageously with her yet it's a different flirting to what I have experienced with her online.

'You okay?' I ask.

'Yeah, just a little unsure what's going on between us.

Being together makes it all real,' she says. She bites on her lower lip, and she suddenly comes across shy, self-conscious, immature, far younger than she is. The words of Keats flood my mind again; *Let none else touch the just new-budded flower*…

'…and there's no hiding behind an emoji or a kiss.'

'Exactly.'

'Aye, so let's just take it one step at a time.'

'Okay.'

'Now, can we actually take books upstairs to the café and read them there?'

'Yes, that's why I like it here,' she says, holding three books in her hand. 'You can leave them on a trolley when you've finished. D'you want another cuppa?'

'I do, yes. And cake…' I lick my lips in mischief knowing I can eat the cake without Sandra telling me off. Maria smiles one of those girl-next-door smiles and it melts me.

'You can read your poetry to me now too.'

'I might have a couple of stanzas on my Instagram account.'

'Aye, you'll have a connection here.'

I choose the last piece of lemon and poppy seed cake; she points to the raisin pastry. I pay for the teas and nod towards an empty table.

I sit opposite Maria but the streaming light coming in from the tall window behind me cuts into her sight line.

'Why don't you sit next to me? You can't sit there. And anyway, I want you near me.' I pat the banquette and she moves seats obligingly. She adjusts her sunglasses on her head, and I sense her relief at not having to squint against the sun. She turns to face me.

'You okay? Is it me?' I ask, trying not to give way to a flutter of dancing fireflies in my chest, conscious of the blood prickling beneath the surface of my cheeks.

'It's what you do to me Alexander,' she says, fingering the pages of one of the books she has brought up to the café with her.

'Please don't be nervous. It's just me. Ordinary Alexander from Inverness.'

'I know. I'm sorry.' She bites her bottom Lip and smiles that infectious smile which fills me with flames.

'So here we are my darling. It's like a dream. It's wonderful.'

'So here we are. Drinking tea. Having cake and a pile of poetry books between us.'

'It's wonderful my darling Maria. And my condition?' I push her for a response, desperate to know what she's thinking. 'Now that you know more about it.'

'Well, talking has highlighted a lot I wasn't aware of, that my research didn't reveal. I think you're amazing.'

'I don't think anyone has called me amazing before you.'

'You have to cope with so much that I take for granted, that people take for granted,' she says in earnest.

'It's a difficult thing to explain. I straddle life constantly from being a disabled man with CP to being invisible to trying to succeed in an able-bodied world. I get tired; use three times' as much energy doing everyday activities ordinary folk would find less demanding on their energy levels. But I can do most things though perhaps a little slower than most.'

'And does it bother you?' She bites on her lip. Is she regretting asking the question? I mean how can it not bother me? My answer seems to surprise her.

'I've lived with this all my life. Whether it bothers me makes no difference. It is what it is. It's a part of me I've learnt to live with. I don't know any different. But it doesn't mean I like it. I put up with it and at times it bothers me a great deal. It frustrates me.'

'I'm sorry. I don't mean to upset you.'

'You're not upsetting me. I like it you're so interested. Nobody asks me. Nobody much asked me growing up either. But as an adult it's a taboo subject. You know, *don't mention CP in front of Alexander*, that sort of thing.'

'I suppose it's like anything people don't understand. They don't want to offend you or embarrass you or themselves, so they don't mention it.'

'But you're just beautiful… sitting here with me, talking about it. You're incredible.'

'Well, C and P are not your initials, are they? Your identity is made up of all of you, the whole of you, Alexander Campbell with the initials A and C.'

'Aye… no.'

'And I'm genuinely interested in it. I don't even know how to refer to it, but in your Cerebral Palsy.'

'Am I your scientific little muse? Your experiment?'

'No, not at all. When you mentioned the erectile dysfunction, I didn't find it threatening or sexual. It was a fact and one I'm not familiar with. I suppose you intrigued me.'

'What about my innuendos and sexual advances?' I ask her, being bold.

'If there were any, I missed them.'

'You're saying I drew you in?'

'I let myself be drawn in,' she says.

'I'm glad you did.'

***

The next two hours disappear like a cloud of misty vapour.

I read silly poems to her; she reads serious poems to me. We discuss their meaning; we laugh leaning into each other. I play with the ends of her hair, lightly touch the back of her neck, stroke her hand. My nerve endings spark. My gaze holds her eyes that second too long. I want to get lost there, not find my way out. She wipes her tears away and blows her nose. She's brave and strong. My aches seem to fade; I have a renewed energy and my bones have a strange lightness to them. She is my anesthetic.

I playfully tease her, and each little brush sends a tiny shockwave through me but I'm tired too.

'Do you like being here with me?' I ask.

'Yes. I do.'

'Me too.'

'I can't believe you're here. That you're real.'

'It's incredibly surreal for me sitting here with you. It's incredibly pleasurable.'

'You're so intellectual Alexander. You know more literature quotes than I ever will. Your mind fascinates me. How you talk and articulate your sentences, your thoughts, your ideas. It's like talking to an encyclopedia.' Her cheeks flush pink again. Her eyes shine and my heart swells; they're shining for me.

The waitress hovers, gives us a ten-minute reminder to closing time. She clears the tea pots and leaves Maria's cup; a pink lipstick smudge on the rim teases me. Around us the crowded space is thinning; people leave for home, a wife's kiss, the hug of a child, a lover's embrace.

30
Alexander

We walk the short distance towards Tottenham Court Road underground. The glow of a long summer night is silhouetted against the high-rise buildings shimmering with the earlier rain… and at the station's entrance I pull her close, one arm around her waist, the other resting on my walking stick, and kiss her. A long passionate, deep kiss; one I've waited all my life to give. It leaves me breathless.

Her response radiates passion, and a hot prickling sensation runs through me. I should be exhausted, close to running on empty, but I pull on new-found reserves and an overflowing energy fills me; my body hiding the part of me which renders me invisible, different.

Maria is so much more than the whole of me and so much more than the part of me plagued by this damn CP. I struggle to contain my feelings, to bury them behind my disability. I push back a realisation so strong it threatens to break me. I have to matter to me because I know how much I matter to her.

She overpowers all my senses. I am utterly in awe of her and utterly in love with her.

'What now?' she asks, pulling away, her words dripping like honey.

'Whatever you like,' I manage to breathe, my voice gravelly. I finger the errant dark lock dusting her pink cheeks. I'm trembling. Not from exhaustion. Elation. I have a new sense of self.

What happens next unfolds in front of me, like an old romantic silver screen movie. She guides me away from the station, her hand satin silk in mine.

Harried commuters seem to open up a path for us along the packed pavement. My heart is pounding and suddenly, against this wonderful woman, London, drab and colourless, is a kaleidoscope of patterns and reflections. A burst of energy carries me, and my debilitating movements disappear. Adrenaline is pumping and pushing its way around my body enabling my limbs to move almost effortlessly and pain-free. I'm in a dream.

I daren't speak and don't for a few minutes, lost in the sights and sounds of London's West End. The rumbling engines of buses, the thundering weight of lorries and screeching brakes of taxis, a far cry from my quiet hometown, fill my senses. A line from a Betjeman poem forms in my head: *"Let's say goodbye to hedges, And roads with grassy edges, And winding country lanes; Let all things travel faster, Where motor car is master, Till only Speed remains."*

Maria doesn't turn towards the station's entrance; she pulls me into a waiting taxi instead. In that instant I am the happiest man alive. My bulge fills my trousers, and I am so full of anticipation I almost want to yell, *step on it* but

I control my urge to spoil the moment despite wanting this journey to defy time and space so that I'm already at the hotel with her.

***

'So?' she teases in her breathy voice, double locking the hotel bedroom door behind her.

I pull her towards me, my hands pulling at the straps of her dress, caressing her neck. She's breathing hard, whispering my name, rushing, undoing my shirt buttons... we both fall back on the bed.

'Ouch.' I yelp, in pain from my hip twisting uncomfortably.

'Oh no. You okay?' she asks.

I try to shift position in an effort to get more comfortable but reality charges at me. Damn. Immobile fool. But my self-consciousness is short lived.

'Have I got you all twisted?' Maria reacts with a sexy nervous giggle; it reminds me of how much I miss being around positive people; her youthfulness and her energy turns me on.

'I've got myself twisted,' I laugh, and an animalistic instinct arouses me from dormancy. It's an instinct I've not given in to for too long. Invincible. I want this woman. I want her in every way. She instinctively kneads my back with her balled fists, lifting me out of pain. She's like an angel, no a goddess.

'That feels so good,' I say, pulling her round to me.

I know I mustn't rush but can't help myself. I'm clumsy. I'm a concoction of adrenaline and progesterone, delirium, and elation. I kiss her with a force lying dormant all my life and she responds, her mouth open, her tongue searching mine. It's surreal yet real. My head buzzes.

Seconds later, in the faded glow of the evening's stolen light, I struggle to focus but the whoosh of her strappy dress tells me she is stripping; it slides to the floor and my eyes find their focus in the semi-darkness. She undoes her bra; slowly, teasing out my every reaction. I undress, clumsily pulling at my clothes, anesthetising the pain in my legs, adrenaline flooding me.

I reach towards her; she pushes my hand away. She slips off her knickers, steps out of them, her movements devouring me the whole time. Within seconds her dappled curvy silhouette moves towards me. Our bodies collide, skin on skin; she lies back on the bed pulling me close.

I lay my palm flat against her bare skin; the sensation sweeping through me forces me to inhale sharply. I'm overwhelmed, mesmerised by her, by what's happening. Every sense of her seems magnified.

I caress her curves and soft mounds. The rush of our breathing is heavy, uncontrolled, a moan leaves me, and I tremble with each new breath.

'You're just as wonderful as I imagined. You're amazing, truly you are.'

'I think you're in a state of shock.' She's flirting, twisting her dark locks around her fingers. 'And you've clearly not felt my fat tummy but thank you.'

'The only shock is lying here with you after so long. You're beautifully real and *nothing ever becomes real till it is experienced,* I say, quoting Keats. I run my hand over the bump of her abdomen, the fullness of her bottom and the curve of her thighs. She tenses and relaxes again. I play with the sapphire jewel in her belly button. Her physical response to me has been, is, incredibly overwhelming. She's lying here with me, completely comfortable in her nakedness. I almost expect her to say it's a mistake, to push me away but she doesn't. She's sweetness and light yet roaring and on fire.

Her urgency tells me she wants me just as much as I want her. It's a vivid awakening into sexual passion. I'm trembling with longing; everything comes at me. This is what we have shared so many times online and now it's happening for real. I suppress my rising panic. I don't want to mess this up. I don't want to spoil it for her.

Her eyes dance like pools in a midnight sky and in that instant, I know I love her. I knew it before but now I feel it; feel it deep in my soul. My love for her is my truth and nothing will change that. I know we are destined to be together, and I can't imagine being without her, never want to be without her.

'So, here we are,' I say, kissing her lips, her neck. I want to explore all of her, to devour her.

'Here we are,' she gasps, kissing me back, full on the lips, arching towards me, pulling me closer to her.

I pull at her hair, I kiss her shoulders, her breasts, drowning in her. She reaches for me and I freeze.

'It's okay,' she mumbles detecting a change in me, a hesitation. The sheet ripples under us; her hand massages me, gently at first and slowly builds momentum, her grip tighter. But it's no use.

'It won't,' I say, a catch in my throat. 'I won't…'

'It's okay. Let me.' Her voice is gentle, loving. Her movements play in the shadows. I force myself to calm down until eventually I lose myself in the imagery, the motion. What she's doing turns me on despite my negligible reaction down there.

My breathing comes hard, and I swallow. My mouth is dry. Watching her heightens my sensation and my imagination. In my mind I am ready to cum. In my mind

I can feel her hand on me and know, almost as if it's real, how that makes me feel. What's Maria thinking? Is she less excited knowing I can't come? Does she realise I won't no matter how excited I am? However hard she tries.

She carries on massaging me. She builds the momentum, suddenly stops. She goes down on me; the outline of her kissable mouth sends me catapulting into a different realm. My mind is an explosion of fireworks and a 100-gun salute. I imagine being inside her, firm and quivering.

I push her down on me.

I change position, try my hardest to slow down but she's equally impatient. We rush. My fingers delve into her most intimate place.

We lie together, the rise and fall of her presses on my chest. I cradle her in my arms, her breasts resting on me, her skin like silk. Skin on skin. I try hard to recall if I've felt like this before. I know I will cherish this moment forever, though I'm desperately uncomfortable in this position.

I can't go back to Sandra, my life in Inverness, to pretend my life is all I want it to be. I'm cheating on Sandra and when I go back to her, I will be cheating on Maria too. What have I turned into?

An image of Sandra in her nightdress invades my thoughts like a moving photograph, a stitched memory of past and present; her spammy white legs and translucent veins along her wrists and hands, her yellowing fingernails from the years of smoking, the creased puckering of her upper lip. I squeeze my eyes in an effort to repel the picture. I focus on Maria; a complete contrast; her warm olive skin and tanned complexion a goddess-like vision, her hands, and feet with painted nails. In this woman, I envisage a new living, breathing patchwork of moments come together.

Suddenly Sandra's voice is calling me to cook dinner. I

shake my head in an effort to expel her whine. I don't want to be thinking about Sandra. I don't want Sandra muddying my moment with Maria.

All that matters, all that exists and is real, is Maria and me, lying here together. She's fallen asleep and I flick on the bedside light. I pull back from her, as gently as I can, my arm's numbed. Her hair drapes in soft folds over her face. I note all her little features, a beauty spot on her left cheek and an errant grey hair. She's perfect in all her imperfectness. I adore her. She fidgets, turns her back to me. I run my fingers over the blue butterfly tattoo on her shoulder. She doesn't wake. I can't tell what is night and what is not but I've changed.

'I love you Maria,' I tell her, stroking her bare, upturned bottom. She's so sexy and all the more so because she doesn't know it. She has this quiet sex appeal which bubbles to the surface when she smiles.

Her aura makes her totally captivating, and she doesn't hide her unashamed longing to be loved, her joy of sex and everything that goes with it. Her almost desperate thirst to please is open and free. She's beautiful. I am invigorated, lost in her… every little part of her. I pull the duvet over her and the cool linen against her bare skin rouses her.

'You're not regretting anything are you?' she asks turning to face me.

'No. Not ever. Are you?'

'I fell asleep, didn't I?'

'You did. Just like you do when we're together online. I knew you would. It's your "thing" and I love you for it. I'm glad knowing you can fall asleep beside me. It's like a physical union outside of us… sleeping together.'

'A bit embarrassing though. I'm sorry.'

'You were only asleep for a few minutes, ten at most.

And now…'

'And now?' She wraps her legs around me, lapping me in hot flames. She kisses me, rouses me. That increasingly familiar and welcome sensation floods me. I'm melting into her. The shooting pain in my leg, across my lower back has gone.

'Let's do it all again. And this time I want to see all of you,' I say.

'You're insatiable Alexander.'

'I am with you,' I say, squeezing her tight. 'Just making sure you're real.' I smile. 'I am. And so are you. We are both real,' she says in a way that touches every inch of me and despite the rush of fireworks bursting inside of me this is where peace lies. Here, with Maria who judges me, not by my physical inabilities, but by my physical abilities, my thoughts, my words, and my mind, and yes, my manhood.

31
Maria

The red brick modern architecture of the British Library looms up ahead of me. My heart's racing, remembering what happened last night. I consciously slow my pace in an effort to calm myself. Come on, I chastise, knowing that after yesterday I shouldn't be as nervous as I am. Or maybe that's exactly why I am.

I spent most of last night thinking about being in bed with Alexander and what we'd done together. He understood why I wasn't staying the night, had to get back for Natalie, though it turned out to be a waste of time. She stayed out... again.

He was a passionate lover, though rather clumsy in his attention. His eager-to-please-me attitude was refreshing. I suppose not being able to means he has to work harder to please a woman and he certainly didn't hold back in coming forward. The heat rises in me, my cheeks burn. I slept with him and enjoyed it despite him rushing to please me, to do everything we'd done online, all in one go.

I skip across the road, my sunglasses shading my eyes from the blaring July sunshine. My skirt's hem rustles, and I hold its folds flat against my bare legs.

The London heat clings to me. I run my fingers through the ends of my hair loosening the curls, crunchy from too much serum. The air brings little relief to the back of my neck, sticky with sweat.

My handbag, lighter than yesterday, knocks gently against my thigh as I pass through the gated entrance into the library's outside concourse. A weightless flutter suddenly dances through me. My nerves, an excited flurry of butterflies, awaken in anticipation of being in Alexander's company again.

I descend the steps leading to the piazza. I spot Alexander immediately; he's sitting on a wall almost opposite the entrance, his strong torso in sharp contrast to his slim legs. Behind him looms the huge banner advertising the exhibition he has tickets for.

He catches sight of me and waves. He eases himself onto his feet, leans onto his cane; a reminder to me he's a disabled man and a surge of something runs through me. Is it a pang of pity? Is it a burst of admiration? Despite his disability he is a man I already admire, am connected with; there's nothing wrong with his mind or his desire to please me. I see his disability but feel his wholeness more.

Would my friends only notice the disabled man, or would they be wowed by his charm, good looks and sensitivity? What they might think bothers me more than it should and the thought presses down on me like a threatening raincloud. Why does it matter what they think?

I wave back and wedge my sunglasses on my head,

approaching him. I lean in for a kiss; sandalwood and musk invade my senses. I want to nuzzle his neck… lose myself in the powdery sweetness of his aftershave.

'Hi. Sorry I'm a few minutes late. Guess it's my turn to keep you waiting…'

'Aye, it is. No, no, it's fine.'

'Sure?'

'Aye, I am now that you're here. And I've bought you a wee gift.'

He hands me a scrunched-up paper bag and I melt; it's the book of poetry we read together in Foyles the night before.

Dear Maria, because you love poetry just as much as I do, love from Alexander xxx

'Thank you so much,' I say, leaning in to give him a kiss on the cheek which turns into an awkward cheek-lips smudge. My mind's flapping and my heart's flipping.

'Our ticket time is half twelve,' he says, checking the printed pages in his hand.

'We could have a drink if you like. I'd love a cup of tea. Or do you want to go straight in?'

'Yes, let's have a drink so I can sit and lose myself in those beautiful brown eyes of yours. Listen to you giggling,' he says.

'Okay,' I say, and an excited quiver shakes my voice. 'I'll get these.'

We each pull up a chair and sit under a huge awning. I lean on the table and it wobbles. Alexander stares straight at me. I pull my lace cardigan across my front and fiddle with the long ties of its pussy bow. My cheeks flush. I listen to Alexander, enthralled; he talks about the history of Russia; Putin and the siege of Leningrad. I'm mesmerised by how his moustache moves with his lips. Around us people are walking past towards the exit, towards the entrance. The melee seems to create a dance, a show of carefree celebration. It sits right with my mood.

A breeze brings a light drizzle of rain and I involuntarily move closer to Alexander. He holds my hand in his and continues to talk as if this is the most natural thing in the world.

Suddenly, the world loses all its sense of reality. Where will this meeting of two people who know each other so intimately end? The reality is miles apart. Alexander's voice flits in and out of my consciousness, as my own conscience nabs at me; a low drone in the background; he's a married man and here I am living it up in London with him. Out of nowhere, my feelings change, are helter-skelter, up, down, high, low. I try to shake them away.

***

We join the queue snaking across the piazza and Alexander puts his arm around my waist.

'Can I kiss you?' he asks, looking straight at me.

He doesn't wait for an answer. He leans in, plants a gentle kiss on my lips. They are soft, his scraggly moustache and his scratchy beard creating contrasting tickly sensations against my lips, my face. Today, the feeling isn't alien. I'd never kissed a man with so much facial hair before yesterday. In the throes of our union yesterday I hadn't noticed the scent of his woodsy beard oil. What am I doing? This is madness.

Not another word passes between us, and we shuffle forward side by side. Alexander holds onto our printed tickets like they are love notes carrying simple love messages, fondling and fingering the paper between his fingertips. I'm tingling inside.

Once inside the entrance hall, Alexander ambles up the wide row of stone steps leading up to an open mezzanine level; he wants to use the toilet. Will he use the disabled facilities?

Waiting for him to return, I turn my attention to the display of Russian Revolution giftware and books, posters, and postcards. I pace around stroking the covers of books and flicking through others; pictures of Leningrad and the Romanovs leap at me, and I recognise a portrait of Princess Anastasia and her brother Alexei. I am pulled into a world of history I know little about, though, many years ago, a documentary about a woman who claimed to be the Princess Anastasia moved me; her ordeal consumed me for days.

I think about Alexander. What sort of a man is he really? He seems placid, gentle, kind; same in reality as he is online. But what would he be like as a permanent boyfriend? Would his desires for me translate more aggressively as his physical appetite consumes him? He says they have previously remained unsatisfied. Did I satisfy them yesterday? Am I enough?

I think about his bulge. Think about catheters and bed-wetting and worse. Do these aspects of his CP repulse me or would I accept them as a part of him? Panic fills me. I text Fabio. Within seconds my phone rings. I wander to the back of the shop, lowering my voice.

'I'm having a panic.'

'What's happened?'

'I don't know what I'm doing.'

'You had me worried, thinking all sorts.'

'Sorry.'

'Relax. Isn't not knowing what you're doing part of the fun?'

'Yes… and no.'

'You can always just run away from him… he won't be able to catch up.'

'Ha, ha. Stop being mean.'

'Sorry. You got caught up in the moment yesterday. It was fun, exhilarating. You don't have to do anything again if you don't want to.'

My mind rushes through the images of yesterday stacked up one after the other; fused and overlapping, they're blurred and running into each other.

'I know… and thank you so much. I'll be in touch,' I say, catching a glimpse of Alexander. I turn round to face him and, in that moment, everything, the panic, falls away like a curtain revealing the sunlight behind it; he's found a place in my head and my heart.

***

At the entrance to the exhibition, Alexander flashes our tickets; they are stamped and initialled. A painted timeline of the revolution dominates the wall opposite us.

As we wander around reading the notes accompanying each showcase, I shake off a flutter when Alexander gently puts his arm around the back of my waist. A heat comes off him and through my top; it sears my skin. I edge millimetres away, but he leans into me again, touches my hand at every opportunity. A faint trembling passes through him; he is excited. It fascinates me and enthralls me and puts me at ease. His reactions arouse me all over again.

Yesterday is brandished on my mind and I don't recognise the woman who was in the hotel room with him, writhing under the sheets, pressing herself into him. How honest I am being with myself? How honest I am being with Alexander?

Alexander holds my hand and this being with him feels natural. I like how his hand wraps around mine… protective. He's an ordinary Scottish man from Inverness, and I crave more of what lies beneath his charm and boyish lop-sided grin. What else is there to experience with him? What else will he reveal the more time we spend together?

I know what going back to the hotel means and a tremble passes through me and a wet sensation seeps between my legs. The forcefulness of my feelings surprises me. Alexander turns me on. It happens undetected, an undercurrent between us. Within ten minutes our taxi is pulling up outside the hotel. Alexander pays the fare and slowly, rather precariously, climbs out using his stick to bear his weight. The doorman holds the heavy glass door open for us and tips his top hat.

I sit down on a cushioned bench. Alexander lowers himself into the space next to me and reaches for my hand. A waitress promptly welcomes us with a smile as dazzling as the bar's polished chrome lighting and shining mirrored panels. It's quiet and instantly I relax. It feels decadent; the beautiful plush surroundings jump out at me from my all-time favourite film, *Pretty Woman*.

'What can I get you?' the waitress asks, smoothing the white apron over her black trousers.

'I think I'm going to have a gin…' says Alexander, scanning the drinks menu. The waitress spouts off the names of special gins available and he orders a double measure of one infused with cinnamon.

'Sounds delicious,' I say.

'One for you too?'

'Oh no… no thank you. I'll have a…'

'…vanilla vodka and lemonade?' interjects Alexander. 'After all it's what you drink isn't it?'

'Yes, that's lovely. Thank you.' Today is a proper date, the practise is over, and I feel the weight of its expectations.

'I want to tell you something else… you asked about my work, my career. I'm no saint. I'm not living a life of luxury working part-time. I resigned from my previous job to avoid being sacked, not because I could afford to work less hours. Far from it. I knew it was on the cards, would be inevitable, had I carried on… I spiraled into a spell of drinking, arriving late to work, missing deadlines and one time turned up to a meeting in a sequined party dress still half-cut.'

'Oh, my darling. I don't care about that just how much you suffered.'

'The decision to leave, in the end, was one of self-preservation but it devastated me, and it was justly unceremonious. I had no partner, no income, a young daughter, and no job to shape my day, my confidence zeroed.'

'But you're here telling me your story. You're strong. You've survived. You trust me enough to tell me.'

'I do trust you.'

'But?'

'Not sure I will survive again though…'

'And you won't have to. There's little chance of falling pregnant with me,' he jokes. 'What else are you not telling me?'

I smile a little smile, 'And now, with Natalie being pregnant,' I say. 'One part of me wants her to have the baby, the other wants her be free, to live her life.'

'What does she want to do?'

'I don't know. She's crippled with indecision. Her boyfriend's young. They're both young.'

'I imagine it's why you've distanced yourself the last

couple of weeks… understandably so, too. She has to be your priority.'

'I suppose that and meeting you, us… everything.'

'She'll come to the right decision. She's got a strong mum. You're incredible, truly incredible. I'm here for you. You can talk to me whenever you want.'

'Thank you.'

'And as for us, we're okay, aren't we?'

The waitress sashays across the swirly-patterned carpet towards us carrying our drinks on a round black-lacquered tray.

'Cheers, Alexander and thank you for listening,' I say, ignoring his question, too scared to say anything, to admit I depend on him.

'Cheers my darling Maria. And thank you for a fabulous day. To us,' he says again, and he holds my gaze while his free hand strokes mine.

I sip at my drink. I'm blushing. Libido seeps through me; a deliciously illicit guest. My heart and mind battle with my emotions. I shift in my seat. His blue eyes hold mine, tempting me where I'm afraid, yet excited, to go again. It is tantalisingly naughty and risky, heightening the bubbling in me all day.

I suck on my straw and pull a face.

'Not good?' he asks, stroking my arm gently.

'It's definitely a double. And Alexander, if we do anything again, this turns from being a one afternoon stand to being an affair. Is that what you want? Doesn't it bother you?'

'Does it bother you?' he asks.

'The affair doesn't bother me, no. Because your wife doesn't deserve you. She doesn't treat you well and you're so nice. You're fun, you're clever, you're a real gentleman and even though this is wrong I can't feel guilty when it's obvious how happy it's making you.'

I'm getting hotter and hotter. My words tumble out. I pick up my drink, give it a swirl with my paper straw, the crystal-clear ice cubes tinkle against the side of the tall glass. I take another long sip, the ice liquid coats my tongue and the back of my throat.

'This is about you and me, the connection we have and the here and now. I don't want to think about going back… not when I'm here with you,' he pauses, laying his hand gently over mine. 'Are you happy with me?'

His voice… so grainy, sexy. I like his temperament… he is calm yet passionate in bed… I blush again remembering yesterday.

'Yes,' I say, though how long for I don't know.

We talk about London, my writing, his job, more about Natalie, our favourite memories of growing up. He orders more drinks. I drink my second glass too quickly; thirsty from the heat of him and what he arouses in me. Intermittently nervous and excited. The afternoon light fades into the evening dusk and I flirt with him. I relish being in these plush surroundings with this man. I want to be with him and walk away at the same time. A dance of pulling and pushing, like a moth fluttering against the bright attraction of a naked bulb on a warm summer evening, fills me.

We eat our lunch and Alexander starts to fidget; he is uncomfortable sitting on the narrow upright banquette and although I want to say let's go where you can be more comfortable, I can't say the words.

***

I sit on the edge of the bed and slip off my lace cardi, vest top, undo my bra. I pull down my leggings and knickers at the same time, discarding them at the foot of the bed. I do it in slow motion, on auto pilot. This is surreal.

'Not getting an erection doesn't mean I can't be satisfied or give you satisfaction in other ways. So, I have to ask you again… would you let me slap your bare bottom, lie across my knee?'

I tense and avoid his pleading gaze. I slip from his arms and put on my top; I feel too exposed. He pulls me back towards him and we lie in each other's arms.

'No pressure. I want you to understand me and my ability to feel. I can feel there… I know what it feels like because my dad hit me with his belt once and it was the most exhilarating yet painful sensation ever. That feeling is the only one below my waist I can feel and a sensation I yearn to feel again.'

I have no words; my heart beats a fraction faster.

'I've imagined you all bare bottom and giggles,' he says, trying to lighten the conversation.

'Not sure I'd be giggling. I've never been slapped before. Not like that.'

'Oh darling. I wouldn't hurt you. Wouldn't ever hurt you.'

'I know. It's just that…'

'It's the shock, the pain, the humiliation all mixed together. It turns me on.'

'Because you can't feel anything otherwise?' I ask, hoping I'm not making a mess of this, hoping I'm not embarrassing him. 'I'd be scared of hurting you. You hurting me.'

'Well, what about the other? For me that's the most beautiful way I can get to being intimate with a woman. I can't penetrate you, but I can use my tongue…'

'Can't we just see what happens?'

'We can, but I don't want to get this wrong with

you... you mean too much to me. I want you to be sure, to understand what I'm imagining and seeing. It's as if I can feel sensations for real even though on a physical level there's negligible evidence I'm turned on.'

'I think I understand... that's like having a fantasy, isn't it? Visualising it all in your head and watching it unfold...'

'And the smacking... it's not about pain. It's about enjoyment. It's that fine line between pain and ecstasy.'

'Well, in that case, maybe we should give it a try,' I say, giggling. I extricate myself from his strong arms and down the rest of my drink.

***

On the tube journey home, I think about what he shared with me. How open he is. He's like a set of stacked domino blocks... one thought leads to another and another. He's convinced I am the woman who can send his emotions falling how he wants, one rippling emotion radiating into another.

I tremble involuntarily against a tremor running through me. The tube speeds through the final leg of the underground journey and the carriage fills with the orange of dusk when it bursts into the open.

32
Maria

It's the night before Natalie's appointment at the birth control clinic.

'Next time this happens, you'll be ready. I promise you, my beautiful girl,' I say to her, and a weak smile creases her face.

'My heart is broken Mum. I messed up and nothing will ever be right.'

'You live your best life and that will be atonement enough.'

I pull the duvet over her in the same way I used to when she was a toddler. 'Sausage roll,' I whisper. But inside my heart is shattering, the splinters piercing me. I rock back and forth, immersing myself in the pain, allowing myself to feel it in every part of me. I can do nothing but let the tears roll silently down my face.

I sit on the edge of her bed for what seems like hours but

is only a few minutes; her eyes flicker under her lids against the light of the bedside table. Eventually they still and her quiet breathing tells me she is in a deep sleep.

In my bedroom, I kneel by my bed, and I pray. I clasp my hands together and I pray the hardest I've prayed since her father left me.

For the first time in months, I don't check my Twitter feed or read any of Alexander's messages. His messages are lined up in my inbox like a row of chocolate kisses but instead of wanting to take each one and taste it I feel sick. I don't answer my vibrating phone. All I want is for tomorrow to come and go and for my Nat to be happy again.

I squeeze my eyes against the threatening tears and recall the words in her diary.

July 26th
"It's 2 days before my appointment and I can't sleep. Mum thinks I'm up working on an assignment. I want to tell her how I feel but can't. I keep touching my stomach, I'm even praying to God to forgive me for what I'm going to do which is madness—do I even believe in God? But it's the right thing, I know in my heart that it is the only thing I can do. Not for me but for him or her... an angel or someone visited me from heaven in my sleep last night. I know that feeling, like someone wrapped their arms around me. I felt warm and safe. I know what to do if I'm brave enough. Whoever it was promised to look after Tom and me."

I vow never to read it again after tomorrow.

33
Maria

'What was it like? I mean you didn't have rompy-pompy,' asks Fabio, cutting to the chase.

'I told you on the phone.'

'No, you didn't. You fobbed me off.'

'No, I didn't… but it was good… a bit of a blur.'

'Oh gosh, tell me you didn't get plastered.'

I chuck a sofa cushion at him and thump him on the arm, giggling through a mouthful of guacamole. 'No. I just remember lying back and… it's blurry. Other parts I remember well… you know…'

'You've made me wait two weeks for this. Spill.'

'He was different face-to-face, surer of himself than I thought he'd be.'

'Different in a good way?'

'I realised he's the sort of man I want to be with, I've longed for.'

'How? Come on, you're a writer. Tell me what you mean.'

'He was considerate, kind. He listened.'

'And sex?'

'He made up for his lack of finesse with enthusiasm. He was urgent, rushing, tearing at me, couldn't get enough of me.'

'Very Mills and Boon. He sounds desperate,' says Fabio, piling his fajita with spicy chicken, red peppers, and crisp lettuce. He rolls it and demolishes it in two bites.

'I think I was a bit desperate too. Desperate to prove myself to him, to myself.'

'To you? Why? What's all that about?'

'I don't know. I just wanted to be good enough for him. Wanted to be the woman he says he's fallen in love with.'

'Fallen in love with? Did he say that?'

'Yes.'

'Wow. He's got it bad. You both have. Do you believe him?'

'I don't know. He seemed genuine. He was so kind and thoughtful, but I feel inadequate…' I say.

'You're good enough for him, you are. More like, is he good enough for you?'

'There was no going back, and I didn't want to go back. I wanted him to, you know, fill up on me. I wanted him to drink me up.'

'Sounds like an adult version of Alice in Wonderland.'

'Stop it. I'm opening myself up to you here,' I laugh. 'I wanted to be adored again. Wanted to be special. He made me feel like that.'

'And was it like you thought it would be after all the messaging and sexting?'

'He touched every part of me, and I will remember it for a long time.'

'Wow. So, no bonky-bonky suits you?'

I pretend to be disgusted. We both fall about laughing. In room 231 I succumbed to Alexander; he had all of me. And I wonder, sitting here with my best friend, whether that was me? I gave myself so readily assuming our meeting was a one-off… that we'd go back to sexting once he was back in Inverness. But now I want more. I wasn't jumping further than the three days we had together, but now I am.

The flat door slams. 'Hope there's food left for me,' Natalie calls out.

'Plenty,' shouts Fabio. She slopes into the sitting room and dumps her school bag. She's flushed, glowing.

'Okay, Nat?' I ask.

'Yeah, just a catch-up session for sociology. Mrs. P is just so fresh.'

'Fresh?' asks Fabio.

'You know On. Point. With. Everything,' she says, mimicking her teacher's high-pitched voice.

'She means exact. Doing her job properly. You should be grateful she's putting in the time to help you,' I say, handing her a plate.

She sits cross-legged on the floor and bum-shuffles up to the coffee table. 'Smells good,' she says, licking her lips. I notice her hand; it rests fleetingly across her belly.

'You're shining,' says Fabio. 'Being pregnant suits you.'

'Oh stop! I'm getting so fat.' She piles double helpings onto her plate, and I want to burst.

'You're going to be alright. The extra baby weight suits you and you know what else? You're glowing from the inside out.'

'Thanks Mum. That's what Tom says.'

We finish the Mexican and Natalie, in a rare show of maturity and consideration, clears the coffee table. I hear the clatter of plates and cutlery; she is loading the dishwasher, haphazardly as anyone with a lack of experience would, but at least she's doing it.

'She's a good girl. You should be proud of her,' says Fabio. 'Unlike her sex-mad mother.'

'Stop it. She'll hear you.'

'Hear what?' she asks as she comes back in, picking off the purple nail varnish she only put on yesterday.

'Actually. It may come to nothing, but a Twitter follower has a contact with a publishing house in Scotland and he's already passed on my manuscript to the editor. I may actually have found a publisher for my book.'

'OMG. Mum!'

'And that's not all. JangleJewels is finally heading towards international success. Orders have quadrupled in less than three weeks… Leo is pulling out what little hair he has.'

'That's incredible. A double celebration. So happy for you,' Fabio says. A question hangs on his lips.

'Me too,' I say with an at once possible and impossible elation, my shoulders shaking. 'Our guardian angels are shining down on us.'

'They certainly are… pass one my way, will you?'

'Always,' I say, smiling so big it hurts my jaw.

34
Maria

'What's happening with your Twitter? You were so excited about it and now you don't say a word,' says Natalie, struggling to iron her jeans.

'Not much, really. Lots of new followers,' I say, leaning back into the couch, stretching my arms up over my head.

'And Alexander?'

Just as she mentions his name a text comes in:

> *Thinking about you. And vodka. You and vodka and you and you and vodka and my lips on yours and your lips on mine and vodka. I'm drunk on you.*

His message brings on a spreading heat. For a split second I pull back from mentioning anything about him.

'I met him in London last week.'

'You met him? Mum!'

'Don't start on me.'

'Is that him now?' she asks, pointing at my mobile. 'Why didn't you tell me?'

'You've had so much going on with school and feeling sick, I wanted to be sure before saying anything.' I blush, knowing I'm not being completely honest with her.

'And do you?'

'What?'

'Have something to tell me? Mum, you've dropped yourself in it. That's what you were talking about with Fabio, isn't it? When I walked in?'

'We spent a couple of days together. It was…'

'Mum… you like him.'

'I do, a lot actually, and he likes me, but it's complicated.'

'My mum had a date with a man she met on Twitter. Whoo-hoo. You're kinda peng,' she says, switching off the iron at the socket.

I smile, a little bit of the old Natalie is back. 'By peng I'm assuming you mean cool?'

'Yes.'

'You've changed your tune… it wasn't so long ago you were giving me a lecture on online safety.'

'I was shocked that's all. Being protective.'

'Oh darling. I love you.'

'So, you like him? And he likes you?' she asks again.

'I like him Nat. I like him a lot, but I don't know where this will lead or if it will lead to anything.'

'Are you meeting again? Can I meet him?' she asks, jumping up and down to get her jeggings on. She's going to need a bigger size soon.

'Woa, hold on. You're getting carried away.'

'No Mum, it's you who got carried away.'

'Darling, I'm so glad we're back on track.'

'Me too.'

'You know how much I love you. And I just didn't want you, and don't take this the wrong way, making the same mess of things that I did.'

'Mum, come on. You didn't mess up. I know it was Dad who walked away. Who left us.'

'And you? Were you walking away from me the way he did?'

'No. Of course not, never. I was just… it's different. I just wanted to do something mad-crazy-stupid for once,' she says, wincing as she hoists the waistband over her neat, rounded belly.

'I know what you mean but being crazy doesn't always work out best in the long run.'

'No, but it has for me. I'm happy Mum. I'm not scared or worried or afraid anymore. Life is what you make it, right? And I'm going to make it right with Tom. We know what we both want even if it's taken a bit of wandering around in the dark to find that out.'

'Oh, darling. You're so much better at all this than I ever was. You're strong and beautiful and just brilliant. I'm sorry I let you down with all my panic and ranting.'

'Mum, it's okay. You didn't. I guess I just had to find my own path and I have. Life isn't meant to be lived in a straight line, right?'

'Talking of straight lines…'

'Yes?'

'About Alexander…'

'What about him?'

'He's got CP.'

'And?'

'And he's different to you and me.'

'Mum, everyone is different to you and me. Everyone is

different from everyone.'

'He walks with a cane.'

'And you can't walk in high heels,' she says, giggling.

'I'm being serious.'

'Mum. If he likes you and you like him, what's the problem?'

'I guess there isn't one.'

'Mum, you can't keep treating me like your little girl. I'm nearly eighteen now.'

'Now that's something that'll never change. Come here,' I say, pulling her close and hugging her tight.

'Mum... the baby. I can't breathe it in,' she says, pulling away, laughing. Her hand goes across her tummy, a protective gesture. My heart swells. She's already a mum and I'm back to being her mum again.

35
Alexander

It's Monday morning. I step into the hallway, after my third weekend shift since meeting Maria in London. Sandra's stifled sobs from the kitchen pound a prickling sensation up my arms and across my neck. She's not cried in all our years of marriage.

My first thought is she has found out; discovered the silly nic-nacs Maria bought me the third time we met in London – the key ring of a brassy Big Ben and a red post box, the Union Jack mug with a giant "A" on it – and her lipstick-smudged paper napkin I sneaked from the table after we stopped for tea and cake in Fortnum & Mason. If she has, will I admit to the affair, all of it, or will I deny it?

My heart races and my thoughts are jumbled. I try to slow my emotions. This may be my escape route, leave Sandra and start over on my terms. Anything to escape this emotionally draining farce of a marriage, but do I have the strength to walk away from the foundations I now know were built on shifting sand? My stomach lurches at the weight of it all.

'You okay, sweetheart?' I call from the hallway, clumsily toeing off my canvas shoes. My feet are soaked with sweat. I should have put socks on this morning.

She doesn't answer.

In the kitchen, doubled over the table, scrunched up tissues strewn over the tabletop, she's blowing her nose. Newspaper cuttings lie in tatters over the floor, in drifts around her feet. My mind is cloudy. What is all this?

A lit cigarette sits in the ashtray we brought back from a trip to Edinburgh, angry curls of smoke waltz around her and distastefully mingle with the unctuous scent of her perfume. I turn away; a tight elastic-band sensation across my chest. I force my breathing to slow, long deep breaths through my nose, and slow exhales through pursed lips. I relax my shoulders and jaw.

'What's happened? Is it Callum?'

'Nothing. Nothing's happened,' she mumbles through the soggy tissue held up to her face.

'For goodness sake. What is it, Sandra? You never cry.' In that second, panic, or is it guilt, tugs at me. I slip my mobile into the back pocket of my jeans. I sit down next to her, and I force myself to reach for her hand. 'Tell me. Tell me in your own time.'

The seconds seem to last an eternity, my thumping heart beats in my ears.

'I want to talk to you. And I think now's the time,' she sobs through muffled words, snot bubbling from her nose.

'What is it?' I try to keep panic out of my voice.

'I know you think I'm cold… that I don't love…'

'What's all this about?'

'I do love you more than you know but…'

I consciously slow my breathing.

'It's about Callum. He's… he's … not yours.'

'What? What do you mean not mine?' I struggle to decipher her words.

'You're not his biological father. I've known it for a long time but forced myself to believe you were.'

'What? What are you saying?'

'I was stupid and naïve and believed Douglas loved me. He didn't, he disappeared the first chance he got…'

'Douglas? Who the hell's Douglas?'

'A man I knew… years ago…'

'Not Callum's dad?' I push my chair back, recoiling from her words.

'No… I…'

'He's not mine?'

'He is yours, he's just…'

'You've lied to me all these years?'

'I didn't mean to,' she manages through a strangled cry.

'You are irrefutably, culpable for the conscious choice you made, Sandra.'

'Douglas didn't know,' she cries.

'But you did.'

'I clung to the notion that the situation was about me all these years. Oh my God. Once we had Callum, it was no longer about me. It was about us, our family.'

'Our family? You say our family after telling me this?'

'Please, Alec. Stop it.'

'You're not the victim here. I am. Callum is.'

'He's still your son. Let me explain…'

'Who the hell is Douglas?'

'A man… just before you… just before we married.' She pauses. 'I thought we would be together. I thought he loved me.'

'And did you love him?'

'Yes… no…'

'Tell me. Which is it, Sandra?' I pace, my legs shaking, my head light.

'I thought he loved me,' she repeats.

'All this time you've wanted him?'

'It's not like that. I liked you. I always liked you. I never meant to deceive you. To deceive Callum.' Tears streak her face, snot trickles over her upper lip into her mouth. The sight nauseates me.

'Liked me? Oh my God. You don't love me. You never have.'

'I didn't say that.'

'You were sleeping with him… while we were together?'

'Once. I promise.'

'Your parents knew. That's why they were always telling us to count our blessings.'

'Mum may have suspected, yes.'

'And I'm the last to know. The mug Alec. Good ol' Alec…'

'Don't…'

'Don't? All these years, I've worried about Callum's health, his development. What a waste of my time, my energy, my peace… and your mum kept her distance unable to face the part she played in all the lies. All your lies.'

A hate fills me from the pit of my stomach, and I don't want to be sympathetic. I want to slap her across the face. But the moment is snatched away by my own guilt, my own wretched lies and deception.

A memory I'd long forgotten comes back to me. Sandra and her once brightly made-up face. She became plainer, no smudges of colour on her eyelids, less bold. The reason why hits me like a hunk of stone; she didn't want to be attractive anymore. Not after being abandoned by her lover.

'I never meant to, Alec. I always meant to tell you but as time went on, I couldn't do it to you. You loved me so much and Callum was a part of what we had. If you knew the truth, I knew you'd leave us.'

'You couldn't do it to yourself, you mean.'

'No…'

'Why are you telling me now?'

'Because I don't want to lose you and I want you to understand what I've sacrificed.'

'Sacrificed? A fantasy love for a man who left you. I loved you, love Callum. I don't understand why you're telling me now.'

'Because Douglas is coming back to Inverness, permanently.' She glances towards the newspaper debris.

I piece together fragments of the newspaper clippings; a bold headline explains it all:

Billionaire Businessman Wins Bid For Inverness
Multi-Million Pound Housing Project

I glare at her and through a strangled cry she says, 'Sorry. I've got to get to work. I can't be late on my third day back.'

The news is shocking. Too shocking to absorb, yet I am relieved she doesn't know about Maria. My own guilt gnaws at me, a different guilt but just as guilty as Sandra all the same. It's all muddled in my head. I sway; lean on the back of the chair. I want to hide. I want to run.

I fling open the shed door and launch myself into my armchair. My hip's aching and my leg's cramping. I wince at the pain. My headache is affecting my sight. I scrunch my eyes shut and will the throbbing to subside but the pressure of squeezing only exacerbates the pain.

The newspaper headline goes round and round in my head. That's it. She's been hiding the newspaper from me for weeks. She knew this Douglas guy was back on the scene. Still kept it from me.

I do the one thing I can to bring myself immediate comfort, relief.

Good afternoon my beautiful Maria. Hold me? Xx

Good afternoon. You okay?

Missing you, my lover. Kiss me? X

Holding your hand, kissing you softly on the lips. How are you?

I'm better now you're by my side, kissing me. Missing you so much. X

Longing builds in me; distant, unreachable. Memories of the one part of my life I was sure of and proud of – Callum – crash and tumble as if on a stormy sea and a deep melancholy drowns me.

I massage my hip; a dull persistent ache comes in surges and seems to coincide with the undulating waves of panic that have a grip on me. I'm disappointed, angry. There's a tension in my head; a wild sea pummeling debris at me. Yet I'm relieved too. Long-buried doubts about me being Callum's dad hurl themselves at me. I chose to ignore the antagonist jeering inside my head. I wanted my life with Sandra to work. But every now and again a sixth sense had left me asking whether he was mine. It wasn't paranoia.

I close my eyes and will an image of Maria to manifest itself. I push back into the armchair and imagine her leaning in to kiss me. I feel her hot full lips on mine and a moan escapes me, pure sexual pleasure. I get a sense of her perfume; smell it and taste it on her. She pops open each button of her blouse and I run my tongue down her front following each one.

I groan and push my hand down my trousers, heat rises within me; like an anesthetic filling me up from my toes to the top of my head. This is a rush of emotions only Maria can bring about; uncontrollable, persistent. My pulse quickens and she undoes her blouse. Her breasts spill over her lace bra…

My phone pings. I read her flirty message. I'm going to explode with lust, with passion, so all-consuming that I'm almost screaming her name. She knows what to say and what to do to get a reaction… she is in tune with my deepest fantasies and desires… sex with her right now is wonderfully soothing, desensitising my pain and pushing me into a state of desperate oblivion. She is as much mysterious and sexy as she is innocent and vulnerable.

Another ping tells me she's on her knees, my trousers slowly slipping down, now scrunched round my ankles and she's doing what I experienced with her for real and a rippling, sensation leaves me tingling.

Our fantasy session leaves me exhausted, but calmer, and the throbbing in my head subsides to a dull ache. I shake my head in an effort to shift that last bit of pain behind my eyes and it moves to my temples.

How was that for you my darling Alexander?

You're incredible. You make me so happy. So fulfilled. I

can't wait to see you again. I need you. X

You need me? Why?

Yes. I need you. You are my breath, my soul, my everything. X

I know how she worries when I express myself in this way and yet I can't stop myself. I want to get away from Sandra. I want to be with Maria, to hold her again. What Sandra has revealed provides me with the perfect excuse to disappear to London again. She can't stop me. My manipulative scheming shocks me. Am I so detached and cold? Where's my empathy? The revelation numbs me, and I cry in agony at how cruel a turn this is yet a tiny throbbing part of me rejoices about seeing Maria again.

36
Alexander

'This is great Sandra, but we have to talk, properly,' I say, spooning a mouthful of steaming potato and leek soup.

'Tell me what I need to do to fix things, Alec. Please.' I finally understand the meaning in her watery eyes; she's afraid of being abandoned again but I toss her tears to the sky, ignore them like a day moon, watch them evaporate in my indifference.

'To fix things? Things haven't been right between us for a long time Sandra and now you think we can right it all by slurping soup together?'

'Why d'you say that? We can sort things out. I'm back at work again… things are getting back to normal.' She picks at the skin around her thumb, and she seems to shrink in front of me.

'Normal? You and me? Our marriage has run on empty for years.'

'Empty? What hasn't been right? What are you saying?' The rims of her eyes are red raw from crying, dark half-moons accentuate her pale pallor more than ever.

'We might as well be at opposite poles of the earth Sandra. There's no love, or happiness in this house since Callum left. And even before he left, what did we share, you and I?'

'We have memories. Good memories.'

'So, you're happy with me?'

'Yes. No. I don't know. I married you, full of hopes and dreams and none of them came to fruition. I thought we'd live a normal life. But you… you aren't normal, and I underestimated that. I don't blame you but didn't plan on being a wet-nurse to my husband, carrying around spare clothes for you and watching you soil yourself… all the time burning under the humiliating stares of others.'

'This is about your boyfriend being back.'

'It's not. Even our friends don't know what it's like to live with your blasted CP. Nobody talks about it. I'm fed up with it all.'

'You can't make this about my CP. You knew long before we married.'

'Not properly.'

'What the hell does that mean?'

'I didn't understand it all. I was young, naïve.'

'Naïve?'

'I saw how you walked differently, struggled to read fluently, tired long before I did when we were out. I didn't think how it would be day in day out.'

'Is that all you saw?'

'No. But over the years it's all got too much for me.'

'Only because you let it. You hid your head behind your hands and didn't look out again in the same direction. You chose to ignore me. You did that.'

'It can't always be about you Alec.'

'But you're saying this is my fault. You're blaming me.'

'I'm trying to explain, that's all.'

'A bit late for that. I can't think straight.'

'We can sort this though, can't we?'

'You don't know what you want. But I do. I'm going to go away for a few days. Maybe London. The distance will do us both good. We can talk when I get back.'

My mind is racing again, and I reach down under the table to stop my knees from trembling. I'm scared to admit I have always had a premonition of what would happen eventually. The yellow greyness has caught up with me and I can't stand it. It's too much to bear.

'London? No, Alec, no…'

'I need to get away, away from you.'

'London? Don't go all the way down there again. I need you here.'

'You're back at work. You've got your friends there. Bet you haven't told them about your secret.'

'Alec, please. Let me explain. Explain properly.'

'I need space to process all this.'

'So now this is all about you?' her voice rises to an unbearable screech.

'You made it about me. But no Sandra. It's all about deciding whether I want to save our marriage and whether it's worth saving. Our whole married life, a farce. It's never been about my happiness or my needs. I've bent over backwards for you to compensate for my lack of ability in the bedroom.'

I did it all because I loved her… but now know what I truly feel. Is *there* anything precious to protect? Not by staying where I am. My comfort zone has always provided a protective wall around my identity, acting like an invisible shield, barring the debris of self-doubt that clouded my sense of purpose. Now I can have a different life; a wider, malleable life and a moveable barrier which I can change and realign with will.

'You and sex. That's all you think about.'

'And it's what you never think about.'

'You do enough thinking about it for the both of us. This is a marriage…'

'And marriage is made up of two parts… husband and wife… but we live separately.' I want to tell her I've entered a whole new world with a woman with an easy laugh, loving words, electrifying touches and tinkling wine glasses and giggly hiccups. But I stop myself. This is about her lies, not mine. My lies are not cruel, haven't made a mockery of our entire married life.

'Are you saying you're going to leave me? That you don't love me?'

'I'm saying we both need time to think this through. This is a huge thing. And if this Douglas is coming back, we have to at least agree the way forward for all our sakes. We don't know what he knows. Damn it! He may even end up meeting Callum at the planning meetings.'

'It's those people you talk to on Twitter making you say that.'

Did she say people or person or woman? My mind mists over and my hearing seems to have stopped working.

'You've changed since you've got involved in all that social media stuff… since your dad died.'

'I'm surprised you've even noticed,' I say.

I exit the kitchen, a storm in me, and stomp up the stairs; my rushed steps jolt my hip out of balance again. I will be paying all night with an incessant ache; like her self-centred moaning and complaining, it will seep into me and erode me bit by bit but only if I let it.

37
Alexander

I lie across the bed, over the duvet, not caring this will annoy Sandra. I think back to when we first met; shy but always smiling in my company and laughing at my jokes. When did I stop making her laugh? When she married me out of necessity and not because she desired me? Her disclosure launches at me with the destructive energy of a torpedo.

My memories charge at me. Persistent and insistent. I think back to her pregnancy. A tough time complicated with preeclampsia and, in the end, after hours of pushing, Sandra delivered by caesarian section. His premature birth took us – no took me – by surprise. I pushed the niggling question around the dates deep inside of me and locked it away. I had a son. I was a father. The world spun on every axis that day.

'Alec, don't shut me out.' Sandra's voice cuts into my memories.

'I was content all those years ago, despite drowning in

nappies and sterilised bottles and timed feeds.'

'Painful breastfeeding, sleepless nights,' she says, sitting on the bed.

'I tried my best but your remorse for not giving birth naturally swallowed the both of us. You didn't want me anywhere near you.'

'My mother suspected post-natal depression... I should have listened.'

'And knowing what I know about the subject now, I think you did...' A wave of guilt passes over me. Could I have done anything differently to support her? The most nauseous pastels fill my mind. Sandra in a cotton nightie, tangled up, on top of me, complaining... I never got her back... emotionally, sexually... and so the downward spiral of containment began.

'What ifs... they don't help us now,' she says, shifting her weight up further towards the headboard.

'Is that why you were spiteful? Your humiliating remarks, your obvious discontent about my performance in the bedroom? Is that why our sex life, all our life, became nothing more than conformity like Callum's bath time?'

'I don't know. I don't care Alec.'

I ignore her insouciance. 'He grew up too quickly. One moment at nursery and the next finishing primary school,' I say.

'It didn't feel like that to me,' she answers.

'I was always working, long hours...' I was popular at work, anonymous at home. 'Did you never appreciate how hard I worked to earn enough to keep the house just as you wanted it... to keep Callum in shoes and a clean uniform?' I asked. 'He had his favourite toys and gadgets, school dinners, never missed a school trip.'

'I know that Alec. You've told me about it enough times

over the years. It was hard work being at home too.'

I sigh. I fell into the background; sank into the wooden bookcases, the flowery wallpaper, the Formica worktops, the moss-strewn grass… lost my confidence, my voice. The cloak of invisibility around me at home slowly seeped into my work life. Passive. Procrastinating. My ambition shrunk in the same way. Control of my home life dwindled. My sexual responses choked.

'In the end your grandiose suburban dreams drowned me, compensated for the lack in anything to do with sex, our sexual closeness.'

'Stop going on Alec… for goodness sake.'

'But I have to say it. I want to say what's plagued me all these years. This is

all wrong and we're here, now, because of things we've both done. I'm stuck in this relationship.' Despite what she's told me I am indebted to her for Callum, our home, our family. 'You married me out of necessity and not love, but I loved you.'

I've used the word love in the past tense. The realisation shocks me to the core. I don't love her anymore. The love has turned to dust. Shifted. Passed on.

38
Alexander

The mundane routine of working, shopping, and sweeping the drifts of magnolia blossom, which always seem to gather in heaps in our front garden, depletes me of energy. My beta blockers are making me unusually more tired than I'm used to. My blood pressure has increased with all the stress. Sandra's suffocating kindness and attention is too much to bear.

The unpredictable nature of the weather this month means I've annoyingly experienced all four seasons, often in one day, and I've found myself repeating a favourite Billy Connolly saying of my mother's: *There's no such thing as bad weather, only the wrong clothes.*

I've come to bed a couple of hours earlier than I normally would in a conscious effort to recharge. I don't have the stamina to keep going or the desire to sit with Sandra, in silence, until bedtime.

I lie on our marital bed; cold, uninviting. The audience

applause and laughter, from Sandra's weekly American sitcom, filters through the relative silence of the empty house, as if mocking, reminding me it rarely feels like our bed because of the number of overnight shifts I do with Danny, and because it was not right between us long before that.

In the darkening obscurity, with only the moon's silvery light casting long shadows, the oak's hefty branches snaking the expanse of the cold room, I listen to my breathing. I close my eyes. Maria fills my every follicle and crevice. I've fallen hard for her, from the moment I laid eyes on her photograph, and it's more than lust. I've fallen for all of her; her mind, her words, her dark eyes, her full lips, her flirtatious conversation and her magnificent poetry.

I've fallen in love with how she physically influences me to "do" all the things I've prevented myself from doing all my life; either of my own choice or through letting others decide for me. Enough is enough. I lie listening to the rise and fall of my chest. The dull ache in my hip creaks and scrapes yet I smile and reach for my mobile in the dark. 10.09pm. It's not too late to message. I've not experienced love like this before… this Maria love. This real love.

Hello my darling Maria. Xx

Hello. Tell me what's happened Alexander.

I will soon. But for now I want to feel you close to me, feel your lips on mine. Xx

I'm as close as I can be, kissing you. How's that?

That feels wonderful. I pull you closer and slide my

hand under your top, undo your bra. Xx

Don't stop Alexander, taking my top off, my bra slips down. I'm all yours. X

My wonderful Maria, I love you so much. Xx

Our messages go back and forth with the ease of lovers comfortable with each passing month. This affair fulfills me to the brim; strangely exciting, familiarly comforting.

We have built on our messages moving forward and since meeting they have assumed a new softer side. Meeting has peeled back a layer and revealed who we are underneath; both seeking love and adoration and a kind of validity.

The bedroom door swings open silently, and I sit up conscious of my heavy breaths and my sweaty brow. The room's cold but I don't feel it; my temperature melts the clouds I'm lost in with Maria, my lover.

'I thought you'd already be asleep.'

'Too much going round in my head to sleep,' I say, concealing my mobile.

'Me too but sleep is just what we both need. Tomorrow's another day.' Sandra, turning away from me, changes into her nightdress.

'For God's sake, Sandra.'

She continues with her back to me, arranging her leggings, sweatshirt and undergarments on the clothes stand at the foot of the bed. Her every movement is rigid, mechanical. She is a creature of habit. She is the antithesis of Maria who's spontaneous, warm, comfortable in her own skin, with her womanliness.

Eventually, with Sandra burrowed in the spare room, I succumb to a fragmented sleep full of jumbled erotic dreams. Maria tangled in the bedlinen, beckons me to lie next to her, her red nail polish glints in the sunlight. Sandra pulls at me from the foot of the bed; I fall back onto a grassy verge, no longer in the bedroom. Her cotton nightie, scrunched up around her waist, reveals her totally shaved nakedness; where's her wiry bush? I look from Maria to her, shaking. They both laugh, Sandra's is hollow, Maria's is full and round. Maria unwinds herself from the sheets, like a goddess, she shines, but her hair falls out, mounds of it cover the ground at her feet. Sandra pushes me towards Maria… I stumble without my walking stick. I'm falling, falling…

When I wake my body is clammy with sweat. I shift onto my side, heaving from the whiff of urine under me.

39
Alexander

Breakfast is as silent and cold as a graveyard in winter despite the sun's hesitant rays warming the kitchen tiles under my bare feet. I pick at my toast. I can't eat. Sandra, it seems, has woken with an appetite as big as a lion's. She chomps at her toast smothered in strawberry jam and slurps black coffee. The bitter aroma hits my nostrils, making me nauseous.

'Where are you going? You haven't finished your breakfast. You have to eat Alec. You're wasting away with all this dieting.'

'It's not dieting. It's a lifestyle change, a choice,' I say, standing and tucking the chair under the table.

'You don't need it.'

'Don't tell me what I need,' I say, counting to three under my breath.

'Let's talk, please.'

'I'm not hungry. I'm going to get started on clearing the garage.'

'The garage?'

'Yes. John's coming over to pick up donations for a charity he's got dragged into collecting for. I said I'd check what I can get rid of... bag it up for him.'

I walk away; her stare pokes me in the back. I should say something but can't. I sympathise with her, but I am annoyed at being taken for a fool. One big ugly lie and I've unfairly absorbed the brunt of it, and her discontent, all these years. Bitterness and anger ooze from me.

Red poppies have pushed through the earth despite Inverness's chilling summer temperatures; their colour is vibrant against the front wall of our house choked with weeds and ivy, reflecting my own strangled, stifled mood. Another job I will have to tackle, and I realise it's not the garden and the weeds I'm referring to.

The neighbour's garden, just as wild and overgrown, reflects the freedom to just be. The row of pots brim with yellow and purple pansies; bright, out of place. Maria would be too in this dull place.

I walk to the garage in the hope that strenuous physical activity, strenuous for me, will distract me. The bars on my phone fade up and down but my message to Maria sends. Everything with her seems so much more poignant now. Has she come into my life to highlight my poor choices in the past, to show me how to change things for the future? I want a different future. I want to find me, the me shadowed by CP, the me shadowed by matrimony, my own cloak of invisibility. I want to find the twenty-something Alexander who could have had so much more had he been allowed, had he been brave enough, had he been man enough. Maria has unleashed another side to me. Or was it buried in me all along waiting for me to entice it out?

I pull a cardboard box from the shelf above the half-open garage door. I struggle to hold the bottom of the carton, the contents too heavy, it spills its load. Dust and a damp, musty smell permeate the chilly air.

'Blast and double blast.'

The concrete floor is a mess of old picture frames, clothes, toys and other long-forgotten nic-nacs. I pop open a telescopic camping chair, and dusting it down with an old rag, I lower myself into it. I lean onto my walking stick for support, picking through the scattered items. There's a sepia photograph of my mother and dad on their wedding day; the frame is bent out of shape, a zig-zag crack running through the glass. I'd forgotten I had it. I wipe the brown smears off with the sleeve of my jumper.

I remember how ecstatic they were with our baby news; Dad thumping me on the back and Mum pulling me close for a kiss on the cheek; both expressing emotions they rarely demonstrated. Did my condition shrink their enjoyment of life too? I've never thought of it that way before, but it must have. I couldn't do what most boys could at any age. My dad didn't have the experience of Sunday morning football, cheering on the sidelines with other proud dads. At least I had that with Callum. I stood and cheered even when my legs ached, at times the bitter pain never faded with the rain soaking through my jeans.

I prop the frame against the foot of my seat and pick up an old Celtic sweatshirt and matching cap. They can definitely go; I only ever rooted for Celtic because it was the team Dad and all our family supported but I was never any good at football and even following it on the TV was difficult for me; the commentating, the camera moving from one player to the other. I found it disorientating. I shudder against that dreadful afternoon with Pete; things have since cooled between us.

An old picnic blanket catches my eye and I shake it open; it's holey, eaten through the middle by moths, past its usefulness. For the next hour, I sift through an amorphous pile of boxes and dusty rubbish bags.

'Tea,' says Sandra, handing me my chipped mug. The weak sunlight creates a halo and her greying hair hangs limply creating an ethereal silvery sheen around her face. For a split second a pang of guilt stabs at me. Loss? A long-forgotten memory? Or is it a little bit of the Sandra I was once in love with?

'Thanks, sweetheart.' The word sweetheart rolls off my tongue automatically, but it stubbornly sticks in my throat, and I want to be sick.

'Gosh, there's a lot of junk in here.'

'Twenty odd years of junk.' I twist the mug around, so the chipped edge faces away from me.

'About time we had a tidy up.' She picks up a tarnished copper kettle and a brass door knocker. 'Why on earth did we keep all this?' The truth lies behind the strain in her voice, wallows in her hollow laugh. And now I recognise it for what it is; a buzz that's existed since we met; the threatening stinger of a persistent lie.

I avoid her gaze. I pick up a broken model airplane, its wing missing, and remember spending a rainy afternoon bent over the assembly instructions with Callum aged five; glue, tiny bits of engine and wheel rims and stickers for the tail, covering the dining room table. Sandra yelled at us for sticking a tea towel to her plastic table cover. I'm picking over the memories; adding to the fresh wounds yet to heal.

I put the model aside. Callum may want to keep it. Funny how he liked putting things together and now he is a surveyor in the planning department.

'Because we hang onto things hoping they will soothe us,' I say. 'Remind us of happier times, but in the end, they just force us to dig up painful memories.'

My words reach her. I concentrate on her melancholic face; her eyes are sad, lightless, her mouth droops into a downward half-moon, blue veins are visible beneath her pale skin accentuating her tiredness. Her shoulders are hunched under a long-tasseled shawl. She used to stand tall, and, with her stiletto heels, she was always at least as tall as I was.

My phone vibrates in my pocket, mechanically I reach for it.

'Who's that?'

'John.' I'm surprised how easily I lie. I never used to, never tried to say an untruth for fear of getting caught. Now it's a challenge. How triumphant to have my own lie, but the mood is short-lived; I'm as bad as her. What I'm doing is just as dishonest. Are there different levels or depth of dishonesty? I decide my lies are less lies than hers, but the decision sits uncomfortably with me, pricks my conscience.

She walks out of the garage. I'm glad she's left me to it. There's little here she will want to keep; most of it is mine. I pick two of the sturdiest boxes and fill them from my sitting position, wedging the football shirts and sweatshirts between items, cushioning the breakables from each other.

I drink the tea; a bitter-sweet trail coats the back of my throat.

Good morning, Alexander. How are you?

I'm feeling excited. Xx

You are?

I'm coming to London to be with you. To see you and hold you and kiss you. Xx

Really?

Can I call you? I want to hear your voice. Xx

Seeing you again is not something I expected to happen.

Me neither. Can I call you? Xx

Now why do you want to do that, dear Alexander?

I want to hear you giggle. I want to tell you I love you. Xx

I dial her number, making sure Sandra's not lurking.

'Hello,' she answers on the first ring.

'Hello my darling.'

'How are you?'

'I'm better now I'm talking to you.'

'Good. What are you doing?'

'Having a clear out. I've escaped from Sandra for a bit.'

'Are you in your shed?'

'The garage. It's unbelievable what I've found.'

'So, shall I warm you up?' she asks with a giggle.

'Yes.' I'm getting hotter just thinking about her.

'When are you coming to London?'

'You okay, Alec?' interrupts John, walking towards the garage, scuffing his shoes on the concrete.

I give him a wave and promptly say, 'No, thank you. And please remove my name from your database.' I end the call.

'Canvasser?' asks John.

'Yes… bloody pushy salespeople.' I'm trembling and cannot stand. I am conscious of my hot face, making me look like I'm having a seizure. I deliberately slow my breathing.

'They catch me in the evenings mainly.'

I cough to mask the strange squeak to my voice, 'Damn nuisance,' I say.

'So how are things otherwise? You do seem a bit stressed. Are you sure you're okay? Shall I call Sandra?'

'No… no, I'm fine.'

'I've known you a long time, mate, and you don't seem fine.'

'Things aren't great actually. Sandra and I… personal issues.'

'I'm sorry to hear that. Sorry for both of you.'

'We're not even sharing a bed anymore…'

'That bad? Can't you work through them?'

'I don't know, and I don't know if I want to either. Maybe this is it. Maybe Sandra will be relieved too.' I resist the urge to grab the phone in my pocket, yearning for Maria to be by my side.

'Don't say that. What's happened?'

'I'm not Callum's dad. A man by the name of Douglas Cox is. I've kidded myself all these years. It's out now and I'm relieved. It explains a lot.'

'The billionaire?'

'Not sure he's a billionaire. How do– '

'The housing development. He's backing it. It's been in the local paper for weeks now. I don't know what to say… how? When? Who is this guy to Sandra?'

'I don't know… but his return has opened up a plethora of family secrets.'

'Because he's back from Australia,' he says. 'I'm so sorry mate.'

'He doesn't know about Callum… Sandra did what she did. What hurts the most is how she's treated me all these years and how she's been hiding the articles for weeks, hiding the newspaper.'

I've blamed myself for our failing and increasingly lonely marriage, yet this secret, wedged between us all this time and now released, like an uncoiled spring, will either set me free or trap me again in its spirals. I suspect though it's overstretched this time and will only return to a permanently deformed shape. Perhaps that's what I'm hoping for, deep down, that there's no return and I can be freed from its tight coils, Sandra's hen-pecking, rigidness and overbearing demands.

'I'm so sorry Alec, mate. I've got to go. Let's talk properly. Any time you want. I'd better get these loaded into the boot. Elizabeth's already at the old dance hall in town,' he says, stroking the greying scruff covering his chin.

With John gone, I tidy the garage as best I can, but all of me is tired now. I fill and stack two boxes. I stand by the open garage door and welcome the smell of the cool summer rain. I've told John about the whole damn mess. I hope I've done the right thing.

***

'So, how are things?' asks John, as we settle opposite each other in the pub.

'Worse than ever, mate. I'm not sure there's anything to even go home for anymore.'

'I must say you look okay on it. Pushing yourself at the gym, are you?'

'No, no… there's only so much I can do, you know… with my legs.'

'It suits you being trimmer,' he says.

'Thanks. The other issue isn't going to be so easily fixed,' I say.

'Talk, get the conversation going. You'll find a way to reconcile.'

'Callum isn't mine. That's not going to change with talking.'

'Oh, Alec, mate… I'm so sorry.'

'Yeah, me too.'

'I can't imagine, but…'

'But what?'

'But… well…' John stumbles over his words and picks up his pint.

'You think because of my CP I should be grateful to be a dad, even if it's not to my own?'

'No, no… come on. That's not what I'm saying.'

'Then what are you saying?'

'I'm saying you're the only dad Callum has ever known and he's the only son you will ever know. Don't tarnish it when it can continue to shine… to be good for the both of you, for all of you.'

'Deep down I know it makes no difference. Not to me. He's mine. But it's the lies. This whole sham of a marriage.' I say the words out loud and want to cry. I want to scream.

'You can make it work. You're good together Alec. Come on.'

'You only know the social us, John. At home we sit like empty shells next to each other and as for anything else, well, a nun would do more.' John shifts in his chair, avoids my eyes. 'I think it's the end of the road for us.'

'You think it's any different for Elizabeth and me?'

'I don't know. All I know is that I don't want the rest of my life to be… empty.'

'Is there another woman involved?' he blurts.

'What?'

'You've changed over the past few months. Even Elizabeth said so. You're happier, lively. That's not how a man fed up at home behaves.'

'No, there's no one else.'

'Because if there is, and she has a chance of making you happy, I'd shake your hand and say good luck to you. Life's too damn short to turn your back on a bit of fun.'

The word fun sits heavy on my chest. Maria isn't only fun. Maria is love. Maria is freedom. Maria is light.

'Sounds like you need to offload too,' I say, deflecting the conversation.

We spend the rest of the night talking work politics, the charity fundraiser and the lack of initiative in school leavers when they enter the world of work. John guffaws at his own tales of pimply interns and how his latest score of 108 at the golf club left his opponent stunned.

We finish our drinks and order another half pint each. We prolong the evening until the bell for last orders clangs across the bar.

'Thanks mate,' I say, and we awkwardly hug. I walk away, fighting the tears. I know what I need to do.

40
Alexander

Work finished, I drive a different route home, the titillation of the afternoon pulls me against my norms, but it soon turns to dread. A twist of nerves builds in my stomach. I can't face going home. I can't face Sandra, her shamefaced expression. I pull over in the supermarket car park; there's Wi-Fi here.

Hello my darling Maria. How are you? Xx

Hello Alexander. I'm great thanks, you?

I'm close to leaving Sandra. Xx

What's happened? Don't do anything hasty... x

Oh, my darling Maria. I've thought of nothing more for

so long.

You are everything I want. Everything I dream of and I can't live this rigid, frigid lie of a life anymore. X

Can I call you? Xx

The next few minutes feel like an eternity and tick by on the car's dashboard: 2.45, 2.46, 2.47... I pull on the seat's lever and push back to give me more leg room, to release the tension in my hip. I stretch out my leg; the ache will probably keep me awake again tonight. The pressure builds. I can't think of anything else but Maria's voice. The phone vibrates in my hand.

'Hello. Hello, my darling,' I say, and suddenly every fibre in me is alive.

'Hello,' she says with a giggle. I picture her smiling and want to tell her I love her.

'I don't think I can stay with Sandra. I can't cope anymore.'

'You're going to walk out on twenty odd years? What's really going on?'

'I discovered Sandra's... dishonesty. I can't forgive her.'

'Can't forgive or won't forgive?'

'I don't want to forgive.'

'What's so bad? Tell me.'

I don't answer. I can't put all this pressure on her. She has enough going on with Natalie. I can't burden her.

'It takes time to digest things, talk to her. You can't say nothing and walk out, Alexander. That's not right. You're her husband. You have obligations,' she says, but her voice is shadowed, lacking conviction.

'I don't love her. Not like I love you. I've never felt like this before.' I can barely hear her breathing. 'Maria, I don't love her anymore. I love you.'

'Your decision can't be made based on us and this... talking in secret, hiding away. I know we've met, and it's been blissful every time, mad, crazy. But who's to say when we'll be together again. How we'll feel next time?'

'I'm coming to London. To be with you again.'

'We've crammed months of thoughts, emotions, fantasies, into a few sporadic days here and there. Amazing days together. We tried to push everything experienced online into reality. Those few stolen days were wonderful, but they weren't real. Picking up all those months of texting and the online sex stuff in real life is impossible to do over a few days.' She pauses and I'm afraid she's going to cry.

She takes a deep breath. 'It's like we've just met, because we have really, and we have to re-trace what we have said and done online to catch up in reality. And as wonderful as it is, it's still not real. Do you know what I'm saying? We haven't had time for our real relationship to unfold the same way it would have had we met face-to-face to start with. You know, had an ordinary relationship, away from Twitter and secret messages.'

'But it's real to me, all of this is real. The unreal in my head has become real and I feel alive. I'm coming to London because I want to be with you.' My temperature rises and a panic threatens to strangle me. I'm not listening properly. My senses have numbed. What is she saying? Doesn't she love me? Doesn't she want to carry on?

'I understand that's how it is for you. But it's not like that for me. This is too sudden,' she says.

'Are you saying you don't feel like I feel?'

'I'm saying it's exciting and still new. But not real. It's all accelerated online but in reality, we're still new to each other. Each time we meet we need time to get comfortable with each other all over again on a different level, not the Twitter messaging level we are totally comfortable with. Time plays out differently in reality with how we feel, how we react.'

'I know that. But I know how I feel about you. I wish I could tell you properly. Tell you that I love you. I love you, Maria. I do.'

'Please Alexander. Think carefully. Is leaving your wife what you want?'

'I do.'

'You're in Inverness and I'm in London. How will that work?'

'I'll come and visit. Come often. I've got my dad's inheritance. I can take a sabbatical until we know what we both want. We can decide together.'

'Why are you rushing this? Tell me.'

'I just want to be with you. Any way I can, even long-distance is better than this. I've had enough of lies.'

'Are you actually going to leave your wife for me?'

'Yes. That's my decision. I want to grab every second life gives us.' I'm being pushy, needy even. Is she slipping away? Are my declarations too much?

'I hear what you're saying but I'm panicking. Making what we have a reality is happening too fast, it scares me.'

'I'm sorry, but that's how I feel and you've nothing to be scared of. I want to more than anything. Please believe me Maria.'

'But I'm being practical. How on earth would that work? I've got Natalie to think about, her state of mind. The pregnancy is life-changing for her, she's fragile.'

'I don't mean to put pressure on you. I'm not. I'm leaving Sandra because what I have with her is broken.'

'We have a lot to talk about Alexander. There's so much I don't have the answers to.'

'Tell me. Ask me. I can help you.'

'Well, I don't know how I'd cope sharing my life with you fully. You're ten years older. This is getting messy. I want to get it right this time. I want to do right by the both of us, by all of us.'

'I want that too. I want you.'

'And how long will that last? How long before you decide it isn't what you want? That you want your wife back?' she asks, rising panic in her voice. 'Just promise to think carefully. Sleep on it. Don't decide now. Not today.'

'How I feel about you won't change now and more importantly I don't want to be with Sandra.'

'What you want for yourself, without me in the picture, has to be your main reason for leaving. I can't be that reason.'

'Okay. So can I kiss you now?'

'You can kiss me now,' she says. Her soft moans waft down the phone for a few seconds and she ends the call.

Behind my closed eyelids I imagine kissing her lips as I have so many times now and everything else we have shared swirls at me in a kaleidoscope of wonderfully erotic images. In my head she guides me to what she wants and how she wants it. Her reactions are full of such passion and open enjoyment I'm rapt in the wonder of her and remember the smell of her perfume.

My hand reaches for my bulge… a more familiar physical reaction now and I can't help but smile. This is what a piece of heaven on earth would be like for me and for those few precious moments I forget the mess my life is in and think about the brand-new page we will fill together. My imagination is gloriously taking over.

***

Sandra steps into the hallway before I have managed to remove my shoes. I avoid eye contact, fiddling with my shoes longer than I have to.

'Where have you been? You had me worried.'

'Sorry… I had a few things to sort out after work.'

'I thought we could go out and talk. Talk properly.'

'What's this?'

'Delivery came for you,' she says, handing me a parcel.

'Oh yes, new boxer shorts,' I say, defiance tinging my tone.

'Well, shall we go out?'

Sandra's suggestion surprises me and evokes an unusual sympathy for her; sadness for her, sadness for me, but talking means I will decide where I go from here. I suppose we both will; the conversation I've avoided is one we have to have.

***

I order us a drink each and Sandra heads for a table tucked next to a mahogany grandfather clock adorned with dried hops and lavender, choking from years of thick dust hiding their once sage green and lilac hues. It reflects my mood; weighed down with the past twenty years' grime and secrets.

'Alec, I never meant to hurt you.'

'But you have, and you can't change that. What's happened has happened.'

'But we can change what happens now.'

'We?'

'Yes, we can move on from this, can't we?' she says, picking at imaginary flecks on the front of her blouse. The blouse I bought her for her birthday only months before. A small stain on the front seems to mock me.

'I don't know that we can. I don't know if I can.'

'Please. I know I'm a moany mare, but we've stayed together this long. We love each other.' Her declaration of love, the mere mention of the word, repulses me. I've not entertained the word love in association with us in a long time. We just floated along and the love we once must have felt for each other, it seems, drifted so far into the background haze I now barely see it, touch it or feel it anymore.

'Do you love me, Sandra? Do you even care for me let alone love me?'

'I do.'

'Well, there may be care but there is no concern, Sandra. None.'

'These past few months you've changed…'

'Now hang on a minute. Don't you dare turn this on me. Don't you dare.' My face boils with festered fury. I thump my fist on the table. It wobbles, our glasses overspill. Even when Callum was growing up, there were many times when my patience was pushed to the edge, more because of my own limits than his behaviour, yet I didn't raise my voice.

Sandra shrinks into the ladder-back chair, her eyes wide with horror. I swallow a gulp of my beer and stand up. I bang the glass back onto the table; the barman's eyes are on me. My knuckles hang white by my sides.

I force myself to sit down again, succumbing to Sandra's pleading eyes within a few seconds. 'I'm sorry. I shouldn't have shouted.'

'No, no… you've every right to be angry. I'm sorry too. Her rounded shoulders and dark circles around her eyes give her away, but her hair shines; she's trying but it's too late.

'I need a break, to think about what all this means.'

'We can't go back. I can't go back… though I have wished it over the years,' she says, a sting of tears pricks the corners of her eyes.

'You've lied to me for the whole of our marriage… for the whole of our courtship.'

'I did. I had no choice.'

'You say you love me, but you have only ever loved yourself. There were times I doubted you loved Callum yet convinced myself how could you not?'

'I've tried to love him… I do love him.'

'You've tried?'

'Yes… it's been difficult.'

'Difficult to love your own child? Your own flesh and blood?'

'Yes, Alec. It's sucked every bit of strength I had to care for him.' Her words tumble out in a flurry of anguish, and I catch the bile in her throat.

'But why?'

'Because… because… I loved Douglas and he abandoned me.'

'You've felt sorry for yourself?'

'No. I look at Callum and all I see, all I ever saw, is Douglas looking back at me.'

***

A few days later, I'm in my shed; the door is propped open with an iron boot scraper caked in mud which belonged to the previous owners. The weak sun is penetrating the violet haze. I can't think straight and flip through an old photograph album of Callum's toddler years.

My response to Sandra goes round and round in my head.

Callum is his own person. He's an adult. He's just as much a part of me as he is of her, isn't he? But the words stick in my throat. Do I believe that? Do I believe in the forces of nature versus nurture? Is Callum mine and a part of me because I brought him up? I push the album away, scattering loose photographs to the floor. I don't pick them up.

Damn it. She wedded me intentionally, manipulating the situation to meet her ends. I'm hanging onto a precipice and the truth is almost too painful to acknowledge.

My whole married life was built on quicksand, and I can't do anything to stop it shifting. In that moment, a mantel of sadness and regret and of lost opportunity engulfs me. I'm beaten. I'm worn out.

Reflections push to the forefront of my mind, unfolding in a tangled mess. What else could she have done? Tell the truth? Yes, tell the bloody truth. I don't want to sound unsympathetic but the sheer cunning of her has unnerved me. Have I never known the real Sandra?

Everything has been a farce, a setup, a staged soap episode, a carefully contrived studio set. The loss is enormous; it leaves a void that can never be filled by Sandra, by Sandra and me, ever again, and my insides, stripped and scraped are bruised.

I sip the smooth green liquid; it warms my throat. I start to relax. Through the open door the sun pours from a break in the swirling clouds and warms my legs.

A hush descends upon me. I discard my socks and twiddle my toes in the pool of warmth. I wonder if I'd known about Sandra's deception, whether her reactions to me, and my hunger for sexual pleasure, would have been different. Would I have viewed sex differently? Gauged it against her displeasing experience of sex? After all I was led to believe I married a virgin; so coy, so shy in the bedroom. An act she played too well.

I can't answer that question but have to believe I would have been sympathetic, loving, and gentle, as always. But she never gave me the chance, the opportunity to prove just how gentle and affectionate I could be. It appears Douglas robbed us both of a loving relationship. It could have been so different. It could have been so good.

I think of all the times I tried to encourage her to try something new with me but she shunned me. She had other memories to fill her mind; she wasn't interested in building new ones with me. I was her second choice, her booby prize. My tears fall unchecked, and I bawl until my eyes are sore and my throat hurts from the raw pain of it. I feel sorry for me, sorry for Sandra, sorry for Callum, sorry for the relationship we could all have had.

Her secret isolated her, kept her from me and my love. Her plan was always her plan. And now it's too late. It's too late for Sandra and me. It's not too late for me with Callum or Maria. My mind is made up.

My eyes stream behind my glasses. I take them off, wipe the tears away. I can't feel sorry for myself now.

***

I'm lying in bed, the mini grandfather clock in the upstairs hallway counting down time; its tick-tock bounces off the walls in the otherwise silence of the house. There are no new messages on my devices.

The weight of everything sits heavy on my chest, like a wrestler kneeling on it. Disconnected from Maria I am like a ship with no sails in the middle of a storm. The clock's ticking is like the drip drip of a leaking faucet; it's usually a comforting sound but tonight it seems out of rhythm. I'm out of rhythm, off-balance.

I've messaged Maria, all yesterday and once in the middle of the night. I sent her a text and risked a call from the shed last night. She hasn't responded. She's keeping away like she said she would; giving me time to think but my mind is made up. And she has her daughter to look after.

I'm weary and worn down by it all; the effort of trying to sort the mess out too much. But I have to admit this is the life I accepted, and never complained about. Now I want to be free of it. My emotions yo-yo back and forth making me dizzy with anxiety and fear. It's an emptiness; loss and numbness associated with exhilaration, mixed with fear of the unknown.

I get up an hour before my alarm is set to go off. A swooning heat of claustrophobia grabs me; I throw the covers off in a hurry. Sandra is cocooned, facing away from me; an errant grey hair on her pillow, a silver thread, highlighted by new white rays coming in through the parting in the curtains. She's getting old, I think. I'm getting old and don't want to; I haven't lived. I haven't loved… until now.

I think about Maria's giggling words I'm too young to be old and my heart leaps like a spring hare at her light-heartedness, her youthfulness. I miss her and can't wait to be with her. I have planning to do but I reassure myself she will wait for me; she wants to be with me just as much as I want to be with her. We will find a way to be together.

In my dressing gown and slippers, I clasp my iPad and mobile as if lifesaving rafters. I don't turn on the kitchen lights, not wanting to disturb Caramel, asleep in her basket, a familiar silhouette. She opens one eye, yawns, stretches, and nestles back. It's too early to be up even for her.

I brew a mug of Jasmine green; its flavour one I've become accustomed to and it's become our tea, mine and

Maria's. I send her another text message saying I love you and adore you my princess Maria and I fill a line with pink hearts and bows and kissy emojis. A few months ago, I would have mocked a grown man for using emojis.

Outside the grass glistens with early morning dew, its sparkle giving me hope, telling me not to give up. It glints in the daybreak's first light, and I trust it's a good sign. Two doves swoop down with long strong wings, and peck at the fat balls with their pointed bills. I read how they usually mate for life. Another good omen. My mood perks. I slurp my tea. My new life with Maria in it will be exactly that, a new life.

I wouldn't claim much. Over the years Sandra chose most of the house contents and she's welcome to them after we sell the property, split the proceeds. Speaking to Sandra about the decision I've come to was only the first step. We still have to tell Callum.

As for the first, well I'm his dad and, for me, this Douglas guy is just a name on a piece of paper. His name isn't even on the birth certificate. Oh my… Sandra registered Callum's birth while I finished painting the nursery. He surprised us three weeks early. I try to recall whether I saw the certificate, but our lives were so fraught with the heady excitement and exhaustion of having a newborn I can't remember. Think Alec, think.

My heart races. I drop my mug. It clatters onto the kitchen table. Caramel jumps and shrieks. I scoop her into my arms and stroke her soft fur, her body's shaking, my body's shaking.

'My pwincess, silly Daddy. So sowwy, my pwincess,' I say, lowering her into her basket when she calms.

I stagger into the sitting room, my legs trembling. I drop into the armchair closest to the sideboard. I dump the pile of folded crumpled clothes, waiting to be ironed, to the floor; its freshly washed smell nauseates me. Where is his birth certificate? Surely Callum would have questioned Douglas' name instead of mine?

'What time did you get up?'

Sandra waddles in wearing her brown dressing gown, at least two sizes too big for her; a January sales' bargain. Suddenly, she's the ogre in the dark fairytales, mean and menacing.

'Where's Callum's birth certificate?'

'What do you need that for?' She appears outwardly calm and for a split second guilt consumes me for being suspicious. She sucks in her left cheek and bites on the inside of her mouth.

'I want to see it,' I say, not telling her the truth of my suspicions even now, after everything. I'm a coward and I'm ashamed of myself.

'In the file with all our important documents,' she says. 'Bottom drawer, left-hand side. Where it's always kept.'

I try hard to conceal my desperation, the overpowering sense of dark secrets hidden in the drawer. I hesitate. Secrets. Too many secrets. I fling open the drawer. Shaking, I grab the top few documents but, in my haste, drop them, sending the loose sheets onto the carpet. 'Damn it and fiddlesticks.'

'Why don't you just ask me, Alec.' She lights a cigarette and blows in my direction. The smoke hovers blue in front of me, taunting me.

'Whose name is on the certificate? Is it mine or his?' My voice is shaking just as much as my legs are, despite still sitting. A sweat builds on my forehead and my hands are moist with anticipation. I scrapple through the scattered papers; house documents, photographs, old postcards.

'Yours. Yours. Alec, you're his dad. No one else.'

I find the certificate as she utters the words; they re-iterate what's registered on the document in front of me. My hands tremble. I finger a photograph of me holding Callum in my arms, the hospital tag around his tiny ankle.

Her words hit me like a bullet in the chest. I stare at the photo. For an instant I don't recognise the sound coming from me; a strangled, desperate cry. It's a strange howling, a desolate sobbing from a person hanging onto their last thread of hope. Sandra takes a step towards me, reaches out to console me, but I lash out at her. She jumps back flinching from my shove. One side of her face is soaked with silent tears, the other is dry, and her eyes are wide, weighted with a confused expression. I flop back into the armchair and put my hands over my face. I cannot look at her; the whole of me is beaten, bruised, broken.

41
Alexander

'Dad, it's okay. I'm shocked but not surprised, please don't worry about me,' he reassures again, pushing his chair away from the kitchen table. He suddenly seems so big with his legs outstretched.

'You're not even a bit upset?' asks Sandra, clearly hurt by his matter-of-fact reaction and level-headed reasoning.

'I've expected this for years. Don't be upset Mum, at least not for me. When Jill and Chris's mum and dad split up, I thought you would too. You've always argued and Mum, you've always picked on Dad. You both have to move on, find a way back to happiness.'

'I am certainly not mean to your dad.' Her reaction doesn't surprise me. It's as if her strict Sunday school upbringing rendered her with an inability to visualise things other than in black or white. There is no in between with her... well I suppose until now.

'Gosh, and how I've worried about telling you,' I say, ignoring her outburst, determined not to shift focus onto her.

'As long as you're not going to disappear,' he says.

'No, we will always be here. Inverness is our home,' says Sandra.

Her denial seeps into me and I shiver against it.

In the end, despite a few sniffles while we reminisce the old days, he doesn't seem that bothered about our split, and he wishes us both well promising us nothing will change as far as he's concerned.

'You'll always be Mum and Dad,' he says and doesn't shy from my display of emotion. I hug him, hitting him on the back in a show of comradery, and tell him I love him. I fight back the tears. I have to be honest with Callum. His life cannot be a lie like mine.

'There's another thing…' I say.

'Your dad and I haven't decided what we're doing about the house, but we'll let you know,' jumps in Sandra.

A festering anger fills me; she's lying again and dragging me into it. A fury like none before shakes me.

'I know the timing might not be great, but I've got good news. I'm now head of planning,' Callum announces. 'My promotion is official.'

'That's good news. That's good news isn't it, Alec?' says Sandra in a high-pitched, shriek voice.

I stumble up to the bedroom. Head of planning. He'll meet Douglas. He will meet his real father. Work with him. Be in the same room as him. I have to tell him. I take the newspaper cutting from the back of my bedside drawer and bring it downstairs with me.

'There's something else, son. Something you need to know.'

'Dad? What's wrong?'

'There's no easy way to say this. To soften the blow. So, I'm just going to say it. I'm not your real dad… not your biological dad.'

'Now you're winding me up.' Callum looks from me to Sandra as if wanting reassurance. 'Mum?'

'I wanted to tell you both,' Sandra says.

'Both? Dad? What? Now this is a joke, right?'

'I've only recently found out myself. I'm sorry son,' I say, choking on my tears.

'But how? Why? Oh my God, Dad, are you okay?' His selfless words and caring push me over the last bit of dignity I'm holding onto, and I break down.

Sandra stands there, tight-lipped, like a cardboard cut-out, and then fusses by the kettle. Typical Sandra, even in the most emotional of situations she is not wired to be demonstrative or show any empathy.

'Your mum can fill in the details. But what we have won't ever change Callum. I promise you,' I say, dabbing at my eyes with a hanky.

'Dad. I love you.'

'And I love you son. You talk to your mum now. But I promise we'll talk soon. Talk properly,' I say. 'And you might want to read this. Talk to your mum. She has a lot to explain to you.' I drop the ink-smudged evidence onto the table and walk out of the kitchen.

I'm relieved I no longer have to be strong and practical; reliable, steady Alec. A phase of my life is ending, and I am ready to face it. Instantaneously a flicker in my chest prickles me. I think about my future, my future with Maria in it. Sadness, anger, disappointment, and excitement play tag inside me. Play tag inside a new Alexander, though my heart is breaking.

42

Alexander

'I'm sorry Danny, but no, Pete won't be coming back. Not any time soon, anyway,' I say.

'He promised me a bun…'

'I can buy you a bun once your chores are done.'

'With swirly cream.'

'With swirly cream, aye.' I wait for him to disappear before turning back to face the regional manager.

'As I was saying, Pete's suspended pending further enquiries.'

'The rumours are true?'

'No one wants to confirm anything without further investigation, but it would appear so, yes. A number of anomalies in his record-keeping, for three of those in his care, were found to be suspicious.'

'Is there anything I can do?'

'Just keep things as normal for Danny.'

'Looks like I was a poor judge of character or maybe I just chose to always focus on the good in him.'

'No, no. You're not to blame… the overtime is sorted. You taking on the bulk of Pete's shifts has really helped. Thank you for jumping in. Danny's lucky to have such a loyal carer.'

Loyal. His words constrict in my chest. And here I am preparing to meet Maria in London. Pete's thieving went beyond the church funds. Either way this has put another strain on me and my plans to end things fully with Sandra and move to London.

I can't stand it at home with her. Maria is just as keen for us to be together and now this. I hope she doesn't think I'm stalling.

***

The weeks pass, the extra shifts separate me from Sandra, and it means the real, practical talking I planned doesn't happen as fast as I'd hoped. It adds to my frustrations and my health is deteriorating; I'm rarely having a full night's sleep and in turn my aches and pains are exacerbated. I am existing as if under water and the only air I will get is with Maria in London. But when?

Danny's new support worker seems nice, competent, and experienced. Danny warms to him better than I'd anticipated which has made my leaving less traumatic, for us both.

I push down the agitation building in me. My breathing is fast. This, for me, is going to be the start of my whole new life, a real life where I live and feel. No more merely existing. I'm like a metamorphosing butterfly and finally, after weeks of agonising, I can escape from the confines of this old life and fly, weightless and free, towards a new beginning.

The scene of us together plays in my head, over and over, like an old cine film. The image crackles and flickers. I envisage Maria's smile and fall into her warm arms as she wraps them around me. For a split second a memory of my mother and dad lights up. I think it was their anniversary. Dad scooped her up in his arms and twirled her around the kitchen to pleas of, *Put me down, put me down you silly old fool,* and I clapped in delight. I hope Dad is smiling down on me. His money is making this possible.

43
Maria

A few weeks have passed since Natalie's clinic appointment. She's tearful; her pregnancy playing havoc with her hormones rather than any regret to keep the baby. It's evidently difficult for her yet a gentle peace reigns; I feel it when she's around. It sits on her shoulder like a cooing dove, embraces her waist like the arms of a lover.

Her telephone calls with Tom are full of chatter and laughter. The ordeal has brought them closer and us too. We talk like equals in a way we haven't done for months, respectful grown-ups, with a new-found trust between us.

I consider all that comes back to trust in my life over the past months. Trust in my own judgements, trust in Natalie to make the right decision; trust in Alexander to do the right thing by me and by him. It all sits more comfortably in me. I support his decision to leave his wife but didn't ask him to leave her for me. Shaken by her years of lying he has, in his words, found strength in our new love and our plans to make a new life side by side.

'Telling Sandra about us was one of the easiest things I have ever had to tell anyone because it felt right,' he said.

'And she accepted it?'

'I think she was relieved she wouldn't have to pretend anymore, or try, or live another day weighed down by guilt and lies.'

'And you? How do you feel?'

'Like I've been freed from a life of being shackled to a past I knew nothing about, a life which had held me prisoner in a cage with invisible bars.'

Our once lustful meetings in London have since taken on a new level of calm, still loving, but with a more realistic measure of how we can create a life together.

I accept our reality is different to our secret online relationship and know I could not have carried on like that infinitely. It was exhilarating yet exhausting. Our love is real and has shown me how sharing more than a bed with someone, how being vulnerable, can make me stronger.

After everything that's happened in my past relationship, and between Natalie and Tom, I have become more realistic in my expectations yet succumb to the universe; it unfolds my future for me, and I trust the vibrations I'm radiating are the right ones. Synchronicity. Alignment. For once want to relinquish control. I want someone else, something else, to decide for me. I am ready to face what comes. No more hiding. No more pretending.

My darling Maria meet me at Euston. I won't let you down. Trust me. Xx

Trust is a big word. X

His ultimatum excites me. It's romantic and exhilarating. It already feels solid and real. This is happening.

'He's coming to London. Like to stay?' asks Fabio.

'That's the plan, from what he's told me.'

'And he's left his wife?'

'Told her it's over, told her about our relationship, there's no going back.'

'It's official. And how do you feel?'

'I don't know. Excited. Scared. Everything.'

'And Natalie?'

'She's been so mature. The three of us have had dinner together twice and she said he feels solid. She accepts he is who I want to be with and has her own plans, to move in with Tom. My relationship won't really affect her that much.'

'Alexander... does he tick all the boxes? You want to be with him?'

'It's always going to be complicated, but yes. I want to be with him.'

He bites into a cream horn and plants a kiss on my cheek. 'Well, there's going to be a lot more horn round here now,' he says, laughing.

'Stop it. You're spraying,' I say, wiping the creamy deposit from my cheek.

'This is what you've waited for.'

'I suppose I have. His declaration that I mean something; this realisation I'm worth more.'

'Oh, darling. You are,' he says, licking his lips and revealing his chewed-up pastry.

'Stop it,' I say.

'You're worth more than online sex and secret phone calls and meetings in London.'

'I know. The secrets and the lies lost their dangerous

sparkle. I've outgrown the sexting and I've grown to know I'm worthy of him.'

'Yeah, you're right.'

'I will be happy. I deserve to be happy… and you know what? This might just be my fairytale ending.'

'You deserve all those orgasms,' he says with a grin on his face.

'You are shameless.'

'Not as shameless as you my little flower.'

'How are things with you and Mattie?' I ask, turning the conversation back to a more serious tone.

'He uses me, I use him. I'm as happy as can be considering he doesn't want to commit to anything long term.'

'So, you're happy seeing each other?'

'Yes, when he's being faithful. When he's plastered all over Instagram with his Enrico and his Tony and his Christian, I want to punch his pretty face in and break his perfect white teeth.'

'Oh, Fabio. What are we like?'

'You've found a way out. Your heart's led you to a man who loves you how you deserve to be loved. Mine keeps finding a dead end,' he says, stroking my arm.

'You will find yours too if you dare to follow a different path.'

'And you've got the publishing deal and JangleJewels is taking off too. You're a magnet for success. Well deserved. But I'm mad jealous too.'

'There's no place for envy. You just need to unlock your luck. Get in tune with those vibrations.'

'Enough about vibrators, I'm all for–'

'Yes, I know what you're all for but I also know what you deserve. You've just got to recognise it too.'

44
Maria and Alexander

That conversation was two sleeps ago, two breakfasts ago, two dinners ago. I'm hiding in the bathroom, perching on the toilet, lid down. My face is caked in a revitalising mask I found in the back of the bathroom cabinet while I paint my fingernails as near a pink gloss to that on my feet.

Natalie's spending the day with Tom. Both strong and mature about the pregnancy, their relationship has grown through their support for each other; they often talk late into the night, their conversations seeping through the thin walls. They have reached a closeness I almost envy, one I'm ready to find with Alexander.

My own relationship with her has shifted gears too; there's a clear preservation of respect. She appreciates me as her mum and as another woman who is going through a life-altering decision; admittedly not the same but telling her about Alexander and our plans to be together created the opportunity to discuss relationships and our expectations. Finally talking about Alexander freed me from the stifling burden of secrecy. It's no longer like a secret stash of counterfeit notes wedged down the side of the couch with lost pennies and sticky sweet wrappers.

'Gridlock up ahead, possibly an accident,' says the taxi driver.

'Of all the days… my sleeper leaves just before nine.' I consider abandoning the taxi and walking, but my legs won't take the stress of rushing and pulling my case too. It would take me ten minutes at least; a fit and healthy person could probably do it in four, maybe five minutes.

'You've got plenty of time… so you're off to…?'

'London,' I reply, slumping back into the seat.

'Long trip? Eight hours?'

'About eleven… hopefully sleep most of it.'

The minutes tick by. I'm hot, a sweat builds on my forehead. I play with the sea glass I found all those months ago; it's cold in my hand but fills me with a fiery heat and an anxious courage. I push it back into my pocket; turn my attention to Maria's last few messages. I'm not feeling right when I should be right, should be feeling more than just right. Being a brave new me is draining. I smile but the smile is forced.

'Good news?' The driver asks, catching sight of me through his rearview mirror.

I nod. The taxi creeps forward, the front of it jutted close to the bumper of the filthy white van in front of us. We inch our way through the tight contra flow set up by the police.

I wind down the window and let in a spike of air, close it within a few seconds; the atmosphere is heavy with fumes, a lorry emits a thick black smoke into our path and the tail of traffic builds in both directions. Is the universe conspiring against me? I stretch my leg; the familiar pain pulls at my hip and digs deep into the socket like a poking finger.

The first song Alexander ever sent me, by Charlie Puth, all those months ago, crackles over the radio. I turn it up and it pulls me back to the time we began messaging each other. Those risky flirty messages seem like a lifetime ago. When he told me he loved me, when I was all at once both terrified and exhilarated. But I knew he meant it. He wrote those words with such a passion I felt it in his writing, and it touched me as surely as if he were standing next to me, telling me face-to-face. And he has since told me again so many times. And I have accepted it to be our truth; his and mine, ours.

I sing along, *I love you dangerously… more than the air that I breathe…* and hum along to the parts I don't recall the words to. I reply to his message with a *x*. My heart leaps like a hopping kangaroo and the next moment I'm sobbing. I can't believe this is happening. I'm half-expecting him to say he can't leave Sandra.

Almost fifteen minutes later we pull up outside the station and I pay the driver, not bothering to wait for the change. I struggle to get out of the taxi and almost lose my balance only just stopping myself from keeling over face down onto the pavement.

'Thanks mate. Have a good trip.' He's already turning the wheel, ready to spin the taxi around, concentrating on the road.

I have less than ten minutes to get to the platform and I'm struggling, the pounding in my ears disorientating me. I lean on my walking stick and wheel my suitcase behind me, stopping every few yards to massage my hip bone but it's difficult when I rely on the stick to keep me upright. The niggling ache continues to taunt me, sitting just under my skin.

On the platform, a guard helps me with my luggage. I'm thankful I've booked first class; not having to share the tiny space with anyone else. It's a quarter to nine, ten minutes after the timetabled departure and the train sets off. Its metallic shriek pains my ears with its acceleration.

I open up my suitcase; place my toiletry bag and book; a library copy of Jackie Baldwin's *Perfect Dead*, on the bed. I'm shaking with anticipation, worried I may soil myself. A long journey, almost over. No more regrets. No more words unsaid. No more hiding behind my failing marriage. For the first time, I am taking control of my destiny. My legs buckle, I lean against the mattress, my breathing laboured. The enormity of what I'm doing comes at me. Will I ever be the same again?

I add a topcoat to each nail; our secret conversations go round in my head. Conversations about love and satisfaction, fulfillment, and respect. His own words and recited verse of Wordsworth and Burns, Pinter, and Betjeman. His words; the words between us. No longer illicit or risky... Alexander's message beeps; he's already left the house, feels closer to me.

His presence in my life has encouraged me to be bold in my thinking and my writing. My work shows a depth missing before; collaborating with the Scottish editor is the most incredible experience. She has heightened my emotional connection to the words on the page; my manuscript surprises me, though it shouldn't... it's emotional, deep, enlightening.

I've questioned myself and my own ideals and morality over the past year. I'm unafraid, ready to face the future and what it promises.

In an effort to shake off my melancholic mood I go

to the lounge car and order a gin and tonic. A man and woman laughing together, leaning into each other, attract my attention. Are they a couple? A tangle of nerves builds inside me, and I urge my cock to stir, Sandra pops into my head instead.

She looked small standing at the front door. Insignificant. Weak. I wanted to yell at her: *Why couldn't you have just told me the truth? You've done this to us.* But I didn't.

Too much has happened. Too much has changed. I've changed.

She's now in a house filled with empty rooms and hollow, fragile memories. Walking out of the front door shook me to the core. The alcohol relaxes me. Pent up emotions I had scrumpled up tight unfurl and explode within me; I hadn't realised they were there until now. Their release is like no emotion I have felt before. It is alien; it leaves me disorientated and off-balance.

I pull my thoughts back to the present and a woman with dark hair approaches the bar and Maria-images swamp me. That bubbling sensation ripples up and up in me… the physical union between us, which is corrupt yet candid, rough yet velvety smooth. I panic. Is this happening? Is this going to work between us? Have I kidded myself? Will this woman want me how she's wanted me before? How I dream she wants me?

I knock back the rest of my drink and wander back to my cabin wanting to be alone, away from the besotted couples. I squeeze by a man and woman kissing in the narrow corridor and all I want is Maria's lips on mine.

Natalie comes in and the muffled steps alert me Tom is with her. He stays over more and more since her father bought her the double bed and given the circumstances I can't argue. It's given them a chance to share their living space before they move in together and before the baby arrives. His parents have paid the deposit on a flat for them which Natalie is excited about. Both are.

Living together isn't the same as drifting in and out of each other's space every few days for a couple of hours and I think long into the night about Alexander. Our union is happening and I'm hopeful about how it will work.

I've worried about the steep staircase leading up to my flat's front door, but he fobbed it off when I mentioned it saying a few steps won't keep him from me. His voice soft and gentle, I mostly imagine us drinking tea and talking. Holding hands, sharing our favourite poetry. I won't ever tire of his conversation, his accent.

I pull the duvet up over my ears and neck. I wrap my arms around me, rubbing them with my hands to warm myself. Tomorrow I will be welcoming Alexander to my home and at the end of the night he will be in my bed. This is the last night I will be sleeping alone. I reach out to the empty side of the bed and shudder. No more being on my own. I text Alexander: *Goodnight*.

I throw my jacket onto the upper bunk and hang my shirt and trousers; there's no one to tell me how to hang my jacket, how to fold my trousers. I lie back, pulling the crisp sheet over me. I wrap the blanket around me and get comfortable.

Only two hours into the eight-hour journey and time is dragging, and I hope I can sleep despite the oppressive impatience smothering me when all I want is to be with her.

Maria's text reminds me I'm an hour closer to her since my last message and I smile. The rocking back and forth lulls me into a dreamy but restless sleep, the train's relentless whining and groaning taking me closer to Maria as every minute passes. I fall asleep with a smile on my lips and the tiniest stir in my groin.

The sound of a police siren merging into the noise of heavy traffic wakes me. It's Thursday. Not any Thursday but the Thursday. It's a sky-blue Thursday. I'm like a child on the morning of their birthday party. I make a mug of tea, humming along to the tunes on the radio, and eat a slice of toast smothered with a huge dollop of strawberry jam. I lick my sticky fingers one by one and let out a giggle. Today is the start of something new; something I never thought I'd find.

'Yes, yes, yes,' I say, and an uncontrollable laugh grips me.

I shower and dress, I strip the bed and change the linen, smoothing out the covers and plumping up the pillows. I want my bedroom to be a welcoming space and I've tried to tidy my make-up and even deep cleaned behind the bed. A golden arc of light highlights the dancing dust motes in the air. I can almost feel the magic. I text Alexander: *So excited and can't wait to see you. X*

I wake with a rumbling tummy and a heavy head. I splash tepid water over my face. I put on a fresh shirt, ignoring the creases. Sandra's not here to fuss about the crinkles, not here to insist on ironing each one out. It's liberating.

The lounge car is quiet; two attendants and one elderly couple slurping at their hot drinks, a large teapot sitting between them. I order breakfast; a bagel piled high with scrambled eggs and smoked salmon and a cup of tea.

I stare at the landscape, whizzing by in a blur of sloping yellow corn and rolling purple fields, exposed brown brick and industrial concrete towers. The weather has improved overnight and I'm thankful for that; the pain in my bones less likely aggravated by rain and cold. The further south we travel, the greater the promise of sunshine.

I have a brief conversation and tell the couple I'm visiting my girlfriend. They don't bat an eyelid and I'm pleased it sounds natural, plausible that I should be doing that. It lifts the melancholy I strived to shake off since last night and I feel lighter. It's the first time I've said girlfriend out loud and it leaves the taste of pure pleasure on my lips and a flutter grazes my insides. Emotional, I turn away from them.

I send Maria a text. She replies with good morning and a kiss. A second message tells me she's excited. I reply: *I'm excited too. This ordinary man from Inverness is almost in London and he can't wait to have you in his arms my darling Maria. XX*

I walk to the tube station only to find it's closed and chaos reigns; commuters push and shove their way onto the replacement bus. My mind convinces me it's a sign, a sign that this will never work. I push the doubts away, but they keep coming at me: he's older, he's got a medical condition, life will be more complicated as he ages, he's got CP, what about all those stairs?

I read his good morning message again and it lifts me. My feelings shout louder and spill over with love; it will work, he loves you, he wants you in his life, he is willing to leave his wife for you, he's on his way, he doesn't care about the stairs, you love him, he adores you, he's coming to London for you.

The train approaches Euston and wracked with nerves and a sudden urge for the toilet I go back to my cabin. I sit the last twenty minutes of the journey with my own thoughts. The weeks and months of getting to know Maria have at last brought me to where I have yearned to be. My unease disperses. The energy of the storm inside me has finally broken; the reality of what awaits me sweeps me into a tearful heap on the bunk.

I slow my breathing, trying to regulate my runaway heart and the sun streams in highlighting the words *AND SO IT BEGINS* on the front pages of the morning paper I picked up at breakfast.

I exhale and close my eyes. The realisation my life won't ever be the same again hits me. It's liberating. I'm bursting to hold Maria in my arms now this second.

At Euston people rushing around in their own worlds, minding their own business, create a moment of deja-vu. I shake off the feeling, wanting to stay in the here and now. I want to keep my head, slow the thumping in my chest.

I only have a few minutes to spare before his train arrives. I reapply my lipstick, check the arrivals board and pick up my pace.

Someone knocks into me. 'Sorry, love,' says the guy in jeans and a dark hooded jacket.

'No, sorry. It's me. I'm not here today.'

'Wherever you are it must be gorgeous with you in it,' he winks at me and disappears before I think of a comeback. His compliment makes me smile.

The platform at Euston is chaos. I shiver against the chill of the shade, and I pull my jacket around me. The crowd dissipates and when there's a clearer path towards the exit, I pull my case up the ramp to the main concourse. I try to pick up my pace and the usual frustration caused by the ache in my hip responds differently. I shorten my stride, relying on my walking stick to steady me as I speed up with each step.

I pass through the exit in a swell of people. In my head I'd expected to see her straight away and my heart drops a little when she's nowhere to be seen. I stop. I check my phone for any messages from her. None since the good morning message earlier and a panic strangles me. I squeeze my eyes, fighting the tears.

I'm running, dodging the crowds, my bag slips off my shoulder; I grip it under my arm with my elbow. Suddenly he's there. In front of me. Alexander. My Alexander. He's got a different stance, more assured and his eyes are saucers of pure love. My emotions catch me off guard.

I'm in his arms, blindly wiping away my tears. I kiss him and kiss him more.

'Hello,' I say, melting into him.

'Hello,' I say, taking in her scent. 'Let's make this real for real. For the rest of our lives.'

THE END

Poetry References

Chapter 3
John Betjeman (1949)
'Harrow-On-The-Hill'

Chapter 11
Samuel Taylor Coleridge (1798)
'Love'

Chapter 12
Percy Bysshe Shelley (1819)
'Love's Philosophy'

Chapter 20
Robert Burns (1794)
'A Red, Red Rose'

Chapter 21
Elizabeth Barrett Browning (1806 - 1861)
'How Do I Love Thee?' (Sonnet 43)
Harold Pinter (1975)
'Paris Poem'

Chapter 29
John Keats (1795 - 1821)
'To Fancy'

Chapter 30
John Betjeman (c1955)
'Inexpensive Progress'

Chapter 33
John Betjeman (c1955)
'Inexpensive Progress'

Message from the Author

Thank you!

It is with a grateful heart that I thank you for reading my book. I would love you to keep in touch and invite you to connect with me through any of my social media platforms. I look forward to welcoming you and hope that you continue to support me on my writing journey.

With much love, Soulla xxx

Website: www.soulla-author.com
Twitter: @schristodoulou2
Instagram: @soullasays

Acknowledgements

I would like to thank the following people: my new publishing team at Kingsley Publishers, my critique group and writer friends, Judith Crosland, Louise Stevens, Mark Glover, Ian Grant and Lee Amoss; you kept me on my toes with your keen eyes and often funny comments in the margin of my manuscript.

I'm especially grateful for the reader notes and encouragement of my two sisters Lia Seaward and Maria Amoss who took the time to read my final copy.

I am especially thankful to my author friends Anne John-Ligali, Jane Lacey-Crane and Jackie Baldwin for their contribution to the final copy and the wonderful love and constant support of my partner Alan Reynolds.

About the Author

Born in London to Greek Cypriot parents, Soulla Christodoulou was the first in her family to go to university and later retrained to become a teacher.

Alexander and Maria was nominated for the RSL Ondaatje Prize 2021.

The Summer Will Come, a book club read in the Year of Learning Festival 2019, is currently under contract for translation into Greek and earmarked as a book to movie project.

Soulla is happiest writing in her pretty garden Writing Room and drinking tea infused with cinnamon sticks and cloves. Connect with Soulla on her website https://www.soulla-author.com/

Instagram: @soullasays
Twitter: @schristodoulou2
She loves to hear from her readers.

The Village House

"Romantic, descriptive, and evocative... The Village House captures the authentic spirit of a Cypriot village." - *Nadia Marks, best-selling author of Among the Lemon Trees.*

Katianna receives a solicitor's letter summoning her to Omodos, a mountain village in Cyprus.

What is at first an inconvenient trip quickly becomes more attractive as she spends more time there. Flooded with many childhood memories, she falls in love with her roots and relishes in the relaxed pace and warmth of her cousin and the Cypriot people she meets. And then there's the simmering attention of the builder tasked with renovating the village house Katianna has inherited from her maternal grandmother.

Grappling with yo-yoing emotions, she returns home. But in London all is not well for her award-winning dating agency; her world is threatened, turned upside down, forcing her to question everything she believes in and has worked so hard for.

She travels back and forth and has to face the fact she has to sell the only connection left to her family.

But can Katianna have everything? Will she find a way to hold onto her business? Or will the pull of her heartstrings and the village house entice her to start over in a place closer to home than she ever imagined.

The Village House

SOULLA CHRISTODOULOU

KINGSLEY
PUBLISHERS

Chapter 1

The building, in the heart of London, screamed success. Katianna relished it. Her patent heels clipped across the marble flooring, the echo bouncing across the bright, open space. She took the green coded escalator to the double-decker lifts, leather laptop case in one hand and designer handbag in the other.

The glass doors pinged opened, closed immediately after her. She pressed the button for the twelfth floor, the location of her dating agency, *Under the Setting Sun*. She looked straight ahead at the control panel; the buttons lighting up the company names as the elevator whooshed past each floor: Investment Management PLC, Kew and Press Lawyers, ARC Project Management, Cyprus Property Portfolio... her eyes stayed locked with the word Cyprus... the letter she had recently received on her mind, still sitting on her desk, but she shook the niggling, invasive thought away, refocused.

In her office, she tucked her handbag under her desk and smoothed out her black pencil skirt. She plugged in and switched on her laptop. She sat facing the glass-walled partition which afforded her with a view of her team and the open-plan workspace beyond. At eight promptly she went through the day's key activities with her PA.

'That's great, thank you Angie.'

'I'll get your coffee,' Angie said, her tight ponytail and wide-legged culottes swinging in time with each long step. Her yellow flat pumps coordinated nicely with the mustard of her trousers and echoed the colours of an uncharacteristically warm July. At almost six-foot Angie didn't need any more height. She towered over Katianna, who at only five foot four considered her own heels necessary, especially at work.

Angie was in her early thirties, a few years younger than Katianna, but her mature attitude and commitment shone through from the moment she said "anything it takes" in her interview five years before. Katianna recognised a kindred spirit in her and despite Angie's patchy work history hired her instantly never regretting it.

A real asset to the company, Angie was efficient, productive, proactive and loyal. She had become a good friend over the years and with life very much tipped towards work, genuine friends were hard to come by for Katianna. The glitz and glamour of award nights and ceremonies were just that and Katianna snubbed her friends' comments.

'Slow down,' they urged. 'Not everything which shines is made of gold.'

But her circle shrunk as she rebuffed their comments telling them everything did in her world.

Katianna's sole purpose to be successful was all-consuming, her single-minded ambition her steed. Eight years before, she had won the court case against her business partner, also her ex-fiancé, to keep the business name. She had since spent every waking hour and every ounce of energy making the business a leader and had vowed never to be indebted to anyone ever again, especially in business. But in love too.

Judged by the UK and European Dating

Awards' independent panel on reputation, success rate, approachability, and customer service, *Under the Setting Sun*, had been favoured many times over.

Framed awards hung in a perfect line across one wall and gave no room for doubt: UK Matchmaking Agency of the Year 2015 and 2018, International Matchmaker of the Year 2015, European Matchmaking Agency of the Year 2016 and 2018.

But achievement had come at a price; the ensuing months of working long hours and at weekends had pushed away the university friends Katianna had in her inner circle. The odd text or phone call was all she had time for now. She recognised a shift once they had husbands, wives, families of their own. She pushed aside the split-second prickle. She had her empire, didn't she?

She swiveled round in her seat to face the London vista laid out before her, the leather squeaking against the fabric of her skirt. This, all of it, she breathed, was worth every minute of working past midnight, waking at dawn, and missed lunches with friends. This is what made life worth living.

Every day she breathed in the success of the dating agency and her innovative approach had kept her ahead of the ever-growing competition and away from negative press increasingly associated with dating agencies and relationship apps.

Hers was different; clients plugged into a network of high-calibre, aspirational, professional singles. Supported by an assigned matchmaker, they worked towards the ultimate goal of a long-term relationship. Their sign-up package included professional photography, Myers Briggs-type indicator assessment which provided information on who each client really was and ID-checks on all members which ensured

safety and security. Her matchmakers had backgrounds in
psychology, counselling, and life coaching. Her newest recruit
was a chartered psychologist and Associate Fellow of the
British Psychological Society.

She took a call from John, her full-time accountant and
finance manager. Running any business effectively relied on
the owner's understanding of costs, money in and money
out, and John handled that side of the agency for her; she
preferred the company of people to figures and spreadsheets
and she was instinctively yielding around him, trusting his
knowledge and expertise implicitly.

John had been working with Katianna for almost seven
years and he had been one of the first people she consulted
with in terms of growing the business. It took off in its
second year, more than tripling her forecasted income.

They rescheduled their monthly meeting around another
appointment that had moved for John and said goodbye.

Katianna checked her emails and looked over the schedule
of client photo shoots and website update meetings planned
with her team; she kept a keen eye on the competition and
read the main broadsheet newspapers and magazines every
day. She followed trending hashtags, Instagram stories and
LinkedIn news, including trends in the USA, Canada, and
Europe.

She turned around, a knock-knock at her door.

'Come in,' she said, already gesturing to Warren, one of
her advertising sales team.

'Have you got a minute?'

'Of course,' she said, nodding towards one of the black
leather club chairs.

'I've got good news and bad news,' he said. 'The Mayfair
Inn, Sherlock Mews and Devi Ahilya India have confirmed
their online advertising for another year. I've increased the

ad fee by 10%.'

'And the bad news?'

'One of the new restaurant accounts has paid for the key spot on our home page for twelve months.'

'Bad news because?'

'The Broadgate Hotel & Spa has already confirmed that spot for three months and paid-up front.'

'Use your negotiation skills to keep them holding on until then… offer them something else for the first three months and then the nine months, or even the year, on the home page.'

'I did that already. They're not biting.'

'Leave it with me. When did you last speak to them?'

'Day before yesterday.'

'Email across the details, your conversation notes, files.'

'I'll do it right now,' he said, making for the door. 'Thanks Katianna.'

She smiled at his retreating back. Warren was good at getting the advertising in but not so good with what she called "being cute"—keeping all sides happy when a pickle arose which thankfully wasn't often.

Her laptop pinged, Warren's email. She read the attachments, nothing to worry about. She was sure she could keep both accounts happy.

She pushed the laptop away and the letter caught her attention; the letter that had been mailed three times to her previous address. It was quite by chance she had bumped into her old neighbour who mentioned she had been holding onto post for her.

Katianna had hated sharing a letter box with Nosy Rosy, as she not-so-affectionately nicknamed her, who never missed an opportunity to ask why Vodafone were sending so many letters or why she received discount offer cards when everyone did their shopping online; her own daughter and three nieces did. Katianna had forced a smile and tightened her lips holding back on what she had really thought of her nosiness even though it was cloaked as neighbourly concern and kindness.

She took the envelope in her hand, felt the weight of it, in more ways than one, ran her fingers over the perforated edges of the Cyprus stamp and slipped out the thick cream sheet. She read the three short paragraphs again. She needed to book a flight to Cyprus when all she wanted was to stay in London, enjoy the rare hot summer and get on with running her business. She didn't have the time to take the four-and-a-half-hour trip to a country she hadn't been back to for years and recalled a client, two years ago, who the agency had successfully paired with a French lawyer. She believed they now lived happily in Paphos.

'Look at it as a well-deserved break,' Angie had said, 'on the island of l-o-o-o-v-e.' Katianna smiled, remembering how Angie had drawled the word.

Katianna had tried dismissing the unexpected wave of wistful affection. Her *yiayia* Anna had been the only grandmother she had known in her life and memories filled her; *yiayia* hugging Katianna tight, pinching her cheeks each summer in exaggerated awe of how much she had grown, plucking juicy purple figs, and picking grapes together.

Was going back to claim her *yiayia's* house a good idea? Her grandmother's passing had been painful, a shock, yet Katianna had not returned for the funeral still reeling from the deaths of her own parents; a stab of guilt poked at her, even more so now that the village house had been bequeathed to her and her parents were no longer here to know it. For a moment, tears threatened to fall but she pushed them away. There was no time for silly sentimentality and regrets. Living in the moment was all she had, and this is what she had right now; a house in the village waiting for her to what? Breathe new life into it? Connect with a life and a culture she had negligible ties with?

Her cousin Savva, who had linked up with her, after more than twenty years, put on the pressure, begging her to fly out.

'You can stay with me,' he said. 'I'm all grown up now.'

She had to go. She could not get out of this. Savva wouldn't take no for an answer and, of course she had to sign the legal documents for the house. Cyprus, it appeared, didn't recognise technological advancements and the solicitor insisted she visit to sign the paperwork in person with her identification: 'We have to have the original documents in front of us,' he repeated, though she wondered whether Savva had anything to do with their lack of enthusiasm to do things online.

Saying goodbye to her team was bittersweet; part of her looked forward to a break, a change of routine, and she had solved Warren's issue, with charm, so she was leaving on a high. Her team was the closest she had to family, yet she held them at a distance, preferring not to blur the lines between her work and their private lives. But she was admittedly going to miss them all as well as the buzz of the day to day in the office. As she left shortly after seven, she quietly relished the idea of disappearing for a few days, remembering her mother's words: *Rest is not an indulgence, it is essential Katianna. How can you be your best self if you don't treat yourself well?* Cyprus was going to bring her the rest she needed, she reassured herself.

Chapter 2

Katianna arrived at Larnaca International Airport exhausted and crampy; the pains in her tummy twisting her intestines with anticipation but her exterior façade portrayed nothing of her inner anxiety. It was nearly midnight by the time she exited the airport even though passport control had been efficient, and the queues had moved quickly. She hoped Savva was still waiting for her.

The flight from Heathrow Terminal 5 had been delayed by two hours because of "mechanical issues". The announcement had left her uneasy and anxiety consumed her entire flight despite the luxury of flying first class. All the while the whiney antagonistic voice in her head said: "You should have stayed at home. Leaving your business and gallivanting to God knows where…"

Katianna marvelled at the modern, bright airport remembering how she used to arrive with her parents and have to queue on the tarmac; the airport building too small to accommodate a full plane of arrivals. She walked out of the air-conditioned building with a renewed bounce.

The muggy heat of the night enveloped her and conscious of a sheen of sweat she brushed her hand across her forehead and upper lip. August, the hottest month of the year. Her clammy hand slipped against the suitcase handle as she dragged the oversized luggage behind her. Trying to keep it upright, she crossed the tarmac, no longer riddled with potholes and cracks as it had been years before, though the intense summer heat was the same. Her ankle doubled over as she caught her red stilettos on the edge of the raised walkway and her designer jacket slipped off her arm. Looking down at the heel, the leather had been shredded. Damn, she thought and gathering the jacket draped it over her shoulders despite the heat.

'Katianna,' Savva called from where he leaned against the shuttered kiosk, the streetlamp casting a harsh light.

She carefully navigated her way between the rows of parked hire cars and minibuses. As Katianna neared him, she took in his dishevelled appearance, yet his stance oozed a quiet, sexy confidence which took her by surprise. He was unkempt yet surprisingly attractive. He seemed bolder, more mature, in real life, not the soft, baby-faced man she saw on their video calls.

He threw his unfinished cigarette to the ground, grinding the stub into the tarmac and leaned in to kiss Katianna's cheeks, exhaling smoke over her shoulder. Katianna, taken by surprise, felt a blush of colour fill her cheeks. She had forgotten how kisses and hugs were nothing to shy away from in Cyprus, especially when greeting friends and relatives.

'I thought you said you were quitting?' she grimaced and then smiled as she waved the tendrils of Savva's cigarette smoke away.

'I was, until a week ago when the thought of my English cousin visiting stressed me out.'

'Very funny. You can't blame me. What's the real reason?'

'Lack of will power.'

'That's it?'

'That's it. Now come here and give me a proper hug.' He

pulled her close.

'You stink like an ashtray,' she said, pulling away and giggling, surprised and delighted with the familiarity between them.

She liked the way she was able to connect with him even though her Greek was inferior to his fluency in English. But the closeness between them, there since childhood, was evident and flooded back like a ribbon-like flow of water, comfortable moving with the force of gravity, unperturbed by any babbles or ripples. They were almost twins; their birthdays only three days apart and it didn't take long for Savva to tease her about being older and therefore demanded respect.

'You haven't really changed at all,' she said.

As children they had been thrown together every summer holiday; they danced together, swam out to the floating raft at Santa Barbara beach despite words of warning from their parents, and as a teenager Savva had escorted her to clubs, keeping a close eye on anyone who dared approach her, ready to pounce with the protectiveness of a lion over his pride.

***

The drive to the village from the airport took just shy of an hour and a half; Katianna took in the silhouetted view of tall buildings and huge lit billboards, almost unrecognisable to the landscape she remembered as a child.

The peaks of the Troodos Mountains loomed darker still behind the buildings, with the stars twinkling like Van Gogh's *The Starry Night.* She recalled a specific camping trip to the Kykko Monastery, a royal, Patriarchal Stavropygian Monastery located in the western part of the mountain range, twelve miles from the highest peak of Cyprus' Mount Olympus.

All those years ago, lying side by side with Savva, sharing the same sleeping bag, the same splintered stars had dotted the inkiest blue expanse which felt so close it was as if she could pluck one from its blanket. Savva had tried to grab one for her, huffing and puffing, exaggerating his efforts. The other campers had been woken by her laughter followed by the smack of the thrashing slaps from their parents; both had hidden inside the lumpy sleeping bag till they almost couldn't breathe, holding hands, their bodies squashed against each other's in innocence, as any brother or sister.

'Almost there already,' she said, disappointed when the car indicated at the final E-road exit for Omodos. Omodos, she thought, coming from the Cypriot word "modos," meaning "taking your time," with tact, carefully. She had found the snippet of information on the in-flight magazine. She hadn't realised how popular a destination her ancestral village had become and felt a sense of pride shadowed by a sting of guilt at not having known it.

As a child, the drive from the airport seemed to take forever, the journey made almost in complete darkness with no lighting along the poorly tarmacked roads, pot-holed and rutted—dirt tracks—unlike the roads now, the majority brightly lit and well-maintained.

They arrived in the village, built at the slope of the mountains, the winding roads narrower than she remembered and the pretty stone village houses, with their tiled roofs and terraces and picturesque upper floors, glowing in the amber light of the streetlamps; those replaced at intervals with brighter bulbs shone at a sharp downward angle and she scrunched her tired eyes against their harshness. The sweet smell of grapes carried on the mid-night breeze as it swept over the vineyards towards the village. A stray cat, not straggly or emaciated like the strays used to be, ran out in front of the car, her shiny coat glinting in the headlights. Savva slowed down and the cat's eyes seemed to stare at Katianna.

Katianna shivered against a little tremor running through her, but she looked upon the cat crossing their path as a good omen and her black fur even more so. She slinked away and disappeared under a parked pick-up truck; battered and missing a back bumper.

***

So where do you want to start today? I've taken three days off work to be your translator, chauffeur, whatever you need.'

'You're a real good sort. How comes you haven't been snapped up?' Katianna wiped her brow, already sweaty from the rising temperature.

'Who says I haven't?'

'Because your house is still a house, not a home,' said Katianna, pointing to the stark walls and clutter-free surfaces of the open-plan kitchen and sitting room.

'How is that observation going to help you sort out your *yiayia's* house?'

'Sorry. It isn't. It's a habit of mine… comes with the job.' She smiled, hoping to take the sting out of her comment. 'Let's start with breakfast and then you can accompany me to the house.'

'Sounds good. I want to know everything that's been happening. There's something different about you I didn't catch on our video calls. I can't put my finger on it.'

Chapter 3

'Black tea with cinnamon sticks and cloves, and a halloumi and mortadella toastie for me, thank you.' Katianna placed her order after Savva introduced her to Sofia.

Katianna had spotted the little café *stafilia kai meli* which translated as "grapes and honey" as they walked arm in arm across the village square and though Savva had tried to persuade her to walk further, Katianna's puppy-dog eyes had won him over.

'How delightful. I haven't been asked for a cinnamon and clove tea in years.'

'It's how my *yiayia* Anna made it. It seems right I should drink it now I'm back,' said Katianna.

'She was a wonderful old lady, so kind,' said Sofia.

'You knew her?'

'She was a grandmother to all of us growing up in the village,' said Sofia.

'I guess she would have been, yes. I wish I'd known her better, especially these last few years.'

'Well, there are many around here who can tell you about her,' said Sofia.

'Just a coffee for me, Sofia,' said Savva, interrupting them.

Katianna gave him a look; one she had perfected in the days of child minding to pay her university fees. Memories flooded her: piles of ironing, scrubbing shower doors until they gleamed, tidying endless toys, sleeping on her side on the edge of a single bed until her arm went numb while Jessica and James fell asleep, working with her laptop balanced on crossed legs on the sofa until after midnight, reading Eric Carle's *The Very Hungry Caterpillar* and Michael Bond's *Paddington Bear* Books over and over until she almost knew the stories word for word. She sighed, and then recalled the heavy hardbacks of J.K. Rowling which the family gifted her when she finished working with them two years later together with a generous bank transfer which put her in the black for the first time in four years.

'What?' he asked, cutting across her thoughts.

'You've taken me back to my nannying days… and not the good ones.'

'What d'you mean?'

'No smile. No please. No thank you.' She paused. 'You could at least acknowledge her. She's lovely and no wedding ring.'

'That's because she's not married,' he said, folding his arms across his chest.

'How come?' teased Katianna. Her lighter tone eased the tension she picked up on and Savva gave her a half smile.

'I don't know. She's always lived in the village, never left. Opened the coffee shop when her parents died,' he said, avoiding eye contact.

'She looks happy.'

'They say happiness can come from the deepest sorrows, don't they?' said Savva.

'You're right. Kahil Gibran said something like, *when you feel joy, look to your heart and you'll find it's only that which has given you sorrow that is now giving you joy.*'

'I guess that's kind of true.'

'And she owns this place?'

'She spent all her inheritance breathing new life into the once derelict building abandoned by the previous owners. She's always here. Working.'

'Working but happy,' said Katianna, Sofia's situation closely mirroring her own.

Katianna sat a while, didn't say anything but her mind was already ticking with anticipation, an idea forming. Back in London and across the industry she was inevitably known as *The Matchmaker* and even though she was single herself she had this knack of pairing single hearts together and matching them fruitfully. With a first in psychology, she knew what made people tick and *Under the Setting Sun* had become more than a simple dating agency. It attracted clients serious about partnering and with a view to getting married, finding a life-long partner and it worked.

Sofia returned with their order served in a mishmash of crockery.

'So pretty,' said Katianna, fingering the pretty floral teacup and saucer.

'Thank you, it meant a lot to my mother who received it as part of her dowry when she married. My intention was to use it temporarily and replace it once the business began making a profit but I'm glad I didn't,' she said, with a faraway look in her eye.

'I'm here refurbishing my grandmother's house and when it's done, I'm hoping to have a little celebration in memory of her life. I wonder...' she said, turning an idea around in her head. 'Would you cater for it and, of course, join me as a guest.'

'I'd be happy to arrange anything you need food-wise, but this place takes up all my time. But thank you for the invitation, that's sweet of you.'

'Don't say no to joining us just yet. Let me get sorted and once I have a date you can decide then.'

'She said, no, Katianna. Leave it,' said Savva.

Sofia's cheeks turned a fiery red. She grabbed the empty plates from the next table and scuttled off towards the serving hatch where Petros, her part-time chef, was already lining up the next round of breakfast orders.

'You embarrassed her,' said Katianna and slurping her tea she focused on its sweet, spicy fragrance to take away the sourness in the air.

'Me? You're the one going on about the catering and the invite,' he said and pulling his mouth with both fingers, stretched it wide, and waggled his tongue at her.

'You're not ten anymore,' she tutted, 'but I guess that's what so loveable about you.'

'Enough of me and how immature I am. Let's talk about you. What are your plans with the house?'

'Spruce it up and sell it. It's not convenient to keep it. I'm like Sofia with work leaching my time. And my life's in London.'

'The house is in pretty bad shape so sprucing may realistically need to be translated as refurbishing and even rebuilding in places.'

'It's been old and run down for as long as I remember,' she said, taking a bite of her toasted sandwich. The nutty aroma of the toasted, sesame-seed bread filled her nostrils. 'This is so good. The bread I buy from the bakery back home is good, Polish bread, but this is just heaven.'

'I'll tell George when I next see him. He's very proud of his baking skills.'

'And so he should be,' Katianna said.

'Eat and then let's get the solicitor out of the way.' Savva took the last swig of his Greek coffee as Katianna picked at the errant crumbs on her plate.

She wondered what the story was between Savva and Sofia, and she knew there was one; she felt it.